AN ORIGINAL NOVEL OF THE MARVEL UNIVERSE

THANOS

DEATH
SENTENCE

STUART MOORE

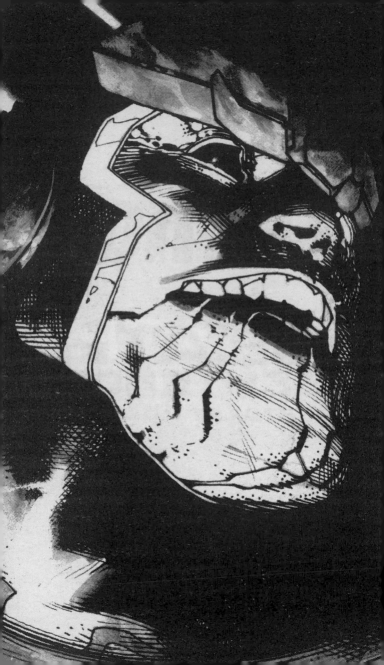

AN ORIGINAL NOVEL OF THE MARVEL UNIVERSE

DEATH
SENTENCE

STUART MOORE

TITAN BOOKS

Thanos: Death Sentence
Print edition ISBN: 9781789092424
E-book edition ISBN: 9781789092431

Published by Titan Books
A division of Titan Publishing Group Ltd
144 Southwark Street, London SE1 0UP

First Titan edition: April 2019
10 9 8 7 6 5 4 3 2 1

This book is a work of fiction. Any references to historical events, real people, or real places are used fictitiously. Other names, characters, places, and events are products of the author's imagination, and any resemblance to actual events or places or persons, living or dead, is entirely coincidental.

© 2019 MARVEL

Interior art: Simone Bianchi and Riccardo Pieruccini
Cover art by Aleksi Briclot
VP Production & Special Projects: Jeff Youngquist
Assistant Editor: Caitlin O'Connell
Associate Editor: Sarah Brunstad
Director, Licensed Publishing: Sven Larsen
SVP Print, Sales & Marketing: David Gabriel
Editor in Chief: C. B. Cebulski
Chief Creative Officer: Joe Quesada
President: Dan Buckley
Executive Producer: Alan Fine

Special thanks to editor Joan Hilty

No part of this publication may be reproduced, stored in a retrieval system, or transmitted, in any form or by any means without the prior written permission of the publisher, nor be otherwise circulated in any form of binding or cover other than that in which it is published and without a similar condition being imposed on the subsequent purchaser.

A CIP catalogue record for this title is available from the British Library.

Printed and bound in the United States

This one's for Jim Starlin, Prince, and the
two Cordwainers: Smith and Bird.
Also for Mimi, who didn't deserve this.

BOOK ONE
INFINITY

He was quick-witted, sharp-eyed, and perpetually dissatisfied. He craved power and wisdom, but not for his own gratification. He was Kronos, first of the Titans, and he dreamed of a better world.

Kronos built a city, a haven, a sanctuary called Olympus. A place of beauty, where the gods lived together in harmony. But Kronos's dissatisfied nature proved his undoing. Bored with peaceful contemplation, he sought to bend the laws of nature. One day he probed too far into the bands of hyperspace, snapped the superstrings, and unleashed power beyond comprehension. The catastrophic explosion shattered Olympus, toppling it from its high peak.

Thus died Paradise.

One of Kronos's sons, a good man named A'Lars, gathered his starlost siblings. He founded a new society on Titan, largest moon of a ringed world called Saturn. Mindful of his father's mistakes, A'Lars ruled over Titan with a careful eye. He hoped to restore the values of peace and wisdom that had been lost in the fall of Olympus.

And so it was for a time beyond mortal reckoning. Until the coming of A'Lars's own son, his deadly seed…

…the Mad Titan called THANOS.

FROM *THE BOOK OF TITAN*
(last known copy destroyed in the First Thanos Genocide)

ONE

THOR was the first to die. A blast of pure cosmic force struck him in the chest, lighting up his muscular form. The Thunder God tensed, arched his back, and tightened his grip on the hammer Mjolnir. Fire burned through him, searing his flesh and peeling away layers of muscle to reveal bones that had fought a thousand battles, endured for hundreds of years. His mouth gaped open in a silent scream.

Thor flared bright against the stars, and was gone. Mjolnir spiraled away, an orphan in the sky, and vanished into the depths of space.

At that moment, a shiver ran up Thanos's spine. The universe shifted; the strings, the bands, the swirls of existence vibrated, sounding a chord of triumph. To Thanos, death was a song, an ode, a lyric poem. It was his art.

He looked down. On his left fist gleamed the Infinity Gauntlet, power radiating from the six Gems studding its surface. The yellow stone—the Power Gem—still flared. A moment ago, it had loosed the bolt that ended Thor's life.

Thanos smiled. The Power Gem was the *least* of the six—and it had just claimed the life of Earth's most powerful defender.

Soon, all existence would bow to Thanos. If he felt merciful, he would grant it the greatest gift of all: nonexistence.

When Thanos spoke, his voice was like granite plates. Shifting and rumbling, jangling the chords of hyperspace.

"LET THE GAME BEGIN," he said.

Half a mile away, in free space, the next wave of Earth's heroes shot forth to face him. Carol Danvers, the energy-powered Captain Marvel. The Silver Surfer, gleaming on his board. The Vision, an artificial being. The cosmic peace officer called Nova.

And their leader, Captain America, grim and determined in a red-and-blue spacesuit flecked with white stars. He motioned to the others, gathering them to him and speaking in low, short tones over the radio in his helmet. The Captain had no special abilities, no invulnerable skin or energy-channeling powers. But Thanos could feel his thoughts in the ether, more focused and intense than any of the others.

Thanos clenched his fist tighter, poured his will into the Gems. His diamond-hard, gray-skinned body began to grow in size, dwarfing his enemies. Already he was as tall as a skyscraper; soon he would be as large as a moon, then a planet. Eventually, all matter in the universe would be absorbed within his omnipotent form.

As he grew, his awareness expanded. He could

sense the bands of hyperspace, an ever-growing range of dimensions, each a glittering string to be plucked and played. Seven strings radiated out from each gem—42 in all, each a window into a unique reality. The strings spread like webs through the stars, wormholes linking all time and space. They could be picked, moved, tied, rewoven, or snapped at his will.

Thanos saw without seeing, perceived multiple planes of existence. Before him, Captain America and Captain Marvel argued strategy, casting urgent glances at Thanos. The word "diversion" fluttered past his awareness, and he laughed.

"YOU SPEAK OF DIVERSIONS," he boomed. "DO YOU NOT UNDERSTAND THAT I SEE EVERYTHING AT ONCE?"

The Silver Surfer's blank eyes went wide. He understands, Thanos realized. Alone among the heroes, the Surfer possessed cosmic awareness.

A small vessel circled nearby, keeping a careful distance from Thanos's ever-growing form. Its engines were strictly sublight, its hull patched together from alien ships and experimental human shuttles. Its pilot, a misshapen creature called Ben Grimm, barked out warnings to his passengers, then sent the ship on a wide-angled course for the outer system.

Thanos cast his awareness wider, surveying the totality of his surroundings. The Space Gem burned bright on his fist, feeding power back into its owner. Several miles off, in a small capsule, a third contingent of attackers waited. This was Captain

America's emergency team, a trio of extremely volatile entities. A green-skinned behemoth; a demon with a flaming skull. A man with cold metal pressed against a hideously scarred face.

Thanos's ship *Sanctuary* floated at the edge of his awareness, out beyond the orbit of Mars. Its crew of space pirates and degenerates was not strictly necessary to his purpose. But he knew: Even a god needs followers.

Exactly one million miles sunward, the Earth floated helpless in space.

"Thanos."

Thanos turned, startled. He'd almost forgotten Captain America. The muscular human floated with his comrades, addressing Thanos directly.

"You have the Infinity Gems," Captain America said. "That gives you power."

The voice was tinged with anger. Over the death of his friend, no doubt. Thanos grinned.

"But power is a hollow thing," the Captain continued.

"YOU BELIEVE SO?"

"I know it." Captain America grimaced. "I've seen the abuse of power—time and time again. It always backfires."

Thanos tuned out the small voice. He was still growing, approaching planetary size. His atoms drew farther apart; he became a specter against the stars. Soon he would engulf this solar system, then the galaxy.

No power—no force of nature or technology—would stand before him. The Space Gem could take him anywhere in the universe. The Soul Gem would break his enemies' will. The Time Gem would grant him access to past and future; the Mind Gem would lay all secrets bare to him. The Power Gem would feed and energize the others.

And if all five of those somehow failed, the Reality Gem alone could shape the universe into any form Thanos desired.

He could feel the power suffusing his form. The universe would kneel before him. It would *become* him.

And yet…

Something nagged at him, casting a shadow over his impending triumph. Yes, the stars themselves had cried out at Thor's death. The trumpets had sounded; the strings had been plucked. Thanos's offering had been heard and accepted.

But something was missing. Some absence tugged at Thanos's stone heart. When the Thunder God perished, Thanos had still been alone. The voice in his heart, the one entity he loved more than any other, had not spoken.

Mistress Death was silent.

In all the universe, only one entity—*one concept*—owned Thanos's loyalty: Death. Oblivion. All his life, throughout countless human lifetimes, he had worshiped her, adored her, sought to please her. She spoke to him in dreams, waking and sleeping, urging him on to slaughter and genocide. Her dark eyes glittered; her scarlet mouth promised peace and a final contentment.

But it was never enough. No matter how many beings, how many worlds that Thanos reduced to cinders, Death had never fully accepted him. Her lips brushed his ear, whispered words of temptation and promise. And then, always, she was gone.

The Infinity Gems glittered on his fist. They were his last chance, his final bid for Death's love. The Gems' power was so great, so universally feared, that they had long ago been scattered and placed in the care of a group of cosmic entities. To accumulate them, Thanos had tricked, trapped, and vanquished the Collector, the Gardener, the Grandmaster, and others he could barely even recall.

Now the power was his. The power to control the universe—to rule it, or to raze it to dust. The greatest gift any being, throughout time and space, had ever granted to Death.

And still she withheld her love.

A burst of cosmic energy blasted against Thanos, disrupting his expanding atomic structure. For a moment, he felt...not pain, exactly. The ghostly memory of the sensation. A whisper of hurt, a flash of anger.

He turned stone eyes to the source of the blast. The Silver Surfer stood astride his board, channeling unimaginable power through his outstretched hand. That power had been granted the Surfer by Galactus, the Devourer of Worlds. One of the few beings whose strength rivaled Thanos's own.

But the Surfer alone could not have pierced

Thanos's enhanced body. The Vision floated nearby, channeling a steady blast of solar energy through the jewel in his forehead. The young hero called Nova gritted his teeth, shooting forth pulses of gravimetric force through his outstretched hands. Captain Marvel thrust forward one fist after the other, sending radiant energy that flared in blinding bursts.

Captain America floated behind them, directing the assault. Eyes wide with alarm.

Again, Thanos smiled. You *should* be alarmed, Captain.

He sent a thought-command to the Power Gem, and the assault simply ceased. The range of energies, of solar and cosmic and gravimetric power, stopped short of Thanos, as if a force field had been erected.

Now, Thanos decided, casting his thoughts forth to Mistress Death. Now the slaughter begins.

The Power Gem flared—and then died down again at his command. Why just kill them all? he thought. Much better to show them the full power of the Gems first. A display, a demonstration to the assembled universe of what was to come.

He turned first to Captain Marvel. She bore a trace of Kree power within her, the legacy of the most fearsome warrior race in the galaxy. Yet she herself was human, mortal. A fragile speck in a large, hostile universe.

The Space Gem pulsed. With the slightest twitch of a cosmic string, Thanos shifted space around Captain Marvel. A moment of disorientation, and she found herself alone and helpless, far from her world, her teammates, her ship. Far from the raging battle.

Somewhere near the orbit of Pluto.

Billions of miles away, Thanos reveled in her panic. She would die in the depths of space, far from Earth, as hunger and thirst inevitably destroyed her human form.

"Close ranks!" Captain America called.

The Surfer, Nova, and the Vision moved closer together, renewing their assault. They couldn't keep this up forever, Thanos knew. It would be easy enough to wait them out, to allow them to exhaust themselves.

But where was the fun in that?

With a quick pulse of the Mind Gem, Thanos swooped inside the Surfer's thoughts. In a millisecond, the Titan witnessed the tortured creature's entire history: his childhood as Norrin Radd on the peaceful planet Zenn-La, his enlistment by the Devourer as herald, and the triumphant moment when he had turned on his master, refusing to scout worlds for Galactus to consume.

Thanos's fingers, each the size of a moon now, twitched. The Mind Gem subsided; the Soul Gem flared. Cruelly, surgically, Thanos reached into the Surfer's mind and altered his essence.

The Surfer stiffened. He looked around at his comrades, as if seeing them for the first time. Then he turned and flew off into the void, ignoring Captain America's protests.

Thanos smiled. The Soul Gem had returned Norrin Radd to a cold, emotionless state, as he had been when Galactus recruited him. This Silver Surfer cared nothing for humans, for love or friendship, for the survival of worlds. His inside matched his exterior: hard, gleaming, allowing no light to penetrate his soul.

The Vision launched himself toward Thanos, his solar jewel blazing bright. Thanos cocked his head, studying the tiny android. Then he raised the Gauntlet and aimed the Reality Gem.

All around the Vision, space went mad. Planets careened and crashed, moons and comets appearing out of nowhere. Captain America's voice in the Vision's ear became a deafening shout, then a gibbering squeak. All directions became one; the Vision scrabbled and flailed in the void, unable to find his way.

The android's strength, Thanos knew, came from the rigid order of his artificial brain. Without that, the Vision was helpless. Trapped in a private hell.

Thanos became aware of a voice breaking his concentration. A faint sound, almost too quiet to make out. Despite himself, his heart surged with hope. Was this Mistress Death? Had she arrived, at last, to share in his glory?

"Uh, guys? Not to complain, but I'm kind of drowning in lizards here."

Anger surged through Thanos. This was not Death's voice. It was a tiny human, a chittering insect he'd faced before. A mote, a speck of dirt.

Spider-Man.

Thanos frowned, seeking the source, then raised an enormous stone eyebrow in surprise. While he'd been occupied with Captain America's assault, Ben Grimm had successfully boarded Thanos's starship, *Sanctuary*. Spider-Man was among Grimm's team.

I'm not yet used to operating on multiple planes at once, Thanos realized. I must learn to divide my attention, to live in all time and space simultaneously. I have been a Titan all my life, but I must learn what it means to be a god.

He swept his fist wide, sending a trail of Gem-power flaring across the orbit of Mars. Captain America and Nova winked out of existence. There was no burst of power, no meeting of weapons in battle. They were there, and then they were gone.

Voices cried out, chattering over suit radios. Thanos folded the bands of space and turned his attention to *Sanctuary*. He thrust his awareness inside, through the gleaming hull, and searched the two wings of the ship until he reached Main Mission, in the thick central section.

A fierce battle raged under the glaring lights and floor-to-ceiling viewports of Main Mission. The Black Panther leapt out, stunning Thanos's officers with his charged gauntlets. The alien crew members fell back, firing lasers. Johnny Storm, the Human Torch, soared overhead, raining fireballs down on the crew.

Captain Styx, a salmon-colored humanoid with white eyes, stepped cautiously into the room. He swept his hand forward, and a horde of enlisted men—most of them recruited from lizard races—swarmed in after him. Spider-Man launched himself into their midst, punching and spraying webbing from both hands.

"This looks kind of…what's that thing that isn't good?" Spider-Man webbed an armed lizard in the face. *"Bad."*

A hatch clanged open, propelled inward by the force of a rocky orange fist. Ben Grimm, the Thing, charged into Main Mission, followed by the muscular She-Hulk. A slim figure followed, soaring gracefully through the air. He wore a space helmet, but unlike those worn by Captain America's team, his wasn't filled with air.

Prince Namor, the Sub-Mariner, drew in a deep breath of water and charged.

Grimm and She-Hulk waded into the lizard-men, punching and jabbing. The Torch swooped up and down beneath the high ceiling, bombarding the enemy with fireballs. Namor launched himself like a missile through the air, mowing down Thanos's officers with his steel-hard fists. The Panther kicked and thrust with his Vibranium claws; Spider-Man cast a web at the ceiling and swung himself upward, then reached down to clog a few laser rifles with well-placed bursts of webbing.

As Thanos watched, an odd emotion came over him. It took him a moment to recognize it as boredom.

The Space Gem flared. In an instant, Namor was gone. He reappeared on a desert world, far across the galaxy—a world with no seas, no lakes, no natural bodies of water.

With the tiniest pulse of the Reality Gem, Thanos

turned Namor's helmet to hydrogen. The last of the monarch's precious water spilled out around him, evaporating as it struck the arid sand below.

Namor raised his head and cursed Thanos. Thanos laughed.

"Um, guys? Prince *Finding Nemo* just kind of… winked out."

Spider-Man again. His voice was like a nail on slate. Thanos vowed to make him suffer.

But first…

Another burst of the Space Gem, and half of Grimm's team vanished. She-Hulk, the Panther, and the Torch all winked back in at the bottom of a deep alien sea. The Torch's flame hissed and died.

This world was the exact opposite of the one to which Namor had been exiled—a planet entirely covered, from one end to the other, with water.

The Panther tore off his mask, struggling to breathe. She-Hulk's eyes began to bulge. The Torch's hands sputtered with flame—but he, too, was helpless. Thanos considered using the Time Gem to slow time, to prolong their agony. But his goal was not to cause suffering—merely death.

Death. Still she tortured him; still she was silent. Thanos clenched his fist. Where was she?

Aboard *Sanctuary*, Ben Grimm winked out, reappearing just outside the ship. Pressure built inside his body; his eyes bugged out, red veins bulging. He exploded into a storm of orange rocks, tiny against the surrounding asteroids.

"Okay, boys." Again, the nagging voice. "Looks like it's just yours truly against an army of green scaly dudes. Now, I may look severely, even hopelessly, outnumbered. I may seem way out of my urban comfort zone here on the Starship Crazypants. But no matter where I am, I'm still your Friendly Neighborhood—"

Thanos thrust his giant fist forward. The Time Gem glowed, with a tiny assist from the Space Gem. Dimensions folded; superstrings struck dissonant chords. Spider-Man rose up, twisted sideways, and warped through space-time.

Thanos smiled. He reached out with the Mind Gem, joining his consciousness with Spider-Man's. He wanted to feel every moment of the agony to come.

Spider-Man felt himself growing smaller, younger. His awareness narrowed, sharpening down to a single, horrific moment. The moment when, with savagery in his heart, he'd held his Uncle Ben's killer in his hands.

The worst moment of young Peter Parker's life.

He pulled the man's face up to his own and remembered: It's the burglar who ran past me. The one I didn't stop when I had the chance. Once again, for the first time in his life, he realized that his own lack of responsibility had brought about his uncle's death.

But Thanos was not finished. He reached out into the 42 bands of hyperspace and caught hold of a single superstring. He twisted the string and tied it closed, into a loop.

As Spider-Man watched in horror, the moment repeated itself. Again he grabbed the burglar, raised him up to view the man's face. Again he felt the first rush of guilt, the shame that would follow him the rest of his life.

Then again.

And again.

Thanos laughed. He withdrew from Spider-Man's mind, leaving the young hero in a hell that would never end.

Thanos's body was the size of Jupiter now. I've only scratched the surface, he realized. The options, the perversions made possible by the Gems—they're endless.

More defenders rushed to tackle him. The Hulk, his furious energy channeled and amplified by a specially designed spacesuit. Doctor Doom, lashing out with a mixture of dark magic and stolen cosmic power. Ghost Rider, his blazing skull a portrait of elemental fury astride a rocket-fueled motorcycle.

From a space warp, a starship appeared. Gleaming, sharp angles—a vessel of war. For a moment, Thanos hoped the Shi'ar had actually dared to challenge him. But when he cast his vision inside, he found only the X-Men. Magneto, Psylocke, Sabretooth, Archangel, Storm, and a strangely young Jean Grey.

One by one, they met their doom. The Hulk's soul, reduced to that of Banner at his lowest state. Storm, trapped alive in a coffin for all time. Jean

Grey, exiled to a deadly time loop of mass murder and endless regret. Ghost Rider confined forever to Mephisto's fiery hell. Magneto returned to the death camps, his great mind crippled along with his powerless body.

Thanos raised his head to the heavens and cried out. "IS IT ENOUGH? NOW WILL YOU ACCEPT MY LOVE?"

A tiny whisper in the night. Too quiet to make out. But it could be her.

He allowed himself to hope.

All around him, the bands were silent. Bodies drifted among the asteroids; shards of spacesuits sparked harmlessly in the night. Captain Styx had resumed command of *Sanctuary*, and was beginning to turn it toward Earth.

Earth. A dot against the sun, a speck of foul matter with a needle-sharp satellite orbiting it. Thanos sensed eyes aboard the satellite, watching him. Plotting a final, hopeless defense.

Those defenders, too, would have their turn. They would find exile in their own unique hells. Or else the Titan would simply kill them, grant them the bliss of nonexistence.

For now, he allowed himself a moment of satisfaction. His mind roamed the dimensions, raced up and down the superstring paths. He watched Namor sink to the pitiless sands, felt Spider-Man cycle through unending grief and horror. Sensed Captain Marvel's growing panic at her hopeless exile, relished

She-Hulk's moment of drowning as water filled her gamma-irradiated lungs.

Each death, an offering. A token of his love.

He was larger than the sun now, vaster than the solar system. Yet still he was incomplete. Still he yearned for her embrace.

And there was something else. Something speeding toward him like an arrow, through the bands of hyperspace. A monster, a weapon, a creature designed and engineered for a single purpose: the murder of the Mad Titan.

Despite his size, despite his power, Thanos felt a twinge of fear. As he tensed, awaiting the attack, a single word bubbled to the surface of his consciousness, taunting and threatening him. A word he hadn't heard for a long time.

Destroyer.

He clenched his fists, willed the Gems to full strength, and awaited the battle to come.

TWO

"WELL," Tony Stark murmured, flipping up his faceplate to view the hologram before him. "Not a bad seat for the end of the world."

"That's your bright side?"

Maria Hill, director of S.H.I.E.L.D., gestured at the three-dimensional image of Thanos. The Mad Titan hovered in space, teeth clenched, fists held out before him. Thanos had grown to enormous size: Stars, comets, asteroids were visible through his cosmically enhanced form. Pieces of destroyed ships surrounded him; bodies, too, though at this magnification they were too small to identify.

"The Gems," Tony said. "He finally got 'em all."

"We knew this day would come," Hill replied.

Tony squinted at the holo. "Wish we could get a better look."

"Richards is working on it." Hill flashed him a glance. "You worried?"

"Not yet." Tony grimaced. "Check back in five."

The multileveled bridge hummed with activity.

Computers buzzed, alarms rang out. Agents of both S.H.I.E.L.D. and its sister agency S.W.O.R.D. bustled around, barking orders and hustling to obey.

The Peak was the satellite command post for S.W.O.R.D.—the Sentient World Observation and Response Department. While S.H.I.E.L.D. handled terrestrial threats, the Peak kept watch on the skies. It hung like a sharp-pointed dart in Earth orbit, surrounded by rings of docking bays, holding facilities, and scientific laboratories.

Under normal circumstances, S.H.I.E.L.D. and S.W.O.R.D. operated independently. But a threat of this level required total coordination. Ships of all nations buzzed around the Peak, preparing to defend their shared world.

"The Infinity War," Tony said. "Or is this the Crusade? I forgot my handbook." He shook his head. "Any word from Fury?"

"He's in Moscow." Hill tapped, distracted, at a tablet computer. "Assembling a multinational military force to make a stand on the Earth. Assuming Thanos gets here."

"If that walking mountain gets here, there won't *be* an Earth. What about Abigail Brand?"

"Coordinating with Fury. She's circling the globe, rounding up Inhumans." Hill let out a long sigh. "We're doing all we can…even launched the new Starcore station ahead of schedule. The nations of the world are actually, sort of, coming together. I've even got a North Korean rep in my office. But against that…"

On the holo, Thanos raised his enormous head, as if responding to some unseen threat. He lifted his fist, and the Infinity Gems glowed bright, one after the other.

"I've fought a lot of bad guys in my time," Tony said. "But this feels different."

"Different?" She paused, lowered her tablet. "How?"

"It feels…final."

He fidgeted, adjusting his armor. He'd been wearing the Iron Man suit for ten hours now; it was starting to itch. He studied the holo, but couldn't make out any sign of Captain America's team.

"Radio contact with the attack teams has been lost," Hill said. "That's not good."

"You're a pessimist." Tony flashed her a humorless smile. "I knew we had something in common."

"How's the plan going?"

"I've built the machine. It's up to the others now." He frowned at the hologram. "Wish I was out there."

"Me, too." She turned to squint, sharply, at the image. "What's *that?*"

"Wide view," Tony ordered.

The hologram zoomed out, the view expanding to include *Sanctuary*. Thanos's enormous form still dominated the image. Tony reached out with both hands, swiveling the view. A green-and-violet streak appeared above the sun, shooting toward the Titan at unimaginable speed.

"That," Tony said, "is the diversion we've been waiting for."

The streak slowed on approach, resolving into a humanoid figure. His body was huge and muscular, marked with fierce red tattoos. His eyes glowed white, and he carried an enormous, jagged knife in each hand.

"Drax," Hill said.

"Any old Destroyer in a storm." Tony shook his head. "Fascinating dude. Dropping out of hyperspace without even a *suit*…that should have ripped his flesh to shreds."

Drax the Destroyer swooped up in front of Thanos. Drax was smaller than the Titan's nose— but for a just moment, a look of fear seemed to cross Thanos's face.

Drax dropped straight down, reared back, and stabbed both his knives into Thanos's enormous chest. Thanos recoiled, his mouth flying open in a silent scream.

Hill frowned. "How can he do that?"

"The Destroyer was created to battle Thanos. *Invented,* if you will. He's a living weapon."

"Can he…you know…destroy him?"

"No chance. None."

"What about the rest of the Guardians? Are they coming?"

"They're busy across the galaxy somewhere. Something about Annihilation Waves, a group of assassins called the Black Order…another front in Thanos's war. Anyway, I'm not sure a raccoon gnawing Thanos to death is our best plan."

"Then what is?" Hill gestured helplessly at the

Destroyer. "If a human weapon created specifically to kill Thanos is useless, what else can we possibly throw against him?"

On the hologram, Thanos clenched his fist tight. A beam of Gem-energy shot out toward the Destroyer. Drax dodged and weaved in space, but the beam grazed his side. He grimaced in pain, his blood bubbling out into free space.

"When the invention fails," Tony said, "go back to the inventor."

He turned to gaze across the huge, circular bridge. A strange machine stood against the far wall, past dozens of frantic S.H.I.E.L.D. and S.W.O.R.D. agents. Its most prominent feature was an irregularly shaped viewscreen framed by a bronze border studded with Mayan and Egyptian symbols. The ancient pictograms clashed sharply with S.W.O.R.D.'s high-tech decor.

A slim, red-cloaked figure knelt before the machine, head bowed. Eldritch energy billowed up from the figure's outstretched hands, rising into the air and feeding power into the glowing device.

"Well?" Hill asked. "Is it ready?"

"Just waiting for Reed's dimensional-turbulence inhibitor." Tony turned, calling out, "Richards! Where are you?"

Hill grimaced. She pointed her thumb at a balcony three stories above.

"You better get up there," she said.

Something in her voice made Tony obey. Not bothering to flip down his faceplate, he triggered his boot-jets with a mental command. As he shot up into the air, he caught a last glimpse of Drax's tiny form, lashing out again at the giant figure of Thanos.

On the upper level, high above the activity of the bridge floor, a balcony alcove had been cleared for Reed Richards's use. The pliable scientist's body seemed to fill the entire space, his limbs stretched and coiled around consoles and machines, fingers absently manipulating viewscreen controls several yards away from his staring eyes. But Reed Richards's stretching power was actually the *least* of his talents. His incredible mind allowed him to adapt any situation, any combination of equipment, to his own needs. That innate problem-solving ability was what truly made him Mister Fantastic.

But as Tony jetted in to land on the balcony, he realized something was wrong. Reed's equipment was studded with screens, mounted at all different heights: small screens and large, square- and oval-shaped, some of them no doubt built for alien use. Reed's long fingers reached out to pinch and enlarge one image, then danced across consoles to the next. His eyes flickered from one image to another.

Every screen showed jagged chunks of orange rock floating in space.

Tony laid a metal hand on Reed's shoulder. The gauntlet almost sank into Reed's pliable flesh.

"Ben," Reed murmured.

Tony nodded. Now he recognized the images on the screens: chunks of Ben Grimm's cosmically altered body, blown to pieces by Thanos.

"Reed," Tony said, struggling to keep an edge of impatience out of his voice. "We gotta close this deal."

When Reed looked up, Tony almost flinched. The scientist appeared older, more tired than Tony had ever seen him before.

"I couldn't save him," Reed whispered.

There's no time for this, Tony thought. His mind shifted into hyperspeed, proposing and discarding a dozen courses of action in milliseconds. Yell at Reed? Commiserate? Pick him up and carry him down to the bridge?

Slap him?

"Reed." Tony kept his voice steady. "Where's Sue?"

"With Fury. In Moscow." Reed shook his head. "They'll never survive against Thanos."

"Let's make sure they don't have to."

Reed looked away.

"Come on, Reed. Don't make me do this. You know I suck at pep talks."

"This is true." Reed nodded. "What do you need?"

"What do I *need?* I need the gizmo! The turbulence inhibitor!"

"That? I finished it ten minutes ago." The scientist held up a small cube covered with intricate circuitry. "I thought you were still working on the portal."

Tony snatched it out of his hands. "Now I *really* want to slap you," he muttered.

"Mm?"

"Nothing." He jetted up into the air. "Let's not tell Hill about this, 'kay?"

"Tony?"

Tony looked back down. Reed's 13-inch finger was pointed at a small screen in the corner of the work alcove. A large chunk of Ben Grimm's body, perhaps a piece of his chest, floated in space. As Tony watched, the spinning hammer of Thor tumbled across the screen, tiny against the star-flecked blackness.

Tony said nothing. With a mental command, he flipped down his helmet faceplate. As his armor's circuit closed, Iron Man's bright, white eyes glowed to life.

"Come on," he said.

He kept the faceplate on during his descent. Tony had built the Iron Man suit to shield himself from attacks, but sometimes it served another purpose. To the world outside, no expression showed on that gleaming gold visage. No tears welled up in those blinding white eyes.

Reed followed, his body extending and contracting, grabbing onto railings and tumbling down levels like a Slinky on stairs. Tony was about to touch down when the station shook with a violent impact.

"Battle stations!" Hill yelled.

Tony pivoted, veering sideways, and came in for a landing next to Hill. She stood before the main holo-display, which showed a large, three-segmented spaceship firing particle beams.

"*Sanctuary*," Reed said. Tony jumped—he hadn't seen the scientist's head and elongated neck swoop up next to him. "Thanos's ship."

"Softening us up," Tony breathed.

"Scramble all fighters," Hill said, pressing a comm button on her shoulder. "S.W.O.R.D., S.H.I.E.L.D., everything we've got. And alert Fury: The battle's come to us."

A small secondary holo-window in the corner of the display still showed Drax dodging and weaving in space, avoiding Thanos's blasts. The image flickered and vanished. A technician turned to Hill and said, "Remote feed lost."

Hill turned, astonished, to Tony and Reed. *"What the hell are you two waiting for?"*

Tony touched Reed on the shoulder—at least, he thought it was the shoulder. With Reed's arms stretched out over half the bridge, it was hard to tell. "You got the dingus?"

"You took it from me."

"Oh. Right."

They crossed the bridge, dodging and leaping around frantic S.W.O.R.D. agents. Another blast struck the Peak; Tony jetted up into the air to avoid stumbling.

When he reached the machine with the Egyptian symbols, Tony glanced back at the main holo-display. A phalanx of Earth fighters—at least two dozen—had surrounded Thanos's ship, firing particle weapons and small nukes. They looked like mosquitoes trying to bring down an elephant.

"Wanda," Tony said. "Ready to make some magic?"

The kneeling figure turned and blinked, as if

noticing him for the first time. Wanda Maximoff, the Scarlet Witch, wore a ceremonial red cloak and tiara. Behind her, a strange pattern of static hissed and flickered on the machine's flat, oddly shaped screen.

"Wanda?"

"I am ready," she said. She turned back toward the machine, knelt down, and fired off a blast of chaos magic into it.

Static flashed bright. A wave of energy swept across the screen and sharpened into an image of fast-moving clouds. Tony couldn't explain it, but the clouds seemed almost alive.

Wanda shivered.

Reed slinked up beside Tony. "Is she ready for this?" he whispered.

"Wanda's proved herself plenty of times." The bridge shook under another impact. "Besides, we're out of options."

The screen shifted again, a fierce wind blowing across it. "I have reached him," Wanda said. "I have located the one we seek."

Tony shot Reed a look that said: See?

Clouds whipped across the screen. Staring into their depths, Tony could feel their power. The winds died down, revealing a hazy, flickering image of a man with mustache, goatee, and piercing eyes.

"Oh," Tony said. *"That* one."

"Doctor Strange," Reed said. "Where are you?"

*"I'm afraid the answer to that question wouldn't...
much sense."* Strange's voice faded in and out. *"I have*

crossed many…sional planes to reach this place."

Another blast struck the bridge. The screen went blank; Strange's face vanished. Tony swore, opened a panel in his gauntlet, and initiated a force-reboot by remote control.

Wanda stabbed her hands out rigidly and poured more energy into the machine. The Sorcerer Supreme reappeared. He seemed disoriented, buffeted about by the otherworldly winds.

"I fear I have…lost myself. The dimensions are shifting…out of alignment. The paths are not as they were."

"I can speak to you, Doctor." Wanda glanced up at Strange. "But I cannot locate you."

"Doc," Tony said. "We're running out of time. You found our boy yet?"

"Yes. He resides in the nether dimension where Thanos … him. But I cannot pierce the turbulence surrounding that realm."

"I have that covered." Reed stretched his fingers around the back of the machine, searching until he located a specific port that Tony had built to his specifications. He plugged in the dimensional-turbulence inhibitor.

"Science and magic." Tony shook his head. "Like bacon and ice cream."

"Bad for the heart, but delicious," Wanda said.

A slight smile had crept onto her face. Despite the tension in the air, Tony smiled back.

On the screen, Strange's eyes grew wide. The amulet on his chest began to glow, rising up into the air. As it took position on his forehead, it seemed to iris open like a third eye.

"The Eye of Agamotto," Strange said. *"Slowly it clears. I…not penetrate the dimensional veil, nor can I yet perceive my own path back. But I can show you the one you require."*

As Strange's face began to fade, Reed stretched forward. "When this is over, Doctor, we *will* find you. We will bring you home."

"May your efforts against Thanos … successful," Strange said. *"I should prefer there be an Earth to come home to."*

"Yeah." Tony blinked. "There's that."

He glanced around. On the Peak's main hologram, Thanos's *Sanctuary* vessel was taking heavy damage. But the shattered hulls of S.H.I.E.L.D. and S.W.O.R.D. ships surrounded it, floating in space. The battle was far from over.

And none of it really matters, he thought. *Win or lose, Thanos will soon be powerful enough to destroy the Earth with a mere thought.*

"Oh," Reed said.

Tony turned sharply. On the machine's screen, Doctor Strange had been replaced by a massive humanoid figure. It floated in a sort of nether-space, alien stars and moons showing through the gaps in its cosmic form. The figure's wrists were shackled with a rusty chain the width of Saturn's rings, each arm bound to a separate asteroid. Its ankles were similarly tied, lashed to bright-glowing gas-giant worlds. An even thicker chain encircled its waist, holding its back arched against a dead, black cinder of a star. The being seemed dead; its eyes stared blankly, mouth gaping open in the memory of a scream.

The image wavered. Tony looked down at Wanda, placed a hand on her shoulder. She waved him off.

On the screen, the enormous figure turned to stare out at them. Its eyes lit up, glowing with the ember of an ancient fire.

"WHO SEEKS KRONOS?" the being asked.

"Um," Tony said. "Uh…"

"We do," Reed said.

Tony glared at him. "Thanks." He turned back to the huge, shackled figure. "Just to be clear here. You are indeed Kronos the Titan? One-time ruler of Olympus, grandfather of a genocidal little creep called Thanos?"

"I AM." Kronos glanced at his bound wrist. "IT WAS THANOS WHO IMPRISONED ME HERE."

Kronos twitched his arm. The chain on his wrist dug a trench into the planetoid, but it held fast.

"Right. Well, here's the thing: We might be able to help with that."

Kronos glowered. "NO EARTHLY POWER CAN FREE ME."

"Ah. But." Tony stepped forward, gestured at Wanda's kneeling form. "This one's power draws directly on…chaos magic, isn't it?" Wanda nodded. "And that magic—as I'm sure you know, being a god and all—is cosmic in nature."

"PERHAPS IT CAN BE DONE." Kronos peered

at Tony. "BUT I SENSE YOU WISH SOMETHING IN RETURN."

"Nothing you wouldn't do for free, I bet. We need you to get rid of Thanos." The bridge shook. "And, uh, fast."

"I HAVE SENT WEAPONS AGAINST MY GRANDSON IN THE PAST. IT WAS I WHO CREATED THE DESTROYER."

"Yes, well, *he's* not gonna keep us out of extra innings tonight. You're gonna have to do better." Tony paused. "We have a deal? This offer *will* expire immediately upon the total obliteration of the human race."

"THANOS WIELDS THE INFINITY GAUNTLET."

"Never said it was going to be easy."

Kronos closed his eyes. "I HAD HOPED THINGS WOULD BE DIFFERENT."

"Hope. Yes." Tony clenched his fists. "I'm sure Thor hoped to be drinking mead in Asgard tonight, too."

"Stark." Maria Hill touched him on the shoulder. "We're down to our last dozen ships. Whenever you're done here, we could use Iron Man outside."

Tony whirled back to Kronos. "I gotta go, Granddad. We have a deal?"

"IF YOU CAN FREE ME," the Titan rumbled, "I WILL AID YOU."

Wanda rose to her feet, straightening up to her full height. She raised both arms in the air.

"I can do this," she said.

Several things happened in quick succession. A

trio of force bolts stabbed through the Peak's hull, shattering the viewport. Air blasted past, escaping through the gap in the hull. Repair crews fastened on their helmets, rushing to seal off the bridge.

Tony heard a gurgle, almost lost in the storm of escaping air. He looked down to see Reed twitching on the floor, 20-foot limbs spread out across the bridge. His eyes were wide, his mouth moving soundlessly.

One of the force bolts had blown a hole in his chest.

Wanda stood her ground, unmoving, as uniformed officers scrambled past them. Facing the machine, she glowed with accumulated chaos magic. Her hands lashed out toward the screen, sending forth a flare of cosmic energy. Kronos's image was lost in the blinding flash.

Reed gasped and went still.

Hill strode back and forth, barking orders into her shoulder. S.W.O.R.D. agents bustled around, strapping on jetpacks. Repair crews struggled to seal the ruptured viewport. Through the shattered glass, Tony could see a distorted view of the huge *Sanctuary* ship, circling around for another assault.

Wanda was barely visible in the blinding light. A crimson silhouette in a storm of chaos.

Tony glanced once more at the dying form of Reed Richards, sprawled on the floor. *I've fought battles before,* he thought. *Desperate battles, hopeless battles. I've made hard calls, lost friends, and come within inches of dying myself.*

Again, he thought: *This feels final.*

Another blast shook the Peak. Metal creaked; glass flew all around. The Peak's hull groaned, threatening to break apart.

Tony Stark, the Invincible Iron Man, closed his eyes and sucked in a long breath. Then he slapped down his faceplate, activated all systems, and raced outside to join the battle.

THREE

"THANOS," Drax the Destroyer proclaimed. *"I am your doom."*

Thanos eyed the tiny green form. Bleeding and broken, the Destroyer fought on. He faced the Mad Titan without fear, without hesitation.

"I have tracked you here," Drax continued, *"across the stars, through the unimaginable depths of space. I was born for this day, evil one, and now at last it is arrived. Now your reign of terror ends—"*

"REALLY?"

Thanos stretched out a finger longer than the diameter of Jupiter. The Reality Gem flared once, and Drax was gone.

"NO CLEVER DOOM FOR YOU," Thanos mused. "NO TIME-TRAP, NO DISTANT EXILE, NO LINGERING DEATH."

Thanks to the Reality Gem, Drax's very existence had been erased from history. Soon his teammates, the self-styled Guardians of the Galaxy, would behold the face of Thanos in some alien sky and meet their own dooms. And even then, in their final moments, they would not remember the fierce, green-skinned fighter who had been their friend.

For a moment, all was quiet. Bodies floated all around—some whole, others mangled and broken. Captain Styx had already taken *Sanctuary* sunward to begin the final assault on planet Earth. That, Thanos knew, was an indulgence: Earth was in no way crucial to his plans. But if Styx whipped up the human race into a frenzy of panic, it would make their obliteration all the sweeter.

Besides, a god should always reward his subjects—and Styx's pirate crew had served Thanos well. He would allow them their measure of plunder and slaughter—before they, too, perished.

Thanos clenched his fist, smiling at the planet-sized Infinity Gems. Soon, every being in the universe would bend its knees to him. And he would cut them down—singly, and by the thousands and billions—giving over each soul in turn to Mistress Death.

Then she would see. Then she would adore him. She would take him in her arms, accept him into her kingdom of skulls. At last she would appreciate the shrine he'd built to her, the love that had driven him to sacrifice every living thing in the universe.

But what if—

Panic seized hold of him. What if Death rejected him again? What if she spurned his offering, turned away from his embrace? What if she *laughed* at him?

He gazed at the bodies: the twisted corpse of the Black Panther; the broken, sparking body of the Vision.

The mangled figure of Doctor Doom, mask hanging loose from his face. The floating swarm of rocks that had been Ben Grimm.

What if it were all a *mistake?* The killing, the schemes, the relentless pursuit of power. A lifetime of slaughter, of deception, of building walls. Of genocide, matricide, even infanticide. What if it was all for nothing?

"MISTRESS?" Thanos appealed to the heavens. "WILL YOU SPEAK TO ME?"

Only the solar wind replied.

"SPEAK." A hint of anger crept into his voice. "GIVE ME A SIGN, DAMN YOU!"

Silence.

"PLEASE." His voice cracked. "I MUST KNOW. LET ME KNOW YOU ARE WITH ME, THAT YOU APPRECIATE MY DARK, ETERNAL LOVE."

At the edge of awareness, a sound. Too quiet to make out.

"MISTRESS?" he repeated.

A voice. A whisper. He recognized a single word, his own name: *Thanos.*

"YES? YES, MY LOVE?" He struggled to keep the emotion from overwhelming him. "IS IT YOU, AT LAST?"

He concentrated, casting his awareness out into the universe. His consciousness rippled in waves past the outer worlds of this system, Uranus and Neptune and Pluto. He probed in the opposite direction, too—through the sun, out into the immense void of interstellar space. He searched Alpha and Proxima Centauri, Wolf and Sirius and Barnard's Star. Then he continued outward, through the millions and billions of suns comprising the Milky Way.

Like a master pianist, he slid up and down the hyperspace bands, tapping each string in an effortless glissando. In the near realms, ships flashed from star to star at unimaginable speeds. In the middle levels, strange beings fought like slow trees and slumbered for eons. Farther up the scale, creatures like the Dread Dormammu held sway over realms too strange for human minds to comprehend.

Voices rattled and shrieked and rumbled. Human and inhuman. Tones that vibrated on a thousand alien planes at once. A thousand billion beings on ten thousand worlds.

But not the voice he sought.

"YOUNG ONE."

His eyes went wide. The voice was close, much closer than he'd thought. He narrowed his vision, struggled to focus on the world that had caused him so much trouble in the past: Earth. No, not Earth itself. The voice emanated from that tiny needle-satellite above it, the one about to crack open under the bombardment from his own *Sanctuary* ship…

Before he realized it, Thanos found himself staring at his grandfather.

"KRONOS," Thanos rumbled. His voice sent shockwaves through the ether.

"GRANDSON." Kronos hovered in space, his

massive ethereal body tensed to strike. Stars, whole galaxies, showed through his torso and bare scalp. His blank eyes were narrowed in disappointment. "I KNOW THAT REASONING WITH YOU IS USELESS."

Thanos hovered in place, possessed by silent rage. *Family,* he thought. *The most vile thing in the universe.*

"YET I MUST TRY," Kronos said.

Thanos jabbed his fist, faster than light, and fired off a burst from the Space and Power Gems. The energy struck Kronos in the stomach and ripped open the fabric of space-time. Kronos cried out, then reached down and thrust both his hands into the warp. His wiry fingers, each as long as a comet's tail, glowed with pinpoint energy gleaned from the stars. In a microsecond, they stitched the rip back together.

Kronos glared at his grandson. "ALL YOUR LIFE," he rumbled, "YOUR ELDERS HAVE CLEANED UP AFTER YOU."

He fired off a blast of cosmic energy, an electromagnetic disruption powerful enough to black out the Earth. Thanos parried it easily, raising the Gauntlet and dissipating the blast with a flicker of the Reality Gem.

"YOU KNOW NOTHING," Thanos said, blasting out again. "YOUR LIFE HAS ALWAYS BEEN ONE OF PEACE."

"NOT ALWAYS." Kronos dodged the blast, allowing it to disperse harmlessly in space. "I, TOO, FACED MY TRIALS. MY OWN TEMPTATION TO ULTIMATE POWER."

"AND YOU FAILED."

"I DID." A barrage of meta-cosmic flares flashed from Kronos's fingertips. "I WAS BROUGHT DOWN BY MY WORST INSTINCTS."

"YOU WERE BROUGHT DOWN BY INCOMPETENCE!"

Distracted by anger, Thanos allowed the blasts to strike him. The Gems flared automatically, shielding him from harm. But the cosmic energy stung like tiny insect bites.

"YOU FAIL TO SEE THE LESSON," Kronos boomed. "YOUR PLAN, TOO, WILL FAIL. YOUR PATH LEADS NOWHERE."

"DO NOT PROJECT YOUR FAILURES ONTO ME." Thanos allowed his rage to build, funneling it into the brightly glowing Gauntlet. "WE ARE NOTHING ALIKE."

"WE ARE MORE ALIKE THAN YOU KNOW."

"FAMILY. ALWAYS I AM VEXED BY FAMILY." He let out a massive blast of power. "NO MORE!"

"IS THAT WHY YOU MURDERED YOUR MOTHER?" Kronos absorbed the energy, gasping as it struck his gigantic body. "WHY YOU—uhh—SOUGHT OUT YOUR HUNDRED OR MORE OFFSPRING—AND BUTCHERED EVERY ONE OF THEM?"

"YOU WILL NEVER UNDERSTAND ME."

Kronos straightened, struggling to face Thanos directly. The last blow had damaged him, forced his unearthly atoms farther apart. Thanos sensed this—he could always sense weakness.

"I SHOULD HAVE RIPPED YOU LIMB FROM LIMB, LONG AGO," Thanos said, using the solar winds to move himself closer to his enemy. "YOU AND MY HATED FATHER BOTH. NEITHER OF YOU HAVE THE STRENGTH, THE RUTHLESSNESS, TO BRING THIS UNIVERSE PEACE."

Kronos's eyes shone bright. The expression in them made Thanos shiver.

"RUTHLESSNESS?"

The elder Titan reached out with blue-black fingers, pointing through the blackness. A pinpoint beam stabbed out, heading toward the sun. At the last moment it veered, zigzagged through space, and circled around the humans' needle-satellite. Small ships scrambled to avoid it; a man dressed in red and gold dodged away, jets flaring bright from his boots.

The beam struck *Sanctuary*, blasting its hull open wide. Captain Styx and his pirate crew scrambled, scrabbled, and finally tumbled into space, gasping for air.

"WE ARE MORE ALIKE," Kronos repeated, "THAN YOU KNOW."

His fingers danced. Five tiny beams shot forth, following the same course sunward. Four of them struck the damaged *Sanctuary*, ripping it to pieces. The final beam engulfed Captain Styx.

All this Thanos saw, his awareness enhanced by the Space Gem. He watched as Captain Styx screamed in pain. The cosmic energy fried Styx's flesh, stripped muscle from his bones. When the flash faded, nothing remained but a bloodstained skeleton, floating in space next to the frozen, agonized bodies of his former crew.

Thanos, the Mad Titan, raised his head and laughed.

"SO," he said. "YOU ARE STILL THE DESTROYER OF OLYMPUS. AFTER EONS OF TRYING, YOU HAVE NOT CHANGED."

"NOR HAVE YOU." Kronos's voice was tinged with sadness. "AND I FEAR YOU NEVER WILL."

Again the Space and Power Gems flashed on Thanos's fist. A funnel of destructive power shot through the ether, toward the sun. It stopped just short of Earth, expanding to cover the quivering needle-satellite in a glistening corona of energy.

"WITH ALL THIS POWER AT MY COMMAND, GRANDFATHER…" Thanos turned to face the Earth. "…WHY WOULD I WANT TO CHANGE?"

He twisted his wrist, and the Peak snapped in half. Bodies streamed into space, joining and mingling with the flow of dead from *Sanctuary*.

Kronos's eyes flared. He stretched his arms wide, fingers twitching. Gravitational fields shuddered in response, shifting and surging into new configurations. A dozen asteroids—barren rocks from the field circling the sun past the orbit of Mars—moved toward him in response. Then a dozen more. A hundred. A thousand.

Kronos reached back and hurled the entire asteroid belt at his grandson.

Thanos smiled. With a thought, he used the

Reality Gem to turn himself incorporeal. The rocky barrage passed harmlessly through him, fanning out into open space beyond.

"OH, GRANDFATHER." Thanos's voice was mocking. "YOU SERVE THE HUMANS. YET IN A MOMENT OF ANGER, YOU'VE DESTABILIZED THE GRAVITATIONAL BALANCE OF THEIR ENTIRE SOLAR SYSTEM. YOU'VE JUST DOOMED THE EARTH TO A NEW ICE AGE—AT BEST."

"I SERVE NO ONE," Kronos replied, his tone icy. "I HAVE BUT ONE PURPOSE HERE."

"NEVERTHELESS." Again, Thanos smiled. "IT FALLS TO THANOS, AS ALWAYS, TO GRANT MERCY."

"NO. NO."

Thanos ignored his grandfather's cries. He turned like a dagger toward the Earth, reaching out with his mind. He drank in the fear of seven billion minds, relished the agony they felt as their champions fell and died.

With a blast from all six Gems, he blew a hole through the world.

Humans died. In the thousands, the millions. Gasping for air, burned alive, drowned beneath madly rushing seas. Frozen in the pitiless depths of space.

The two Titans glared into each other's blank eyes. All around them, asteroids careened and shot madly through space. Planets screamed out of their orbits, wobbling madly, atmospheres hissing into space or catching fire. The Earth was a cinder, hollow and dead.

"YOU CANNOT MATCH MY FURY," Thanos said. "KILL TEN SOULS, I WILL KILL TEN THOUSAND IN RESPONSE."

Kronos clenched his fists. "I TRIED TO AVOID THIS," he rumbled.

He began to grow. Larger, vaster, his atoms pushing farther and farther apart. He reached out and drew power from the sun, sending solar flares rippling across its surface. He stretched his arms wide, spanning the unimaginable distances between the stars.

Thanos gritted his teeth and sent a mental command to the Space Gem. He felt the rush of expansion as the Gems fed power to each other. Soon he overtook his grandfather, dwarfing the old Titan's enormous body. The Reality and Power Gems surged, creating an enormous, funnel-shaped gravimetric field stretching light-years from end to end. With a twist of his hand, Thanos gathered up a yellow star and flung it at his enemy.

Kronos's eyes went wide. His essence grew thinner as he willed his body to become immaterial—but it was too late. The yellow sun struck his dark, star-spattered face and burst into a thousand flaming pieces. He cried out, blinded, his form wracked by heat and gravitic stresses. Bright embers burst forth in all directions, cooling as the remains of the star scattered into interstellar space.

Only then did Thanos realize: The star he'd flung was in fact Earth's sun. That world—and Titan, as well—was now gone. Nothing remained of the solar system that had birthed him.

And yet…

Still Death was silent.

Thanos clenched his fists and grew larger, ever larger. The hyperspace bands closed in, crowding his awareness—an inescapable feature of his newly expanded consciousness. He saw a realm where all stars, all galaxies, formed sharp-angled cubist shapes. Another was filled end to end with Trans-Dimensional Nexuses: glowing spheres linking together an infinite number of probabilities. A third realm formed a single enormous city of machines, cold circuitry pulsing in a flow of electronic impulses.

In a corner of his awareness, Thanos sensed his grandfather—regrouping. Gathering power. Preparing for another attack.

The last of my family, Thanos thought. He will die. He will die soon.

Thanos reached out to the machine city. The Gems pulsed, drawing power into themselves. The machines did not cry out; they were not built to cry out. They resisted, hoarding and channeling their power, attempting to close off circuits. But there was no resisting the Infinity Gauntlet. The machine city sparked, darkened, and died.

Thanos funneled the power down the hyperspace bands and fired it in a narrow beam. His grandfather stiffened, screamed, and tumbled backward. His ethereal body passed through the entire Milky Way, scattering stars in a pinwheel pattern.

Billions died. The hyperspace chords throbbed in agony, in disharmony.

And still Thanos grew. Stars dwindled and faded from view, too small to be perceived. Galaxies shrank to disks of light. Hyperspatial planes became visible in their entirety, webs of worlds captured and enslaved by the Mad Titan's immense power.

He looked down at his hands. On the left, the Gauntlet throbbed with power. In his right palm, cradled like coins, rested a local group of galaxies. A dozen glittering disks—the last survivors of a devastated corner of the universe.

Soon, he thought. Soon, Mistress, I will snap my fist shut and deliver these billions unto you.

Thanos glanced up. Above and around him, space seemed to curve. With a shock, he realized: I've reached the edge of the universe. This is it. This is all there is. All the strings, all the chords…everything ends here.

He could sense the heartbeat of existence… of Eternity, the all-pervasive being whose body *was* the universe. Thanos had expected resistance from Eternity, some effort to prevent the Titan's expansion. Yet Eternity was strangely quiet.

Something stirred in Thanos's hand. He looked down in alarm, focusing his senses on one of the small galaxies. This, he saw, was the domain of the Shi'ar, a proud warrior people. He sensed their ferocity, their rage at their own impending extinction. Their helpless determination to battle till the end.

Thanos's hand began to close…

Something was wrong. The Shi'ar were being slaughtered, he realized; their collective will was being drained, their life-force seeping up and out of their galactic refuge.

But not by him.

Who? he thought. Who is doing this?

"FOOLISH BOY," Kronos said, and fired the entire life-force of the Shi'ar race into Thanos's brain.

Thanos's scream shook the realms. He staggered, pummeled by the searing anger of a billion sentient beings. Their universe had been shattered; their lives had been taken. This was their revenge.

Time passed—a day, a thousand years?—while Thanos struggled to banish the Shi'ar. Kronos maintained the assault, blasting the souls of a dozen more races into Thanos's mind. The savage Badoon, the warlike Skrulls. The ravenous Brood, driven only by instinct. Old Ones, serpentine creatures from the depths of space who had inspired the darkest legends of the sea.

How? Thanos wondered, reeling under one attack after another. How is my grandfather doing this? Where does his power come from?

"YOU WOULD SACRIFICE ENTIRE RACES?" Thanos demanded. "BILLIONS OF LIVING CREATURES?"

"TO STOP YOU," Kronos replied, "I WOULD SNUFF OUT EVERY SUN IN THIS UNIVERSE."

"YOU ARE…MORE MONSTER THAN I COULD EVER BE."

"AS YOU SAID, I HAVE NOT CHANGED."

The sadness in his grandfather's tone infuriated Thanos. "YOU SHOULD HAVE SNUFFED *ME* OUT," he growled. "EONS AGO, IN MY CRIB— AS MY MOTHER SOUGHT TO DO—"

The burned-out cinder of a dead star hurtled toward him. Thanos ignored it; it could not harm his cosmically enhanced form. But as the star grew near, it suddenly blazed to life and seared his hand.

Through his pain, Thanos realized what had happened. Kronos had snatched up the star, hurled it through space—then bent time around it. By the time it reached Thanos, it had reverted to its blazing, fusion-powered prime.

He struggled to think, to purge the screeching Badoon and screaming Shi'ar from his thoughts. What Kronos had done was impossible. He had no power over time. Unless…

Thanos shot a glance at the Infinity Gauntlet. The Time Gem pulsed bright. The Space and Reality Gems glowed; the Power Gem added its power to the others'. The Soul Gem surged with the essence of the Skrulls, the Kree, the Shi'ar.

"THE GAUNTLET," Thanos exclaimed. "YOU'RE USING THE GAUNTLET!"

He looked around, panicked. He could sense Kronos everywhere, a presence echoing across the surviving stars. But the old Titan had vanished.

"MORE ALIKE THAN YOU KNOW," Kronos intoned.

His voice was coming from the Gems.

"NO," Thanos said. "IMPOSSIBLE."

Voices screamed through his body. He sent laser-impulses throughout his own gigantic form, desperately trying to burn out the invading souls.

"I NEEDED YOU ANGRY," Kronos said. "I NEEDED YOU DISTRACTED."

"THE GAUNTLET IS MINE." Thanos tightened his fist. "THE GEMS DANCE FOR *ME!*"

The Gauntlet was growing hot on his hand. Searing. It was overloading.

"ALWAYS YOU SEEK POWER," Kronos said. "BUT YOU NEVER UNDERSTAND: POWER IS NOT A GLOVE ON YOUR HAND. NOR IS IT SALVATION."

Thanos held up the Gauntlet and stared at it in alarm. The Reality Gem quivered; the Power Gem surged. The Space Gem began to smoke.

His lips moved in a silent prayer. *Mistress Death,* he mouthed. *Aid me now. If* ever *you loved me—*

The Space Gem flared bright. Thanos shrank away, blinded. He felt a tugging, a wrenching of gravimetric fields, all centered on his left hand. The Gauntlet burned white-hot—and severed the dimensional strings.

Thanos tumbled away. He was conscious of a lightness, a burden being lifted from him.

When he looked up, Kronos stood facing him, huge against the remaining stars. The elder Titan wore the Infinity Gauntlet on his own ethereal hand.

"POWER IS HOLLOW," he said.

Rage surged through Thanos. Every fiber of his being yearned to slay his grandfather, to rip the old Titan to bloody shreds. Nothing else mattered—not the souls he'd planned to sacrifice, nor the being whose love he'd hoped to win. Not even his own life.

But he knew it was useless. He had lost the Gauntlet. Already he was shrinking, regaining his meager status as a Titan in a world of gods. Kronos towered above, looking much as the old man must have in ancient times, when he'd ruled Olympus with a velvet fist. The elder Titan reached out and fanned his gigantic fingers, sending Gem-power glimmering out through the remains of the shattered universe.

Thanos's anger began to fade. A terrible jealousy rose up to take its place, a pain rooted in loneliness. He tried not to think of *her*—of the love he'd dared to seek, the gift he'd hoped to bestow. The dream that had now died.

The last thing he saw on Kronos's face was a terrible look of pity.

FOUR

KRONOS reached out with the Gauntlet, across all the realms, through the mists of time and the farthest bands of hyperspace. With the Space Gem, he restored the worlds and galaxies that had been rent asunder. The Reality Gem restrung the strings, restoring the universe to its former shape and character. The Time Gem straightened loops, unknotted paradoxes, restored worlds and creatures to their proper life-paths.

The Soul Gem released the Shi'ar, the Kree, the Badoon, and a dozen more races, repairing their worlds and their bodies. The Mind Gem healed terrible memories, granting peace to the universe's billions. The Power Gem pulsed bright throughout, fueling Kronos's act of universal healing.

He saw a smoking black world and with a thought made it blue again. Sought out a billion scattered atoms and in a single heartbeat reshaped them into a fierce, needle-shaped satellite: a guardian to the planet below.

Kronos paused. He owed a debt to the humans, who had freed him from his prison. He wielded the

Reality Gem like a laser, stitching and knitting their lives back together.

In a bar called the Gravity Well, on the lowest level of the Peak, Reed Richards welcomed his friends, Ben Grimm and Johnny Storm, with open, extended arms. The Avengers—Iron Man, Captain America, Thor, Captain Marvel—shared a victory toast. The Vision and Wanda, the Scarlet Witch, enjoyed a more tentative, but no less heartfelt, reunion.

Namor, the Black Panther, She-Hulk, the Silver Surfer, Spider-Man: All were returned to their lives, with only hazy memories of the battle just fought. Maria Hill supervised the arrest and exile of Captain Styx aboard *Sanctuary.* Even Drax the Destroyer, the simple-minded weapon that Kronos had forged long ago, was restored to his proper place alongside his comrades half a galaxy away.

As a final kindness, Kronos located the astral form of Doctor Strange, lost and tumbling amid the windswept realms. He plucked up the startled sorcerer and deposited him in the Gravity Well among the Avengers, a large glass of cognac overflowing before him.

When the work was done, Kronos looked down at the six Gems. They glowed, casting patterns of light across the back of his hand. They seemed to say: We are ready. Use us, now. Use us to create the universe *you* want.

Kronos felt the temptation. The same lure had led him, eons ago, to the rash actions of his youth. In that horrible moment, all unwitting, he had destroyed Olympus—and set in motion the diaspora of gods that ultimately led to his grandson's rise.

"NO," he said. "NEVER AGAIN."

With a flick of the Gauntlet, he tore an arc-shaped rift in the fabric of space. Six separate warps appeared, each leading to a different band of hyperspace—to the farthest, most remote corners of existence.

"GO."

The Gems popped out of their casings, hovering for a moment in free space. Then they fanned out and vanished, each into a different warp.

Kronos's Gem-granted abilities were fading. But as an Elder of the universe, he retained enough power to thrust his consciousness outward. He saw the Shi'ar galaxy, restored to its proper position in space. The machine city; the cube galaxies of the remotest hyperband. The blue planet Earth, crackling with costumed, powered beings.

All restored. All as they had been.

Only Thanos eluded Kronos's gaze. Perhaps he was dead, reduced to his component atoms. If not, the humans would have to deal with him themselves. Kronos's task was done.

The arc-warps hovered in space before him. He reached out and waved a hand through the rift. The warps vanished.

Kronos was tired. He thought of the confession he'd made to his grandson: I HAVE NOT CHANGED.

Maybe I have, he thought. Maybe now, at long last.

He took one last look at the little blue world, then turned and warped space one final time. Returning—of his own free will this time—to his quiet exile.

○━━━━━━━━━━○

AT THE exact center of the universe, between an uncharted nebula and an enormous naked singularity, a small figure floated. Its granite form was inert, unmoving. Alone in defeat.

Thanos did not sleep, but neither did he move. There was no hope left in him, no will, no thought for the future. He had achieved his greatest dream, wielded ultimate power—and lost it. He survived, but in a purgatory of his own making.

How long will I live? he wondered. How long will I be haunted by this failure?

As he drifted, still as a stone, a tiny sound encroached on his consciousness. A familiar voice, deep as a growl but light as fallen petals. His heart leaped in anticipation.

"My darling," the voice said. *"Come."*

His eyes opened. Was it her, at last? Was this Death?

Something warned him that he had entered a new paradigm. A new reality, different from any he had known before.

"Come to me."

INTERLUDE ONE

THE SENTENCE

THE CASTLE floated in space, three stories high and a quarter-mile wide. Frozen jewels shone from immense stone columns; enormous gargoyles stared down from the turrets. Twin carved faces—a huge skull and a beautiful young woman—flanked the thick wooden door that stood atop a stairway of worn slate. Smaller skulls spilled from every window and ran up and down the walls, creeping across the stone façade like ivy.

Thanos docked his wheezing single-flier ship and launched himself out of the cockpit, into open space. Cold stones cracked as he landed on the flat-carved meteorite that held the castle.

He rose to his feet, staring up at the huge carvings. Two faces of Death: the destroyer and the comforter. Age and youth. Horror and beauty.

He allowed himself a moment of hope. He had built this castle with his own two hands, as a gift to his dark love. Now she had summoned him back here. Did that mean she forgave him his trespasses, his failures? Could it be that she did love him, despite everything?

"Master?"

Thanos whirled, annoyed. At the edge of the castle wall, a small humanoid figure stood watching him. The figure wore a thinsuit and oval-shaped helmet, fitted to his elongated head. One of Captain Styx's lesser officers; as he shifted nervously back and forth, Thanos struggled to recall his name. Nil. That was it.

"I received your message," Nil continued, a slight quiver in his voice. "I'm afraid the, uh, the rest of the crew aren't coming. Even the ones that escaped. After the business with the, erm, the uh-uh-uh Gems—"

Thanos turned away, raised his hand, and without looking loosed a plasma blast in Nil's direction. Nil didn't even have time to scream. One moment he stood before the looming castle; the next, he was a wisp of vapor.

Thanos turned and strode up the stairs, leaving the last of Nil to waft off into space.

Inside the heavy double doors, the castle's main hallway was filled with air. Thanos allowed himself to breathe. He didn't require oxygen, but his senses felt stunted, limited without the Gems. He craved input: a sound, a taste, a stray scent.

A stench of mildew and decay washed over him. He looked around at the high, green-tinged walls, built of stone blocks weighing half a ton apiece. Thanos had salvaged them from the planet Agathon, from the oldest castle in the galaxy. The last Agathonian had watched, bloody and dying, as Thanos hauled away the stones one by one.

He reached out and touched the wall. It flaked and chipped against his finger. Slivers of stone fell slowly to the ground, hesitant in the meteorite's low gravity. He frowned. How long ago had he built this place? Not long enough, surely, for it to have fallen into such a decayed state?

He continued down the narrow corridor, past guttering torches mounted high on the walls. As he approached the throne room, his doubts grew. Was it truly Death who had called him here? He'd only heard her voice a few times before, on the rare occasions she'd deigned to address him. Could this be someone else? An enemy, perhaps?

Come to me.

He paused before the doors, willing his fear away. He had already lost ultimate power today. What more could an enemy do to him? What punishment, what fate could be more painful?

When he thrust open the double doors, his breath caught in his throat.

The room held hundreds of skulls. They lined the walls, covered the fixtures, even the columns reaching up to the distant ceiling. A rack of ancient weapons sat against one wall: knives, slingshots, heavy-gauge energy swords, dueling pistols salvaged from some backward world. The bones of long-dead foes littered the floor, cleared only to form a small pathway leading to the throne itself.

Mistress Death sat atop the high throne, resplendent in deep viridian robes.

Thanos stared, struck speechless by her beauty. The throne was constructed from a set of teeth and jaws 12 feet high. Thanos himself had pulled out the creature's heart and skinned the flesh from its bones.

Slowly Death turned dark eyes to stare at him. She uncrossed her legs—a divine, graceful motion—and rose to her full height. With quick, gentle movements, she began to descend the pile of skulls forming the throne's base.

He stood still, stricken with doubt, paralyzed by her beauty. Her skin shone white as marble; her face was flawless—eyes dark as pulsars set above perfect cheekbones, all framed by a regal silk hood in dark cerulean tones. Her lips were pale but full, with just a hint of blood pulsing beneath. She was as tall as Thanos himself and as slim as a single-stemmed rose.

We're alone, he realized. That was unusual. Death normally traveled with a guard of demons and animal-men.

"Mistress," Thanos said. "I come to you in a somewhat diminished state."

She stared at him with a blank, enigmatic intensity.

"I had hoped to present you with a great bounty," he continued. "An offering, a gift of billions of souls. But my grandfather…"

She stopped and held up a hand. Her eyes narrowed, as if to say: *No excuses.*

"Of course. Yes. I merely wish you to know: I have not abandoned you. I will never stop trying to win your love."

A slight smile tugged at her lips.

"Already I have begun setting new plans in motion. Masterworks of slaughter, weapons that will shake the stars." He clenched his fist. "I *will* be worthy of you, Mistress. I…"

Mistress Death held a slim, black-nailed finger up to her lips.

"Mistress?"

Her eyes locked onto his. Thanos found he could not look away. In her gaze, he saw worlds colliding, a massive starship punching a hole through the stars. Gray steel planes, bombs with fins, cities reduced to ash. Bodies torn apart; a woman's flesh melting from her face.

She stepped closer.

Thanos held his breath. Was it possible? Did she love him after all? He had come here empty-handed, his life's work in ruins. But he had *tried*. Had that proven his devotion? Was the mere attempt enough?

He reached out to take her in his arms. She was cold and warm, vacuum-death and starfire. Her flesh was paper-thin, her muscles wiry. Her hands reached out to encircle his neck.

This, he thought. This is everything. I will never stop, Mistress. I will bring you the stars, the soul of every sentient being that has ever lived.

Her lips parted. He closed his eyes and leaned in for the kiss.

Cold teeth bit down on his lip. Bone sliced through rocky skin, digging deep, drawing blood.

Thanos cried out. His eyes shot open to see Death's true face: a grinning skull, stark white against her deep blue hood. He could almost hear her cruel, silent laughter.

He struck out in anger. When he slapped her face, he expected to hear the clatter of bone, the shattering of enamel. But instead he felt flesh—the flesh of a woman, warm and yielding against his savage blow.

Thanos howled with rage. Psionic energy poured out of him; cosmic beams blasted from his eyes, fanning out in waves through the room and out into the halls of the castle. The stones of Agathon bent and cracked under his assault.

He was oblivious, lost in a raging blood fever. His lip ached, but that pain was nothing compared to the pain of betrayal. His love had spurned him, rejected his offer. Returned his affection—at the moment of his greatest vulnerability—with a vicious, personal attack.

She would pay, he vowed. He would bring her to her knees, hear her bones crack beneath his powerful fists. Then...then maybe she would understand...

He shook his head, his vision clearing. The room still stood, but in his rage he'd cracked the high throne in half. Skulls tumbled onto the floor, mixing with grains of rock that spilled down from the ceiling.

And Death was gone.

He turned sharply at a creaking noise. A heavy wooden door swung open on thick hinges. The room beyond was dark and indistinct. With a shock, he recognized it as Death's bedchamber.

A woman's hand appeared from within, finger curled, beckoning him inside.

He paused. Remembered the feel of Death's cheek as he struck her, the impact of his granite hand against soft flesh.

He strode to the door, crushing skulls beneath his feet. A strange excitement, some terrible masculine urge, came over him. If she awaited inside that room, if this were all some twisted game, he would force her to confront what she'd awakened. He would make her feel his power.

The room was dark, windowless. Skull-patterned wallpaper, just beginning to peel, lined the walls. In the center of the room, dominating the space, stood a high, canopied Victorian bed. Dark crimson curtains surrounded the bed, suspended from posts carved to resemble ancient snake demons.

He walked to the bed, his heavy steps shaking the room. He leaned forward to place his knee on the bed and thrust the curtain aside.

Nothing. No one here. He was alone.

Consumed by fury, he ripped and tore at the bedcovers. He yanked a curtain down, rending it from end to end. He snapped a post free of the bed, cracked the carved serpent in half, and flung its severed head across the room.

He sank onto the bed, struggling to clear his head. A strange sensation came over him, a deep fog of unreality. As if he'd entered into a fever dream, a sort of cosmic delirium. He almost laughed. Was there such a thing as an Infinity Gem hangover?

Then his thoughts grew dark again. Death was gone. She had *lured* him here, to this chamber that he himself had furnished. Everything in this room, all the trappings of the castle, were tributes of his love—

No. Not everything.

He crawled to the edge of the bed, swept aside a half-torn curtain, and stared back toward the door. A large wardrobe stood against the wall, its polished mahogany surface carved into four segments: two thin, hinged doors in the center, and a larger mirrored panel on either side.

He walked to the wardrobe, examined it. He had never seen it before. He stood before one of the mirrors, studying his image. His blue-gold battlesuit was torn; his boots were stained with mud. His lip was red with blood.

But still he was Thanos.

A movement in the mirror. Behind him, on the bed, something stirred. He whirled around, eyes wide. Could it be…?

"We have to kill it," a voice said.

A shiver ran up Thanos's spine. The voice belonged to a woman—but not his beloved. This woman was smaller, with short-cropped dark hair. Pale like Mistress Death, but with a wide, lush face. She perched on the edge of the bed, staring at him with disturbingly familiar eyes.

"We have to kill it before it grows," she said.

The words seemed to drill down into his brain.

He had heard them before; it was his very first memory. And he recognized the woman who had said them, years ago, as she'd stared down at the newborn baby in her arms.

"Mother?" he asked.

She nodded, those intense eyes still fixed on him. She sat back on the damaged bed, swept away a fallen curtain, gathered a few pillows together. Then she smiled—a cold, condescending smile.

"Will you join me?'

Once again, rage took hold of Thanos. He remembered that smile, remembered his mother's icy demeanor throughout his childhood. A visceral memory rose to his mind: the feel of her still-beating heart as he ripped it from her living chest.

"I will," he rumbled. He advanced toward her, fists clenching open and closed.

She watched him, calm. "If you harm me," she said, "she will never speak to you again."

He stopped.

"That's better." She patted the bed. "Sit, won't you?"

He felt trapped. Again, the dreamlike fog seemed to envelop him.

"I'll stand."

"As you like." She shrugged. "You've had quite a day, Thanos."

At the sound of his name, he shivered again.

"You have failed," she continued. "Failed yourself, your allies—and your Mistress, most of all. She is displeased."

He glared at her, struggling to keep from trembling. "So she has sent you in her place?"

"Don't pout, Thanos. It ill becomes you." Again, the disturbing smile. "My little monster."

"My mother is dead," he said. "You are but a shade, a projection of my own consciousness."

She looked around at the wardrobe, the fallen bedding, the torn curtains. Shrugged again, as if she knew something he didn't.

"Why are you here?" he hissed.

"To grant you another chance."

He blinked. Peered at the mother-shade, searching for a sign of ridicule. But she seemed serious.

"If my Mistress will accept my love," he said, "I would pluck the stars out of their firmament, one by one, and lay them at her feet."

"Very poetic. But that's not what she has in mind."

She stood up and walked past him. She was small, shorter than he remembered. When she reached the wall, she turned and gestured.

"Behold the Infinity Wardrobe," she said.

He followed her to the mahogany structure. Its mirrors reflected his image twice, evoking the twin Death's heads mounted on the exterior of the castle.

"Her message to you is this: You may yet win her love. *But.* To do so, you must abandon all you hold dear."

He looked up at her reflection, past his own. "I have already lost everything. The Gems, my ship, my power. All that I owned."

"The Gems were *taken* from you. Along with

all trace of the battle just fought." Her accusing eyes bored into his. "If you wish to change, you must renounce your birthright, your ambition, your powers as a Titan. You must start over."

He stared at his own image, thoughts whirling in his brain. Abandon everything? Renounce his birthright?

"You must renounce Thanos," she finished.

"Even if I agreed to this..." He turned to her. "How could it be done? How does a man, a god, anyone—how does one leave one's *self* behind?"

The mother-shade gestured at the Infinity Wardrobe. Its doors snapped open with a click. The mirror-panels swung wide on hidden hinges.

Inside the Wardrobe, cosmic forces swirled against darkness. The shade reached out, sweeping the energy from side to side. Images began to appear, fanning across the space like pages of a book. Figures: some humanoid, some unspeakably alien. A fierce Skrull warrior, green chin wrinkled with scars. A tall, strong human woman. A living Brood starship, large as a moon, swimming the seas of space.

"Within the Infinity Wardrobe, there are many skins," the shade whispered. "Many bodies to be worn."

Thanos stared, mesmerized by the display. A humanoid cat-being appeared, hissing and clawing. A squat creature with hoofed feet and two thin, snaking heads. A winged hive insect with hundreds of jagged teeth.

"I must become something else?" Thanos asked.

The shade nodded.

An oval-headed alien with silver-mirror eyes. A wraith-like being, bristling with weapons. A squid-like creature from the dawn of time.

"You," Thanos began, "you expect me to start over—"

"She expects it."

He turned away from the display. "And then?"

The shade stepped back. Her image seemed to flicker in the dark room.

"Then we will see what path you take."

"I must win her love?"

"You must become worthy."

For the first time, Thanos realized: I don't know how to do that.

The shade smiled, as if reading his mind. "Perhaps you will learn. Perhaps not."

"No. I refuse." He shook his head. "Without my power, I am nothing."

"You are nothing *with* it."

He turned back to the Wardrobe and watched as the image of a thin, blank-featured humanoid flickered past. Then a short creature with a limp. A squat worker-drone with thick, calloused hands.

Was that what he would become? A small creature, planet-bound and helpless, laboring all its life to scratch out a meager existence?

He turned back to the image of his mother. His resentment, the old rage he held toward her, had faded. Perhaps, he thought, I am changing already. Emptying out like an upturned pitcher.

"Tell me one thing." He struggled to keep the pleading tone out of his voice. *"Does* she love me, deep down? Behind all the masks, the games, the cruelty? Does she care for me at all?"

For just a second, the shade seemed to flicker and change. Her cheekbones grew more prominent, her skin paler. Death's eyes bored into his, defiant and cold.

There would be no answer to his questions, he knew. Not today. He glanced from his Mistress over to the Wardrobe, then back to the pitiless skull of his true love. She had only one message for him, and he knew it as surely as if she'd spoken it aloud:

This is your last chance.

He felt as if some greater power were at work here. As if all his actions had been decided long ago.

When he blinked, the mother-shade had returned. She took hold of one door of the Wardrobe, folding it back to reveal the mirror. She cocked her head at him and raised one questioning eyebrow.

Thanos took a last look at his reflection. At the stone-skinned conqueror who had sought to topple the stars. The destroyer of Titan, wielder of the Infinity Gems. Villain, reaver, slayer of civilizations.

Then he reached out, flung open the Wardrobe's doors, and stepped inside.

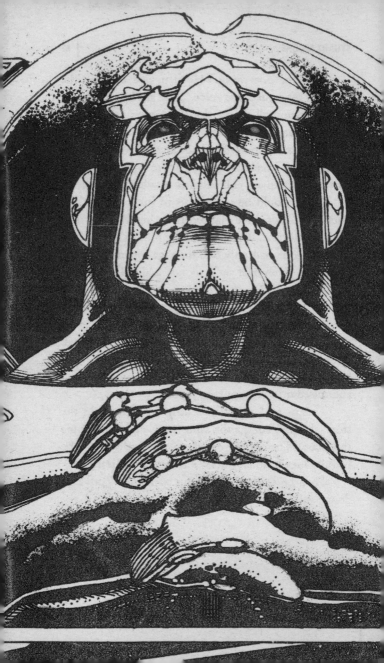

BOOK TWO
SACROSANCT

The planet Sacrosanct, home of the Universal Church of Truth, may be the galaxy's greatest example of religious idealism gone sour.

The Church was launched with noble goals of raising up the poor and disenfranchised of the universe. Its founder, the enigmatic Magus, supervised the construction of the settlement surrounding the Palace on Sacrosanct. The city was designed in the shape of an ankh, the Church's holy symbol of life. The Palace itself sat at the very top of the ankh's oval—the "head"—and was partly constructed within the holy Mount Hiermonn.

But internal corruption and the Magus's disappearance led to a general decline within the Church. This rot was quickly reflected in the surrounding city: The bulk of the oval became a reeking, corruption-filled bazaar. Church-funded housing within the two "arms" of the ankh decayed into slums and shanty settlements. The Church focused its efforts on defending the road to the spaceport, which stretches down the extended "leg" of the ankh shape; and on building higher and deadlier fences around the Palace to keep out the rabble and criminals populating the bazaar.

As for the Church itself, it maintains a strong presence on Sacrosanct. But its glory days of spiritual exploration are long gone, along with its charismatic Matriarchs. Once a vital religious power in the galaxy, the Church has become an aimless, soulless corporation—an engine of profit for a scattered coalition of shareholders, devoid of any purpose, calling, or higher meaning.

GALACTIPEDIA

FIVE

" **NIL! MOVE** your skinny arse!"

Thanos stared up at the merciless, bloodred sun. He leaned forward on his shovel and wiped sweat from his brow.

"NIL!"

The foreman's lash tore into his bare back. Thanos cried out in pain and dropped the shovel. As he bent down to retrieve it, the chain around his waist strained and clanked, knocking the man bound to him off balance. The man swore and elbowed Thanos in the side.

Before Thanos could pull himself back upright, the foreman brought the lash down hard again. Pain lanced through Thanos. He could feel the wet blood running down his back, mixing with sweat.

The foreman stood before him, glaring. The man was old, with dark red skin and white eyebrows. He wore lightweight robes; the chain around his neck held a tarnished metal ankh—the symbol of the Universal Church of Truth.

"You must be the stupidest press-ganger I've

ever seen," the foreman growled.

The others laughed. They'd all stopped to watch: ten men and women in all, representing a variety of humanoid species. All were tied together at the waist, loose chains dragging in the sand between them. Before them stretched a half-dug pit, almost ready to be filled with the electro-quantum fence posts piled up beside the work site.

Thanos grimaced up at the sun. The desert was ruthlessly hot, devoid of shade. Fierce carrion crows, much larger than their Earth counterparts, circled above.

"Well?" the foreman said. "Don't you know your own grud-buggered *name?*"

I'm not sure if I do, Thanos thought. Not anymore.

Part of him wanted to blast the foreman, to strangle him with these chains, to take that crimson head in both hands and twist until he heard the satisfying snap of his neck. That was what he would have done less than a month ago. It was what Thanos, conqueror of worlds, would have done.

But he wasn't Thanos anymore. He looked down at his hands: thin and green, the long, tapering fingers wrapped tightly around the shovel's handle. Those hands were dirty and rough. More calloused than when he'd arrived, three weeks ago.

Nil's hands.

"Sorry, sir," he said. "My mind was elsewhere."

The foreman snorted and spat on the ground.

The other laborers stepped away, snickering. All but one, Thanos realized. The woman on his immediate left was studying him with a serious expression. She was thin and blonde, with bright eyes and a pale complexion. She seemed an unlikely candidate for a chain gang.

"Listen up, you mudgrubs!" The foreman held up his chain, displaying the ankh symbol. "You've all committed offenses against the Church—which, in its infinite benevolence, has allowed you to atone this day."

Thanos followed the foreman's gaze over to the Palace of the Universal Church of Truth. It gleamed in the distance, its high stone walls broken by golden spires. Behind it loomed the high, rocky cliffs of Mount Hiermonn.

"Your labors will keep the Church safe, not only from the scum and lowborns of the medina…" The foreman gestured toward the teeming city a half-mile to the south. "…but also from the nomadic sandgrubs. In security there is faith!"

A few of the chained workers repeated the words, halfheartedly.

The foreman circled behind the group, snapping the lash in the air. The man beside Thanos thrust his shovel into the ground. On his other side, the thin woman lifted a load of sand into the air.

"As for *you*…" The foreman's voice hissed in Thanos's ear. "…here's something to focus your mind."

Pain exploded across Thanos's back. This time, he managed not to cry out. He lifted his shovel and began to dig.

"Better smarten up," the thin woman said when

the foreman had moved out of earshot. "The Church loves discipline. Any excuse to inflict pain."

He spoke slowly, choosing his words with care. "I'm used to being on the other end of the lash."

She raised an eyebrow. "Keep digging."

He frowned and thrust the shovel into the sand. He wasn't yet accustomed to this physique, which was slimmer than his old body. "Nil" was wiry and strong, but his muscles worked differently.

"What did you do, anyway?" the woman asked. "To get sent here?"

Thanos glanced around. The man on his other side was ignoring him, jabbing his shovel viciously into the sand.

"Boosted a shipment from the spaceport," he said. "I thought…I don't know. I thought it might give me a stake, somewhere to start from on this world."

"But you chose the wrong target."

"I didn't realize the shipment was intended for the Church."

She nodded in sympathy. "They get your whole crew?"

"No crew. It's just me." He strained, lifting the full shovel. "Had a one-man flier, but it fell apart the second I landed. So I figured, let's see what Sacrosanct has got. But the Knights caught up with me on the road to town. I'm pretty fast on a hovcycle, but the shipment slowed me down."

"That road's a death trap—perfectly straight, no hiding places. The Church designed this planet, you know." She laughed. "You've got a lot to learn about Sacrosanct, Nil."

A flash of anger passed through him. Was she making fun of him?

"Was the shipment valuable at least?"

"That's the worst part," he replied. "It was just a crate of Belief Fonts…those cheap religious trinkets they sell to the rubes. Practically worthless."

The trench was about three feet deep now. The foreman snapped the lash and motioned toward the Palace. The group climbed out of the trench, chains clanking, and moved along. When they'd reached their new position, the foreman gestured for them to begin digging again.

"What about you?" Thanos asked. "You don't look like a typical Sacrosanct criminal."

A cautious look entered her eyes.

"What's your story?" he persisted.

"A high Cardinal took a bit of an interest in me." She grimaced. "He tried to entice me into the deep Palace chambers, the ones built into the mountain. I told him to, let's say, pleasure himself with a mnemonic flail."

"And he sent you here."

"Like I said." She rattled the chain linking them together. "They're into discipline."

He studied her for a moment. She was quite lovely. Thanos the Mad Titan would have pursued her, sought to break her spirit and make her his own. But Nil…

What *did* Nil want?

Again, the foreman moved the group along. They drew closer to the Palace, to the line of fences and towers separating it from the rest of Sacrosanct. The main gate came into view; guard towers flanked the wide metal doors, manned by quantum-rifle snipers stationed high above. A narrow road stretched down from the gate, toward the bustling marketplace a half-mile south. A small merchant hovercraft, piled high with silks and rich-colored blankets, chugged slowly up the hot desert road.

"I'm Felina," the woman said. "Felina Shiv."

He couldn't place the accent. "Where are you from, Felina Shiv?"

She didn't answer directly. "You're new to Sacrosanct?"

"I'm new," he said.

"What are *you* doing here?"

He hesitated. "Rebuilding."

"You're off to a pretty crap start." Again she jangled the chain connecting them. "How long ago they catch you?"

"Four days." He grunted, digging with the shovel. "That mudgrub in town has probably rented my room to someone else by now."

"You didn't pay him up front, did you?"

Thanos frowned.

"Never pay up front. First rule of Sacrosanct." She smiled, a playful look stealing over her delicate features. "Tell you what. You help me, you can bunk with us for a while."

"Us?"

She turned away, an enigmatic smile on her face. Along the road, maybe 60 feet away, the merchant hovercraft was approaching the Church gate.

"Wait," he said. "Help you with *what*—"

Felina raised her fingers to her lips and let out a shrill, piercing whistle. As the foreman and gangers turned to look, a small animal darted out from under the blankets on the hovercraft. It shot toward the chain gang, a galloping blur of motion.

The foreman whirled toward Felina. "What the flark?"

"Spike!" the chained woman called out. "Diversion!"

The animal slammed to a halt. Now Thanos could see: It was a house cat. A pet tiger, with fierce claws and sharp fangs. It raised its head and hissed.

The foreman motioned the chain gang back. He stalked toward the cat, snapping his lash on the ground.

"Little tabby," he snarled. "You'll be meat for the Church dogs tonight—"

The cat leaped up, claws slashing through the air. It landed on the foreman's face, cutting and swiping. He screamed, dropped his lash, and reached up to pry the animal off. Together they tumbled to the ground.

The chain gang turned to chaos. Prisoners yanked at their chains, knocking each other over. Thanos barely maintained his footing as his male neighbor pulled their chain tight, trying to snap it.

"Avia!" Felina yelled.

The merchant hovercraft drew to a halt a short

distance from the gate. The blankets flew off, and a small, muscular woman took off at a run, heading straight for the chain gang. Her skin was dark, her hair cropped short. Her eyes met Felina's, and she nodded.

"Who's that?" Thanos asked.

Felina smiled. "That's my sister."

The foreman writhed on the sand, his face drenched in blood. He punched and swiped at the cat, but it held fast, clawing his forehead and scalp.

A jostle of chains threatened to knock Felina to the ground. Her sister—Avia—arrived just in time to steady her. Avia was shorter than Felina, with strong arms and less glamorous features.

"Hot day to play in the sand," Avia said, gesturing at the ditch.

"I wanted a tan." Felina lifted her chained arm. "You take care of this?"

Avia tested the chain. She almost lost her balance as the man on Thanos's other side pulled his chain again. The prisoners had fanned out in several directions. Some of them were trying to escape, while others had stopped to watch the foreman's battle with the cat.

"I've taught you how to break these," Avia scolded, waving the chain at Felina.

"I'm crap at fighting." Felina twisted her mouth into a pout. "You know that."

"Excuse me," Thanos said. "If you *can* break these chains, I think you should do it now."

Avia glared at him. "Who the flark are you?"

"He's a friend," Felina said, "and he's got a point."

Avia followed her sister's gaze to the foreman, who was crouched on the ground. He held the cat at arm's length now and was calling for help on a shoulder radio.

Shaking her head in disgust, Avia turned to the heavens and yelled, *"HENRY!"*

Thanos heard an answering squawk and looked up. With a flash of wings, a fierce orange-feathered hawk plunged down out of the blue sky, headed straight toward him. He ducked.

Avia laughed—a warm, harsh sound. Felina's laughter was lighter, more girlish.

As the hawk approached, the other chain gang members scattered. Prisoners on either side of Felina and Thanos dropped to the ground, but Avia held the chain steady. The hawk glided in to land on Avia's outstretched arm. Its head twitched, sharp beak slicing the air as it turned to stare into its mistress's eyes.

With her other hand, Avia held up the chain binding Felina to Thanos.

The hawk fluttered once, rose up, and dove for the chain. As its beak moved furiously, Thanos caught a quick glimpse of steel teeth snapping open and closed. He turned away, forcing himself not to flinch.

With a loud metallic *tick,* the chain snapped apart.

The foreman was on his feet, holding a dagger. He circled around the cat, moving closer. But every time he lunged, the cat leaped back a few paces and hissed again.

The next few seconds were a blur. The hawk seemed to be everywhere at once, snipping and breaking the web of chains. The chain gang scattered, most of them running across the desert toward the medina. Others headed south to the low houses, where poor relatives could hide them from the Church authorities.

"Come on," Avia said, grabbing her sister. "Let's—"

Howling with anger, the foreman slashed his dagger at Felina. She sidestepped gracefully, but he recovered his balance and moved forward again. Avia reached for her sister just as the hawk whirled in midair and started down.

"No, Henry!" Avia yelled. "You might hurt her!"

A movement to the north caught Thanos's attention. A squadron of the Church's Black Knights had burst out of a side entrance of the Palace and were headed toward the chain gang on foot. They were almost half a mile away, but their deep purple robes cast an unmistakable shadow on the desert landscape.

Swearing, Thanos dropped low and ran. He grabbed hold of the foreman's robe and wrenched him away from Felina, then jabbed a fist into the man's stomach. The foreman doubled up, blood dripping from his injured face onto the sand.

"I'm focused now," Thanos growled.

As the foreman looked up, Thanos punched him savagely in the nose. The man whimpered and collapsed in the sand.

Thanos stared at his own hand. Once, he would have blasted an opponent with plasma-charged cosmic energy. Now, he thought, I'm just a thief, struggling for my life. Like everyone else on this depraved, pitiful world.

He looked up. Four sets of eyes stared down at him with almost identical amused expressions. The hawk again sat on Avia's outstretched arm; bizarrely, the cat had assumed a similar position on Felina's. The little tiger must have weighed 15 pounds, but the slim woman held it with ease.

Felina raised her other arm. Hissing, the cat scampered around her neck and onto the far arm. With her free hand, she reached to help Thanos up.

"What do you say, Nil?" she asked. "Feel like joining up with the Shiv Sisters for a while?"

He glanced over at the Knights. They were drawing closer; he could make out the heavy proton pistols they carried. They'd be here in less than a minute.

"Hell yeah," he replied.

"All right!"

And then they were running across the desert, toward the medina. Toward the huge marketplace, the center of the city, full of stalls and pubs and hiding places. The underbelly of Sacrosanct, outside of the Church's control.

Thanos caught Avia staring at him. Her sharp eyes were suspicious, careful. But as they ran side by side, she slowly nodded at him.

"You know how to fight," she said, and clapped him on the back. He winced as his lash wounds reopened.

The sun baked down, the Black Knights drew closer, and his back stung in agony. Carrion crows circled overhead, watching for any sign of weakness. But somehow, as his now-thin legs pounded across the sand, Thanos—Mad Titan, onetime conqueror, master of armies and worlds—found himself smiling.

SIX

THE SISTERS led him to their home, a single-story shack located in the western arm of the city. Some of the surrounding houses were built of stone or oak; others were barely more than canvas tents. Tiny patches of grass, poor excuses for yards, were marked off with low fences made of wood and scavenged metal.

As they approached the door, Avia's hawk took to the air. Its wings flapped wildly, and it was briefly lost in the glare of the sun. Then it glided back into view, coming to rest on the low roof of the shack.

Avia gestured at the hawk, perched like a guardian above the door. "Best burglar alarm you can buy," she said.

Felina raised an eyebrow. "Long as he stays outside."

Avia aimed a thumb at her sister. "They don't have carrion birds where she comes from."

It was clearly an old argument.

Felina held out her arm, and the cat, Spike, leaped to the ground. Spike trotted up to the door and pushed it open. Felina followed it inside.

Thanos paused in the doorway and cast a glance

around. An elderly blue Kree woman stood in the next yard, hanging laundry on a line attached to her trailer. She glared suspiciously at Thanos.

He felt strangely at home.

The cramped kitchen was a portrait of chaos. Dirty plates, forks, and knives were strewn everywhere. On the small table, a half-dozen partly dissected mice lay sprawled out in different states of mutilation.

Felina wrinkled her delicate nose. "Do you have to do that here?"

"Unless you want Henry preying on the neighbors' pets."

"I'll clean up here. *As usual.*" Felina snorted and gestured toward the back of the house. "Why don't you take our guest to his room."

Avia gestured. "Come on."

The room measured less than six feet on a side; it was barely more than a closet with a tiny window set into the far wall. A crude radio sat atop a pile of wooden crates next to a gamma-coil lamp. Clothes lay in heaps on the floor.

"Ain't much," Avia said. "But you aren't exactly in a bargaining position."

She swept aside a pile of jackets, revealing a child-size bed. Thanos started to protest: The bed would surely collapse under his weight. Then he remembered his new body. He perched tentatively on the edge of the mattress.

"It's fine," he said. "Where is she from?"

Avia paused in the doorway. "What?"

"Your sister. Where they don't have hawks."

She frowned.

"Okay," he continued. "Where are *you* from?"

"I was born on Sacrosanct." She shrugged, as if dismissing the matter. "They say nobody's from here— everybody comes looking for something. But I am."

Then he noticed: The wall behind Avia was covered with swords. They hung in neat rows, at least a dozen of them. Some looked very old, a few had gleaming jewels implanted in the handles.

He gestured at the swords. "Yours?"

Avia nodded.

"You any good?" he asked.

"I've won a few duels."

Still standing in the doorway, she took a long look at Thanos. Then she reached into her pocket and threw him a sheet of paper: a map, crudely drawn in pencil. It showed a squarish building with various arrows indicating doorways.

"It's a meatpacking plant," Avia explained. "On the edge of the medina. Felina's been planning a heist." She shrugged. "See what you think."

He nodded, studying the map.

"Might get a few steaks out of it, anyway." She frowned. "But no more Church capers. That's asking for trouble, on this world."

"You know…" He paused. "You don't have to do this. For me, I mean. The Church might come after me."

Avia laughed, a harsh sound. "They don't give a flark about a couple escapees from a chain gang. Not worth the trouble."

She turned and started to leave. Then she paused and pulled one of the swords off the wall, a thin-bladed model with an ornate carved hasp. She thrust it in the air, feinting and lunging in the small room.

"You fence?" she asked.

He sat still, unflinching, as the sword tip passed an inch from his nose. "Never took the time to learn."

"I could teach you."

There was something in her eyes, under those hard, dark features. He stared back at her, trying to read her intentions.

She shrugged, tossed the sword on the floor, and left.

He sat on the bed for a long time, the map held limp in his hand. The air was thick and stuffy. Through the window, the muffled sounds of an argument drifted over from the Kree woman's house.

What, he wondered, was Avia's game? She was very different from her sister. Felina's appearance was meticulous, her manner graceful and calculated. Something about her screamed *highborn*. Thanos found her alluring, yet strangely distant.

Avia was rougher, more muscular—clearly the fighter of the pair. In his earlier life, Thanos would have shoved her aside to pursue Felina. But he'd felt something odd when Avia looked at him. Was she interested in him? Or was this all a business proposition, an offer in exchange for some unknown service?

The answer came to him in a single word, whispered in his mind. Perhaps by the mother-shade, or by his own subconscious. A truth so simple, so alien to his experience, that it had never occurred to him.

What was Avia becoming to him?

A friend.

ON TUESDAY they pulled their first caper. A modest effort, to see whether they could work together. In the sweltering bazaar, Felina flirted with a silk vendor, running her hand across a fine Antaran scarf. At a wordless command, Spike the cat let out a loud meow and leapt up on the merchant's table, claws scrabbling. While the merchant panicked and Felina apologized, Thanos and Avia lifted a box of Aesirian silks from the far end of the table.

Afterward, they celebrated at a bar called T'Spiris. It was a spacious hole-in-the-wall with a long, curved oak bar scavenged from some long-dead world. When Felina drank too quickly and tipped her mead over, Thanos mopped up the spill with an Aesirian scarf worth ten thousand credits. The Sisters laughed.

WATER, Thanos learned, was scarce on Sacrosanct. The desert world was plagued by droughts, and the Church snatched up most of the clean water for its ceremonies. Ale, mead, and wine actually sold for *less* than a pint of drinkable water—and were more popular among the lowlifes and pirates who frequented the city.

ON WEDNESDAY they took down a hovercraft delivering brandy to the northern quarter of the medina. The heist didn't go smoothly. Avia tried to carry too many crates at once, which slowed her down. The driver managed to disarm Felina and put a knife to her throat. Thanos had to restrain the cat from going to its master's aid, a task that gained him quite a few scratches.

The hawk, Henry, distracted the driver long enough for Avia to run him through with a short dagger. Felina escaped with a few cuts and a sore neck.

After that, they resolved to plan more carefully.

ON THURSDAY Avia began to teach him swordplay. She handed him a small, thin sword, barely a foil, and asked him to "show me your moves." As he whipped the blade around his small room, she placed one hand under his arm and the other on his waist. Under the light pressure of her fingers, he straightened his spine and slowed his movements.

The sword struck the gamma lamp, shattering it in a shower of sparks. Avia rolled her eyes and declared the lesson finished for the day.

ON FRIDAY he bought an old Earth blanket for his room. He stood among the open-air stalls of the bazaar, holding the blanket, relishing the soft burn of the wind on his healing back. The medina teemed with life: spacers, merchants, thieves, men and women and nonbinary sentients. All moving in their own patterns, buying and selling and grifting, or just begging coins to survive.

A smell of spiced meat reached his nostrils, grilled in the next stall by a Shi'ar commoner with faded plumage. Thanos smiled, mouth watering, and reached for a few coins.

ON SATURDAY they decided to try the slaughterhouse caper. This time they played to their strengths. Felina kept lookout while the hawk screeched and flapped outside the entrance, drawing the workers' attention. Thanos and Avia lifted one huge Vacabeast on a hook apiece, carrying them out on their backs through the rear entrance.

Afterward, they had a good-natured argument about cooking techniques.

IN THE oldest sector of the city, adjacent to the spaceport, the old, green men drank away their days. They talked in slurred tones of ancient times, before the powerful Magus had come to Sacrosanct. It was called Homeworld in those days. The only world the green people knew.

The Magus had decimated their people, then

enslaved the survivors. It was their labor that had built the Palace, one massive stone at a time. Their descendants who scratched out a living in the spaceport and the medina. A few lucky ones became Black Knights.

Thanos had never had much use for religion before. But, hearing these stories, he couldn't help admiring its power.

○————————○

ON SUNDAY Avia took him to a huge tent where beings of various races competed in fencing contests. They watched as two huge Ba-Bani fought with laser-mounted épées. By the end, both had multiple raw burns covering their bodies. They bumped fists and hugged before leaving the tent.

Avia paid for a practice ring and tossed Thanos a sword. He held his own for almost three minutes before she disarmed him. He was learning.

"Spare credits, mister?"

○————————○

SPARE credits, mister?"

Monday. Thanos stopped at the edge of the bazaar and turned to see two green-skinned children looking up at him. They were of a stocky race—Froma, probably—but their cheeks were sharp from malnutrition. He tossed them a few coins, and they ran off.

He gazed back at the bazaar, at the teeming stew of humanity baking under the bloodred sun. For the first time, he considered the incredible poverty suffered by most of the residents of Sacrosanct. The fragility, the precariousness of their lives.

Did most of the universe live that way?

He realized he was changing. He enjoyed the heists, the weapons training, the thrill of robbery and success. But something was missing; some flame had been doused. His all-consuming ambition, the urge to conquer and dominate all those around him, had been snuffed out.

With a shock, he realized it had always made him miserable.

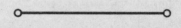

ON TUESDAY, they sat in an outdoor café plotting their next heist. Late-afternoon clouds rolled overhead, threatening a rare shower. Felina stabbed and scratched with her pencil, sketching out the approach to the road, while Spike lapped up a bowl of milk on the ground.

"Carnelia," Thanos said.

Felina looked up sharply. "What?"

"You're from Carnelia."

"How did you know that?"

"I finally placed the accent."

Avia cocked her head. "Somebody's been around."

"One of the wealthiest worlds in the galaxy," Thanos remarked.

Felina glared at him for a moment, then shrugged and smiled. She had a pretty smile.

"I hated Carnelia," she said. "Well, I hated my father. First chance I got, I jetted off-world with a pretty thief. She had milk-white skin and a very dark attitude."

"*That* worked out poorly," Avia said.

"Yeah," Felina acknowledged.

"I found this one cryin' on the spaceport tarmac. Took her in." A thoughtful look came into Avia's eyes. "My own folks are long gone. Mom worked at the spaceport; Dad was a Black Knight. The Church still took the Knights' vows *very* seriously back then... fraternizing with the locals was a complete no-no. One day, when I was 16, they were both just...gone."

"The Church?" Thanos asked.

Avia shrugged.

"I'm glad you found me." Felina rested her head on the larger woman's shoulder. "Even if you are a townie."

Avia punched her on the arm. Felina winced in mock pain.

"So I take it..." He paused. "You're not really sisters."

They both laughed.

"Your turn, Nil," Avia said. "Where do *you* come from?"

He started to answer, a lie forming on his lips. Then some subconscious instinct made him turn his head. He looked around at the crowds, the robed merchants and armed spacemen. A troop of Kree on shore leave marched by, lips curled in disapproval of the Sacrosanct masses.

When the Kree were gone, Thanos saw her. Deep-blue skin, fierce eyes, dark-painted lips. She wore a plain black shift and no headgear, but he recognized her immediately.

Proxima Midnight. Assassin of the Black Order—the onetime elite guard of Thanos's conquering army.

She turned, catching his gaze. Flashed him a sneer, then whipped her head away and walked on.

She doesn't recognize me, he realized. Of course not. I'm different now.

"Nil?" Felina asked.

He barely heard her. Beneath his feet, the ground seemed different. The wind had shifted.

Within him, the flame had flickered back to life.

SEVEN

"**DID YOU** see the look on that Strontian's face?" Laughing, Avia slammed her glass down on the table. "He never even saw what happened to those minidrives."

"I thought he was gonna cry." Felina giggled. "You were right. I thought the spaceport would be too exposed for a heist."

"Nobody cares." Avia poured another glass from the pitcher. "That place, everybody minds their own business."

Thanos took a long draft from his glass. He felt restless, angry. The Arcturan brandy was weak and tasteless.

Midevening in T'Spiris. The crowd was midsize: locals with extra cash, a few hookers not trying too hard to line up work. A group of teenaged Zatoans sat laughing around a table, their wispy, red head-fins waving in the thick air, a pile of bows and arrow quivers stacked up beside them.

One of the Zatoans pulled out a sharp arrow to show the others. The bouncer, a thick-bodied crimson Sakaaran, glanced sharply at him from the door.

Spike the cat wriggled in Felina's lap. She lifted him up and let him crawl onto the table. He lapped up the last few cheese puffs from a plate, then nosed his way over to Thanos, searching for more food. Thanos pushed him away.

"Hey." Felina touched his arm. "Those hyperdrives are small, but we can unload 'em easy. I know a couple lone fugitives looking to get offworld."

"Slow down, girl," Avia said. "Gonna get yourself killed."

"You gotta take some risks." Felina rolled her eyes. "Or do you just wanna scrape by all your life?"

"Tell you what: You learn to handle a knife, I'll take more risks."

Thanos ignored them. His attention was focused on the bar. A troop of Kree soldiers in green-and-white uniforms stood joking with the bartender, a beanpole-thin Earthman with a bad combover.

"That mudworm is watering down the drinks," Thanos rumbled.

"Harry?" Felina glanced at the bartender. "Sure. He always does that."

"What do you expect in this toilet?" Avia asked.

Thanos squinted at the bar. The chandelier above it was half burned-out, its three remaining tachbulbs casting dim shadows. A lone Skrull sat slumped at one end of the bar, his chin shriveled and flaking from alcohol-related dehydration.

The Kree drifted over to one side of the bar, revealing another patron: a tall, elegant, blue-skinned woman. Proxima Midnight drank alone, alternating sips from a bright orange cocktail with puffs from a Dolenzian sniffing jar.

Thanos spat the last of his drink onto the table. "Not worth the effort to urinate this back out."

Avia frowned. *"Somebody's* in a mood."

One of the Kree soldiers glanced at Proxima, raised an eyebrow, and swaggered toward her. She glared at him with blank white eyes. The Kree stopped as if he'd hit a force field, shrugged, and turned back to rejoin his friends.

"Hey, check this out." Felina reached into a bag beneath the table and pulled out a small proton rifle. "I boosted it from the Strontian's locker."

Thanos could feel the bouncer's eyes on them now. Weapons weren't exactly uncommon in T'Spiris, but things could get out of hand quickly.

"What d'you say, Nil?" Felina mock-aimed the rifle at Thanos's empty glass. "Want me to teach that watery drink a lesson?"

Avia snorted. "Shoot off your pretty eyelashes, more likely."

Thanos couldn't sit still anymore. Something about Proxima's presence made him anxious, impatient. Stirred up ideas, plans, memories that he'd been trying to ignore. He pushed his chair back, stood, and started toward the bar.

The bartender looked up. "'Nother?" Thanos glared at him and kept moving.

Proxima didn't acknowledge his presence. Her

nose hovered over the sniffing jar, inhaling the thick red smoke.

"I was wondering," he began.

"Keep wondering." She let out a little cough. "Keep walking."

"Wondering what a member of the *Cull Obsidian* was doing in a pit like this."

She froze. Took a quick sip of orange liquor and turned to face him.

"Haven't heard that term for a while," she said.

"But you know it."

"I never liked it."

"Sometimes what we *like* doesn't matter."

Her eyes narrowed. Overhead, another of the chandelier's tachbulbs flickered and went dark.

Thanos stood his ground, feeling oddly detached from his actions. Provoking Proxima, he knew, was a suicidal act. Under Thanos's former command, she'd murdered whole civilizations, slain armed combatants with only her black-light spear and her bare hands. Without his Titan powers, Thanos was no match for her.

Yet something spurred him on. The flame, burning brighter now.

"I think we could work together," he continued.

"I've seen you around the medina. You've been following me." Her voice was strangely even. "Do I know you?"

"Maybe." He leaned on the bar and pushed her drink aside. "Maybe you'd like to know me better."

He ran long fingers along her cheek. It was

smooth and hot, as if lit from a blue fire within.

He didn't see her move, but all at once her hand was clamped around his wrist. Her grip was like iron, but he didn't flinch. She leaned in to whisper in his ear.

"Should I see you again," she hissed, "I will paralyze your spine with three precision-aimed pulses of black light. Then I will strip you nude, chain you to the wall, and force you to watch as I carve obscene words into your body. Not too shallow, not too deep. Each time you begin to pass out from the pain, I will inject you with a stimulant and twist your neck to view the next incision point." She paused for breath. "Your castration will be slow, unhurried. Every few minutes I will pause to pull out another few feet of your intestines. I hope I won't be forced to tape your eyes open—I've always considered that a crutch."

He glanced at the table. Felina and Avia watched, frowning. They looked uncertain.

"And *then*," Proxima continued, "if I am feeling cruel…unusually, unnaturally cruel…"

She released his arm and threw her drink in his face.

"…I will turn you over to my *husband*."

Avia was already on her feet. Thanos turned and motioned her away. The bartender paused in the act of wiping a cloth across the bar. The other patrons tensed, waiting to see what would happen next.

Proxima ran her eyes across the group and let out a silent snort. Her far hand, he noticed, held her spear half-concealed beneath the bar.

Thanos reached up with a thin hand and wiped the sticky liquid from his face.

"You might like to know," he said. "He's watering down the drinks."

Proxima stared at Thanos for a moment. Then she turned blank eyes to the nervous bartender. She held up her glass, examining it in the dim light of the chandelier.

"This tastes like Brood spit," she said.

The bartender took a step away, toward the group of Kree. "No refunds," he said.

One of the Kree glanced at the bartender and nodded, a signal that meant: *Got your back*. He'd donned his warrior helmet, Thanos noticed.

Avia and Felina stood at the table, keeping their distance. The cat sat along Felina's outstretched arm, licking his lips. Behind them, the Zatoans stood watching, bows held loose at their sides.

Proxima kept her eyes on the bartender. "Is my friend correct?" she asked, gesturing at Thanos.

The bouncer took a step forward, hefting a thick, wide-bladed axe in his enormous hands.

When the bartender ducked down, Thanos moved instinctively. He leapt up and swung himself down behind the bar. He analyzed the cramped space in an instant: shelves of bottles, glasses, a metal trough filled with ice. And the bartender, reaching for a Shi'ar hunting rifle.

Thanos reached out and snapped the bartender's wrist. As the man howled in pain, Thanos backhanded him in the face. The bartender crashed into a shelf, shattering a row of bottles. The smell of sour whiskey wafted out as he tumbled to the floor.

Thanos paused, breathing hard. His heart was racing. He felt alive, energized, reborn by this small act of violence.

A shadow fell over him. He glanced up—to see Proxima Midnight crouched on the bar, looking down. She held her spear poised to strike; it crackled end to end with energy.

She's studying me, he realized. *Taking my measure.*

A group of Kree soldiers approached her from behind, their weapons raised. One warrior leaned over the bar and pointed down at the bartender on the floor. Another reached out to grab Proxima's hair.

Without turning, she jerked her arm back and thrust her spear through his chest. Black light blazed out from the weapon, covering the Kree in a dark, crackling shroud. He gasped and fell to the floor, dead.

Proxima leaped off the bar, her spear whirling. The Kree fell back, eyeing their fallen comrade, and drew their weapons. As they struggled to aim, Proxima flew over their heads and crashed down onto the Zatoans' table, shattering it along with their drinks.

One of the Zatoans held up his bow and let out a battle cry. They looked around for Proxima, but she was already leaping to another table.

Thanos jumped back over the bar. The Sakaaran bouncer caught sight of him and stalked forward, swinging his axe. Thanos dropped low as the blade whistled over his head.

The bouncer swung the axe back, preparing for another blow. Then he cried out in pain as a thin metal blade burst through his stomach in a gout of blood. Thanos looked back to see Avia yanking her sword free. The bouncer swiveled in agony to face her.

She brings those swords everywhere, Thanos thought.

Felina stood behind her sister, holding up the Strontian proton rifle. The Zatoans closed in on her, pointing and taunting. She let out an energy burst, but her aim was off. The beam struck a barstool, splintering it to pieces.

Avia whirled to help Felina. But the bouncer was still on his feet. Clutching his wound with one hand, he jabbed out with the other to punch Avia in the stomach. She stumbled back and turned to face him again.

"Nil!" Felina cried.

Before he could reach the Sisters, a deafening screech filled the room. Thanos saw a blur of wings, and a sharp beak plunged down into the lead Zatoan's neck. Blood spouted from his artery. The other Zatoans scattered, nocking arrows into their bows. They fanned out, struggling to aim at the flapping, furious hawk.

Proxima stood against a table, smirking at the assembled Kree warriors. She bent her finger, beckoning them forward. They advanced cautiously, glancing at each other for support.

A pale white finger descended on the shoulder of the rearmost Kree soldier. He stiffened, as if an electric shock had run through him, and turned. A thin figure in gray and gold, with alabaster skin and an almost unnaturally long face, stood smiling at him.

Thanos ducked down, below the fray. He recognized the newcomer: the Ebony Maw, another member of the Black Order.

The Maw whispered in the soldier's ear. "This is pointless, you know." The man twitched, staring straight ahead. "Your *life* is pointless."

Thanos held his breath, watching, as chairs flew over his head. He struggled to hear over the noise of breaking glass and splintering bones.

"You don't belong here," the Maw continued, snaking around to speak into the paralyzed Kree's other ear. "You should really kill yourself."

Thanos heard a sizzling noise from Proxima's direction. He turned and saw a trio of black beams stab out from her spear, enveloping three more Kree in cold, deadly sheaths of energy.

"NIL!"

He didn't even see Avia toss him the sword. But he grabbed it out of the air by reflex, whirling it around just as a young Zatoan took a swing at him. Thanos was too slow; the blow struck him on the side of the head, stunning him.

Anger coursed through him. The boy fell back, taking aim with his bow and arrow. Thanos growled, thinking: Too short-range for that weapon, boy. Besides, your hand is shaking.

He thrust his sword forward, snapping the

boy's bowstring in half. The Zatoan yelped and scrambled away.

The other Zatoans gathered around their friend. They glanced at Thanos's glaring eyes, then at the strange sight of the Maw's long fingers wrapped around the head of the mesmerized Kree. They turned to see Proxima crouched atop another Kree, stabbing her spear into his heart. Over and over.

Eyes wide, the Zatoans ran for the door.

Thanos looked around. Felina had taken cover behind an upturned table. A trio of kitchen staff appeared from behind the bar, watching in horror. Spike the cat leaped up on the bar and hissed at them. They retreated out of sight.

The Sakaaran bouncer staggered to his feet. His hand was clenched to his stomach, holding in his bleeding guts. But he turned to Avia, brandishing a small proton gun. She whirled—just a bit too slow.

Thanos lunged, spearing the bouncer in the back of the knee. The Sakaaran howled and dropped his gun. As he started to fall, Avia spun on her heel and plunged her sword down through his heart.

She staggered over to Thanos, breathing hard. They stood together, leaning on the bar, as the Sakaaran gurgled his last breath.

Avia looked over at Thanos. "You're learning."

A blast rang out. The last Kree soldier dropped to the floor, his skull shattered by the blaster in his own hand. The Ebony Maw stepped gracefully away, twining and untwining his fingers in the air.

Proxima stood above a heap of her victims. The Maw nodded at his partner, then gestured at the dead man at his feet.

"He was sad," the Maw explained.

An uneasy quiet settled on the room. Tables lay broken, glass and blood mingled with spilled drinks. A puddle of blood spread out from the bouncer's unmoving body. The smell of cheap liquor mingled with sweat in the humid air.

Avia moved toward Felina, coaxing her out of hiding. Henry the hawk screeched over to join them, and Spike leaped up easily onto his mistress's arm. Together, like a bizarre family, they stared across the long room at Proxima and the Maw.

Proxima climbed up on top of the bar and surveyed the room. Only one patron remained: the old Skrull at the bar, gazing up at her with liquor-fogged eyes.

"This establishment," Proxima cried, "is now the domain of the *Black Order!*"

She fired her spear straight up. The black beam struck the chandelier, sending an arc of energy between the two remaining tachbulbs. They sparked and went out.

The Ebony Maw glided across the floor, avoiding the fallen bodies. He paused to glance at Felina and her cat, then at Avia. Then he turned to study Thanos.

Thanos opened his mouth to speak—then whirled at a dull thudding sound. The old Skrull had collapsed, headfirst, onto the bar.

Proxima laughed. She leaped down to the floor, clapped Thanos on the back, and gave her partner an enigmatic nod. Then she crossed behind the bar and kicked the bartender's limp body. He groaned, then lapsed back into unconsciousness.

"I could use a drink," Proxima said, reaching for a bottle. "Anyone else?"

EIGHT

"HE WAS born a Titan," the Ebony Maw said, "with all the power of his royal heritage. From birth, his strength and reflexes were extraordinary. He could endure the heat of a star or the cold of space without flinching. His strength was the equal of any species in this galaxy.

"But that does not *begin* to describe the being called Thanos."

Two hours past midnight in the medina. The last merchants had packed up, folding their tables and vanishing into the dark. Beggars scoured the dirt pathways, seeking discarded crumbs of food and the occasional lost coin.

"Even in his youth, he craved conquest. And knowledge. Knowledge with which to better serve his dark mistress, his Oedipal appetites. The persistent drive to entropy lodged deep within his psyche."

Twin moons struggled to penetrate the nighttime haze. The last hovershuttle of the night rattled down the long road to the spaceport, ferrying drunken spacers back to their ships.

"So he sought more power. And as that power grew, he recruited followers. Builders, Reavers, Blood Brothers. Advance scouts, who reveled in slaughter and the honor of serving the most savage conqueror the universe had ever known."

The bars still shook with laughter and music. Locals spilled in and out of the perpetually crowded Chariot, which served the cheapest drinks in town. At the south end of the bazaar, off the spaceport road, Nachie's served ale and fatty foods to hardy spacers. The usual crowd of off-duty Black Knights sought comfort and sin at the Pig and Barrister.

"We of the Black Order were the first among his soldiers. Some of our number paid the ultimate price, giving their lives in support of his dream."

Of all the taverns, only T'Spiris was silent. The bodies of Kree soldiers, piled up outside the main entrance, were enough to deter even the thirstiest resident of Sacrosanct.

Inside, the Ebony Maw finished his tale. "Thanos devoted his existence to Death," he said. "Now he is gone. And we survivors, we unlucky few—"

"We must rebuild," Proxima said.

She walked toward the table, a bottle of Shi'ar whiskey in her hand. As she passed the body of the Sakaaran bouncer, she paused to give it a sharp kick.

Avia watched, nodding, as Proxima refilled her glass. Felina paused in the act of scratching Spike's neck to cast a suspicious glance at the blue warrior-woman. The cat let out a tentative hiss.

Across from them, Thanos leaned back in his chair. He was barely paying attention. His thoughts were a whirlwind, plans and ambitions rising and falling in his mind.

"I've heard of this Thanos," Avia said, sipping her sake.

"That was his face in the sky last month." The Maw studied her reaction. "Didn't you see?"

Thanos looked up sharply. The Maw was referring to the battle between Thanos and his grandfather. But those events had been erased from reality—rewritten by Kronos with the aid of the Infinity Gems. As far as Thanos knew, only he himself retained those memories.

He studied the Maw's elongated face and pure sea-blue eyes. The Maw had always been different from his comrades in the Order: dedicated to Thanos's cause, but possessed of a sharp, elliptical intellect that made his actions difficult to predict. His perceptions, too, seemed to transcend time and space in some strange manner.

Did the Maw fully comprehend the degree to which time had been rewritten? And how much of that knowledge had he shared with the rest of the Order?

For that matter, Thanos wondered, does he know who I am? Can he see through this false skin?

Felina turned to the Maw, hesitant—skeptical. "I didn't see any face."

"You were drunk last month," Avia laughed. "All month."

"You're drunk *now.*"

Proxima eyed the Maw from across the table. "I don't recall that, either," she said. "I haven't seen Thanos for over a year."

"Ah." The Maw leaned back in his chair, studying the light patterns in his drink. "Different bodies, different perceptions."

Proxima yanked out the last chair and sat down heavily. "Solipsistic nonsense." She took a long drink of dark whiskey.

"They used to talk about Thanos on…on my world, too," Felina said, slurring a little. "But I always figured the stories were exaggerated."

"In his youth, Thanos was a restless soul," Proxima said. "So he traveled with pirates, killers, rapists…the worst scum of the universe. And he lay with women. Many women."

Avia and Felina exchanged a glance.

"Thanos sired a dozen children, then a dozen more. Several hundred in all, on dozens of worlds." Proxima paused, took another long drink. "And then he murdered them."

Thanos bolted upright in his chair.

Felina frowned, leaning forward over the table. "All of them?"

The Maw smiled. "Every one," he whispered.

Confusion surged through Thanos. Was it true? Had he actually committed this genocide, snuffed out the lives of his own offspring?

Of course he had. He remembered each incision, every blow, the sight of each tiny face as its life ebbed away. But the memories seemed like snapshots, distant glimpses of another life. A book of atrocities written by someone else.

He looked down at the bouncer's body, the overturned chairs, the remains of the chandelier. Finally he turned back to the table, observing the body language of the four people seated around it. Felina was clearly alarmed, either by the Order or by their stories of genocide. Or both. Avia seemed troubled, but in a drunken, distant way.

Proxima and the Maw leaned back in their chairs, their manner apparently casual. But Thanos realized: They're studying us. We've passed some initial test, and now they're trying to see what kind of people we are.

At the same time, the Order's presence had solidified Thanos's determination. They were deadly warriors, killers on a whole different level from the petty thieves he'd met on Sacrosanct. He'd fought alongside Proxima in the past, had witnessed the destruction she could accomplish. The Maw had no physical powers, but his twisted intellect had been known to wipe out cities. Here, on this backwater world…could two of them be enough to help Thanos accomplish the goal that was, even now, beginning to gel in his mind?

And if so, could he persuade them to do it?

"He was your god," he said. "And now your god is dead."

Proxima and the Maw both turned toward him.

"Thanos spent his life chasing Death," the Maw replied. "Perhaps he has found her at last."

"Then what is your purpose?"

"The universe reveals these things. In its own time." For the first time, the Maw seemed uncomfortable. "We seek a new path."

"We seek to *rebuild our ranks*," Proxima snapped.

The Maw bowed his head in deference. "As you say."

"You're recruiting?" Avia asked. "Here on Sacrosanct?"

Proxima gave her a condescending smile. "Think you could serve the Black Order, girl?"

Avia shrugged. "Maybe."

"We've got our own thing going," Felina said. Her gaze strayed to the door.

"What about you?" Proxima said to Thanos. "What have *you* to offer?"

Thanos hesitated.

"You said you wanted to work together," Proxima continued. "What work did you have in mind?

"I'm a thief," Thanos replied. "Perhaps jewels?"

Proxima let out a snort.

"Perhaps a *lot* of jewels?" he prodded.

"How many?" the Maw asked.

"The complete treasury of the Universal Church."

They all turned to stare at him. Henry the hawk fluttered over to land on Avia's arm.

"Go on," the Maw said.

"It's all stored here," Thanos explained. "On Sacrosanct, I mean. In a vault deep within Mount Hiermonn. The greatest thieves—the most notorious cutthroats in the quadrant—have tried and failed to get hold of it."

"But you know a way in."

"I know *half* a way. For the rest, I need…"

Followers, he thought. Reavers. Advance scouts.

"…friends," he finished.

"The Church vault." Avia stared at him. "You been holding out on us, Nil?"

"I've acquired a map of the Palace. Just this week, from a merchant who didn't know what he had." He reached into his bag and pulled out a small memory module. "I wanted to make sure it was real before I told you."

Felina frowned at Avia. "You always said we should steer clear of the Church."

"Unless the prize is big enough," Avia said, staring at the module.

Thanos snapped the module onto a holo-mount in the middle of the table. He tapped the mount twice, and a hologram rose up into the air. It showed a schematic of the gold-spired Palace, cut away to reveal pieces of the structure hidden within the mountain.

"It's fairly detailed," he said, pointing. "Includes the inner sanctums, the chambers built into the mountain. The treasury room is here. You can see the—"

"No," the Maw said.

Everyone turned to look at him.

"You're lying," the Maw continued. "You're not interested in jewels."

The air seemed to turn cold. The Sisters exchanged alarmed glances. Spike the cat let out a low growl.

Again, Thanos wondered: Had the Maw seen

through his disguise? Was the Order playing some cruel cat-and-mouse game with him?

Proxima poured herself another whiskey. "The Ebony Maw is never wrong," she said, her voice deceptively casual.

Felina touched Thanos's hand. "Nil?"

Thanos glanced at Proxima, then at the Maw. For a moment he considered coming clean, revealing his true self. After all, the Order had pledged themselves to Thanos once before. If they believed him, they would follow him again.

But why should they believe? "Nil" bore no resemblance to the Titan they'd known. And he had no way to prove his identity. He'd renounced both his innate powers and the enhancements he'd accumulated over the years.

No—better to use subterfuge. It wasn't Thanos's way. But maybe it was Nil's.

"All right," he said. "Okay."

He reached for the whiskey.

"In my youth, I did things I'm not proud of. Treated women poorly; used men and cast them aside when they served no purpose."

Proxima nodded. The Maw just stared at him.

"Along the way, I guess I lost faith. In…everything I'd always believed." He drew a deep breath. "I didn't come to Sacrosanct to be a thief."

"Why did you come?" Avia asked.

"I heard stories. About…about the powers of the Church Matriarchs."

"Belief energy," Proxima said.

Felina frowned. "What's that?"

"The power they use," Thanos said. "In order to gather followers."

The Ebony Maw sat back in his chair. "The Matriarchs are a thing of the past."

"But their power…the 'belief energy' they wielded…it's still there." Thanos turned away. "I can feel it in the air, whenever I'm near the Palace. I have to find out if it's real."

"Hold up," Avia said. "You want to break into the Palace—risk your life—just to find this mystical power that might or might not really exist?"

"And if it *does* exist," Felina said, "might not even be here anymore?"

Thanos bowed his head. He counted out three seconds before he spoke.

"I'm…searching for something," he said. "Without faith, a man has nothing."

"Or a god," the Maw mused.

"Or a god." Thanos looked up. "I meant it about the jewels, though. They're real. If you help me, you can have them."

"If. We help you." Proxima enunciated each word carefully.

Thanos nodded.

Avia whispered something to Felina. Proxima, stoic, sipped her drink. The Maw moved his head up and down, side to side, studying Thanos closely.

The hawk squawked at the cat, who hissed back.

"I've…spoken…with some of the Church cardinals," the Maw said. He turned to the hologram and jabbed a thin finger into the image of the mountain. "The Church's inner sanctum is guarded by a quintuple-redundant series of quantum alarms."

"Yes," Thanos acknowledged. "Someone has to get in and cut the power—"

"—which is controlled from a hidden junction room somewhere deeper inside the mountain." The Maw ran his hands over the hologram, shifting its image, zooming in and out. "I don't see that room marked on this schematic."

"I know. I was hoping that together, we could figure it out."

"Faith is a fragile commodity." The Maw snapped off the hologram. "It certainly won't get one past a quantum alarm system."

"There is our other member," Proxima said.

The Maw turned to her. He seemed unhappy with the suggestion.

Thanos raised an eyebrow. *They're talking about Proxima's husband*, he thought. Corvus Glaive, leader of the Black Order. One of the most fearsome creatures in the galaxy—a warrior who had led his own people to slaughter for the glory of Thanos.

"I hesitate to call on his services," the Maw said.

"Then I will."

Proxima rose from her chair, pulling out a comm unit. She crossed to the bar and began speaking in low tones.

For the first time, Thanos allowed excitement to rise within him. *This might actually work.* With the combined power of the Sisters, Proxima, Maw, and Corvus Glaive…

"He's on his way," Proxima said, striding back toward the table.

It was a volatile alliance. But if he could keep it together just long enough…

Felina and Avia sat huddled, whispering. Proxima poured herself another drink. The Maw just leaned forward over the table, his unblinking eyes fixed on Thanos.

A sudden, sharp smell of ozone. Above the bar, a glowing yellow rift had appeared in the air. Thanos recognized it instantly: teleport energy. Had Corvus Glaive gotten hold of a *teleporter?* That could be useful…

The energy faded. In its place, a small, hairy figure stood atop the bar. Shaggy red hair, pointed ears, a stained loincloth and boots. He looked around, surveying the group. His eyes came to rest on the Skrull, last of the former patrons of I'Spiris, who still slumped unconscious at the bar.

"Need a snort?" the newcomer asked him, producing a bottle from his pack. The Skrull snored, but didn't move.

"Pip the Troll," Thanos said, staring at the bar.

Proxima turned to Thanos. "You know our new recruit?"

Stupid, Thanos thought. Yes, he knew Pip. In times past, he'd kidnapped the troll, tortured him, wiped his depraved mind, and restored it again. They'd also fought side by side, much to Thanos's distaste.

But "Nil" wasn't supposed to know any of that. With one slip, he'd endangered his cover.

The Maw glared at the bar. "Clearly Pip's infamy has spread far."

Well, Thanos thought, *that covers it.* He breathed a sigh of relief.

Pip leaped off the bar and trotted over to the table. He grinned at Proxima and touched a finger to the end of her spear. "You rang, P? Ow." He shook his hand in pain and turned away. "Maw. Maw. MAWWW! Why the long face? Get it?"

The expression on the Ebony Maw's face indicated that, not only did he get it, he'd gotten it from Pip several times already.

"And what's this? Ladies! Of a classier sort than we generally find in these parts, for sure!" Pip cast his eyes from the cat to the hawk. "Tell you what, fellas. I'd like to talk to your girls here. Why don't *you* go eat *him?*"

Grimacing, Avia gestured for Henry to take flight. Felina lowered her arm, and Spike sauntered off with a parting hiss.

"Alone at last." Pip jumped up on Avia's lap, startling her. "What you got under those tights, baby?"

Avia pulled out her sword.

"Right! And *you.*" Pip leaped away, swiveling to take Felina's hand. "Didn't I meet you in a flesh-pit on Degenera?"

"No." Felina frowned. "Well, maybe yes."

Avia turned to her. "You never told me about that!"

Thanos cleared his throat.

All eyes turned to him. The Maw leaned back; Proxima took another drink. Pip let Felina's hand slip free and turned to approach Thanos.

"This mook is your other recruit?" Pip asked.

This was the real test, Thanos knew. He'd spent much more time in Pip's company than he had in the Black Order's. Would the troll recognize his gaze, his manner—even in this new body?

"He looks like a silk merchant," Pip snorted.

Avia laughed; Proxima shook her head.

Felina was staring at the door again; she seemed profoundly uncomfortable with the proceedings. She's the weak link, Thanos realized. The least likely to go along with the plan.

"Pip." The Ebony Maw touched the holo-mount on the table, causing the Palace schematic to reappear. "Perhaps you could take a look at this."

The troll climbed up onto the table and circled around the display. It was as tall as he was. "Sorry, guys," he said. "I've never been inside the Palace. I've been inside other palaces. One time this lady in a tiara tied me up with a lasso and took me to her island…"

Thanos ignored the troll's chatter. Once again, destiny had dropped an opportunity in his lap. Pip was an irritant—a petty criminal and an unreliable ally. His familiarity with Thanos made him an even bigger risk than the others—and to top it off, he smelled terrible.

But he had one thing none of the rest of them did: He was a teleporter.

"Oohhh," Pip exclaimed. "Check this out!"

He strutted inside the hologram and arched his back, wiggling around until the largest minaret on the castle seemed to protrude upward from his crotch.

Thanos sighed and poured another drink.

NINE

"THESE are the Church's confession booths," the Maw said. "Many of them are equipped with electroshock and waterboarding equipment, for reluctant converts." He paused. "Religion is a competitive business."

Thanos frowned at the hologram. "That section is open to prospective converts," he said. "We need to get *much* farther in than that."

They stood behind the bar, which had been broken up, its sections rearranged to serve as a command center. The only working holo-mount had been removed from its table and reinstalled on the bar; it now displayed the Palace schematic, with more detail filled in after a few days' investigation.

"I bet they got a hell of a wine cellar," Pip said. He was perched on the edge of the bar, drinking from a bottle of whiskey.

"That's the treasury room," Thanos said, pointing. "Right there. With your combined power, you should be able to reach it."

"No, we won't."

They all turned. Proxima Midnight sat alone

at a table, polishing the end of her spear with a tiny sparking implement.

"There's no way to get that far unless you cut the alarms. And we still don't know the location of the junction room."

Proxima took a long drink and turned back to her spear. The gadget in her hand emitted a small spray of viscous liquid; on contact with the spear, it sparked into a flash of black-light energy.

She never gets drunk, Thanos thought.

"Alarms!" Pip snorted, then wiped whiskey from his mouth. "I could 'port in there."

"And face the entire Black Knight army on your own?"

"Like I said, there's no way to get in without cuttin' the alarms."

"I got it! *I got the location!*"

Thanos turned along with the others. Avia stood in the doorway, out of breath, with Henry fluttering at her shoulder.

"The junction room?" Thanos asked.

Avia nodded. Henry flapped across the room, coming to a halt on the bar in front of the Maw. The hawk opened his jaws, screeched, and spat a memory module onto the bar.

Thanos snatched it up and plugged it into a free port in the holo-mount. The hologram fizzled and turned to static. Slowly it resolved into a much more detailed, higher-resolution image. Bare outlines sharpened into detailed schematics showing individual confession booths, sanctuary spaces lined with pews, and a large central cathedral.

"I knew it." Pip scuttled across the bar, pointing. "Wine cellar."

Proxima rose to her feet, staring at Avia. "How did you get this, girl?"

Avia walked unhurriedly to the bar. She was hiding it, but Thanos could tell she was nervous.

"There's this hava vendor in the north quarter," Avia began. "A Mephitisoid woman. Her aunt used to look after me when my mom was…busy at the Church. Anyway, she's dating a Knight."

"And he supplied the schematic?" Thanos asked.

"Nah, he doesn't have that kind of clearance. But he plays poker with some higher-ups in the Church, including a Bishop with a bit of a gambling problem."

"So the *Bishop* gave the Knight the plans," Proxima said.

"Nope. The Bishop owes a lot of money to this Shi'ar ex-warrior who converted to the Church just last week. The Shi'ar was still undergoing his Rites of Flagellation when an elderly Cardinal took a liking to the shape of his fin. The Shi'ar's training kicked in, and he snapped the Cardinal's neck without even thinking. Right there in the cathedral." Avia paused for breath. "So the Shi'ar called in the Bishop's debt. The Bishop agreed to help him get rid of the Cardinal's body, and the Bishop hired the Knight to help him. The Knight was in a confession booth making out with Alz'beta, the Mephitisoid hava vendor whose aunt used to babysit me, when the Bishop contacted him. So she went along."

Thanos shook his head, bewildered.

"While they were burning the body in a Cleansing Pyre, this fell out of the Cardinal's pocket." Avia pointed at the memory module. "Alz'beta grabbed it, but she didn't know what it was. She came by while I was out, but Felina traded her a Skrull lantern for it."

"Where is Felina?" Thanos asked.

"Ah, that's the trick. She also had to agree to cover Alz'beta's hava stall for the day. 'Beta couldn't wait to meet up with the Knight in his chambers." Avia shook her head. "Death really makes some people horny."

The Maw stuck a hand inside the hologram. His long white finger probed through the outer chambers, the sanctuaries, and the confession booths. He paused at the Vault, then pushed farther.

"There," he said. "That's the junction room."

Thanos studied the hologram. A series of colored lines denoting electrical circuitry converged on the small chamber indicated by the Maw's finger. The bulk of the mountain rose up around the little room; it was deep within the rocky confines that hid the Palace's darker secrets.

Thanos reached out and pushed at the hologram. Behind the junction room, solid rock stretched into the mountain. That room seemed to be the last, deepest chamber of the Palace.

"Nil," Avia said. "A word?"

He allowed her to lead him to the far corner of the

bar. Behind them, Proxima approached Pip and the Maw. The Maw tilted and pushed at the hologram, studying it from every angle.

"I'm down with all this," Avia whispered, eyeing the Order nervously from a distance. "But…"

"But *she's* not," Thanos finished.

"She's worried." Avia shrugged. "You know how she is. But, well, they *are* galactic assassins. We're just petty thieves, man."

Thanos studied her. They really look out for each other, he thought. Like real sisters—but even more closely, with greater devotion. He remembered Avia assisting him in the bar fight, the look on her face as her sword burst through the Sakaaran attacker's heart. And for the first time, he realized: They look after *me*, too.

"Let me talk to Felina," he said. "You're meeting up later?"

Avia nodded. "Alejandro's."

"It'll work out." Thanos touched her on the shoulder. "You're going to be rich."

"I like the sound of that." But she didn't sound sure.

When they returned to the bar, Proxima cast a pointed glare at Avia. Pip lay on his stomach on the bar, staring at the hologram.

"Well?" the Maw asked.

"I think I can get in there," Pip said. "But…"

Thanos frowned at him. "What?"

"I'm *definitely* stoppin' at the wine cellar first."

○━━━━━━━━━○

HALF AN HOUR later, the plan was set. Avia's doubts seemed to have evaporated. She looked enthusiastic—almost dazed.

"Tomorrow," she said, heading toward the door. "I can't believe we're doing this. You comin', Nil? Drinks are on me."

"Free drinks?" Pip looked up from the bar. "I'll take that action."

"Actually," Proxima said, "we would speak with your friend a moment."

Thanos turned sharply. There was something dangerous in her tone.

Pip vanished in a burst of teleport energy and instantly reappeared at Avia's side. He grabbed her hand, and she gave him a savage glare.

"You realize we're going to meet my sister," she said.

"In that case," Pip replied, "you ever heard of a Troll Sandwich?"

"I'm interested."

He looked up at her, astonished.

"If I get to bite the troll's head off first."

"That solves a problem," the Maw said, watching them leave. The hawk followed in a flurry of wings.

Thanos felt a tremendous sense of relief. He hadn't realized how badly Pip's chatter was wearing on him.

"Nil," Proxima said.

At the sound of his name, the relief vanished. Proxima had arranged three stools in a semicircle around the bar, all aimed at the holographic display. She gestured for him to take the middle seat.

Thanos lowered himself onto the stool, feeling wary. It wasn't like Proxima Midnight to act the hostess. As she and the Maw took up positions on either side, he felt the pressure of their stares.

"As Midnight has said," the Maw began, "we are recruiting."

Thanos nodded. "The troll."

"Pip is…a question mark," Proxima replied. "I'm not certain how that will work out."

"I am *fairly* certain," the Maw said.

"You seek the aid of the Black Order. But this…" She waved her hand at the Palace display. "…is of minor importance to us. Our first priority is to rebuild the Order itself."

Suddenly, Thanos was weary. A sense of fragility, of the fleeting nature of existence, came over him. No more games, he thought. Let's see what they know.

"The Order," he said, "which formerly served Thanos."

The Maw's eyes bored into him. "Interesting that you mention that name."

A long moment passed.

"Thanos selected us for a mixture of skill and ruthlessness," Proxima said. "But that wasn't sufficient. Each of us had to prove ourselves through sacrifice."

"Corvus Glaive's sacrifice was the greatest," the Maw added. "He condemned his entire race to death, all for the glory of his new master."

Thanos nodded. He couldn't tell where this was going. Did they know…?

"You're a skilled fighter, Nil," Proxima said. "And you're quick-witted. In theory, you would make an excellent recruit to the Order."

"But we don't *know* you," the Maw said.

He touched a control on the holo-mount, and the Palace faded from view. A face, greatly magnified, rose up in its place: a pale blonde woman with heavily mascaraed eyes.

Thanos frowned. It was Felina. He turned sharply toward the Maw.

"Kill her," the Maw said.

Thanos blinked. He whirled around to see Proxima studying him closely with those chilling blank eyes.

"Why?" he asked.

"You seek our aid," she repeated. "You must prove yourself."

"But…" Thanos's mind whirled. "The break-in. We need everyone to make that work. Felina's—she's not a skilled fighter, but—"

"She's a pretty face," the Maw said. "That will not get us past a quantum security system."

"She's also a strategist."

"I'm a strategist. You're a strategist." Proxima laughed. "The Maw is the finest strategist on a hundred worlds. We don't need another."

Thanos stared at Felina's face. He'd become fond of the Sisters, had come to enjoy the long drunken evenings in their presence. They weren't conquests to him, or even pawns. They'd become something else.

Suddenly, he realized: I haven't killed anyone on Sacrosanct.

"Even…" He shook his head. "Even if you don't want her on the job, there's no need to *kill* her. I know Felina…she'd never betray us to the Church."

A touch on Thanos's cheek made him jump. The Maw had risen from his stool, silent as a shadow, and crept around behind him.

"As we cleansed the worlds," the Maw whispered, "as we traveled with our lord, reaving and scouring and bathing the galaxy in blood, we came to realize there was another reason he had chosen us. A faith we shared—a god who gave us meaning."

Proxima touched the holo-mount. Felina's face changed, without flickering, to a glittering, grinning skull.

"You said you were searching for something," Proxima said.

"'Belief,'" the Maw said. His hands danced along Thanos's cheeks, making the Titan's skin crawl. "This is *our* belief."

Thanos tried to look away from the hologram, but it was impossible. The skull's blank eye sockets seemed to follow him, accusing him of crimes he'd committed. And even more damning: of crimes he *hadn't*.

He stumbled off the stool, twisting away. One of the Maw's sharp fingernails caught him on the cheek, drawing a small trickle of blood. He didn't remember crossing to the door, but he felt his hands pushing it open.

"Tonight," the Maw hissed, in a voice that seemed to echo in Thanos's mind. "It must be tonight."

TEN

THANOS staggered through the medina, his mind reeling. He pushed past dealers folding up their tables, electric-gartered hookers seeking their evening trade, spacemen drunk too early. Night was falling; the air reeked of smoke and spices, perfume and sweat.

A small lizard-boy brushed up against him. Thanos felt cold fingers probing in his pocket. He grabbed the boy's wrist and pulled away. The boy shot him a look of pure hatred and shook himself free.

Thanos stared at his own hand. Thin, pale green, run through with blue veins. He'd almost become used to it—but now it seemed strange, alien.

He whirled around. Tried to take solace in the chaos, the sights and sounds and smells. But the huge red sun, low over the tents of the bazaar, seared his eyes, blinding him. The air was thick, devoid of wind. Nothing held meaning anymore. Nothing made sense.

Probably nothing ever had.

Then he was in his room. Alone. Avia's swords lay scattered like straw across the small floor. Some of the blades were bent, chipped. He didn't remember doing that.

He brushed aside the foils and crawled to the bed. It looked even smaller than he remembered, as if it belonged to a small boy. He knelt before it and closed his eyes.

"Mistress," he said. "Do you hear me?"

No answer. Even the distant shouts of Sacrosanct seemed to vanish into the thick air.

"I've done what you asked," he continued. "I renounced all I owned. I gave up my power, my body, my life. I became something else."

He glanced around at the broken lamp, the cracked swords.

"I have plans. I have schemes. I am cultivating followers." He felt a surge of panic. "But now I face a choice—a terrible choice. And I don't know what to do. I am your servant, your slave. I would slay a thousand worlds for you. But I don't know what you want.

"There are no rules. I need rules." The fear began to turn to anger. "Am I Thanos, bringer of destruction? Or Nil, a humble thief? I will be either, or both, but you must *tell* me. What do you *want?*"

No answer. Just the Kree woman shouting next door, her voice muffled through the wall.

As quickly as the anger came, it departed. He collapsed on the bed, head first.

"Mistress," he murmured. "Beloved." Then, burying his head in the grimy sheet: "Mother?"

Still nothing.

He straightened, wiped a tear from his eye. *Very well*, he thought. *I am alone, as always. I must forge my own path.*

He snatched up a thin-bladed sword and strode out of the room, his footfalls heavier than before.

HE STALKED through the dark market, past shuttered stalls and loaded-down hovercrafts, until he came to a large outdoor cantina, a late-night bar strung with q-lanterns. He wove through the close-packed round tables, ignoring a query from a waitress in a bustier and low heels.

At the last table, just before the bar, Avia and Felina sat drinking with Pip. The troll tried to push his way in between the Sisters, but Avia slapped him away. All three of them laughed.

Felina smiled at Thanos, shouted a greeting. They all turned toward him. Pip was the first to register alarm. He let out a yelp and vanished in a burst of teleport energy.

Avia leapt to her feet, pushing Felina away. "Nil," Avia began.

She knew. He could see it in her eyes. She had taught him the way of the blade; she was faster, sharper, more agile than him. Yet she hesitated.

He lunged forward and thrust the sword through Avia's heart.

Someone screamed. The crowd rose to its feet and scattered.

Avia gasped and sputtered. Reached for the sword, her trembling hands closing over his. He kept a tight grip on the ornately carved hasp and pressed forward, pinning her to the chair.

He stared deep into her eyes, feeling nothing, until those eyes went blank. Then he yanked the sword free.

People were running in all directions, grabbing their belongings. The proprietor, a short bald woman, watched from behind the bar, shaking her head. She seemed more angry than shocked.

Pain slashed down Thanos's back. He whirled just as Felina drew back a thick hunting knife, dripping with his blood.

"I knew," she said. "Somehow, I knew."

He took a step toward her. She retreated, holding up the knife before her.

"I've been practicing," she said. "I know more moves than she thinks. Than she *thought...* "

She glanced at Avia's body, bleeding on the chair. When she turned back to Thanos, there was shock in her eyes.

"Why?" she whispered.

"Because she wouldn't have let me live," he replied. "After I did this."

He pulled out the Strontian proton rifle and shot her. Point-blank, close range. Felina's skin sizzled; her nervous system shorted out. She was dead before she struck the ground.

A hideous screech filled the air. Thanos whirled

to see Henry the hawk diving at him, jaws wide with murderous fury.

He raised the rifle and fired again. Henry seemed to freeze in midair, feathers catching fire as he died. He twisted, his claws grasping hold of a string of lanterns and dragging them down with him. He crashed into the table, splintering it.

Thanos looked around. The patrons were gone, the tables empty. Even the proprietor had fled— probably to call some private security force. It wouldn't do to stay here long.

A hand touched Thanos's shoulder. He whirled to see the Ebony Maw, watching him with cold eyes.

"Our most vivid days," the Maw said, "are those on which our gods die."

Thanos looked down at the fallen hawk, the sparking lanterns, the broken table. The smell of charred flesh filled the air. Avia's body had slipped to the ground, blood seeping from her chest. Felina lay beside her, united with her sister in death.

"How did that feel?" the Maw asked.

Thanos stared at Felina's pale face, frozen forever in a mask of shock.

"Easy," he said. "It felt easy."

The words seemed to strike some chord within the Maw. For the first time, doubt flickered across his pale countenance.

A small figure crawled out from behind the bar. Spike the cat loped up to his mistress and sniffed Felina's cold, shriveled hand. Then the cat looked up at Thanos with blank, almost expectant eyes.

Thanos pointed the sword down at him. With one thrust, he could run the cat through. Another loose end tied off, another tiny offering. Another step along the path.

He hesitated. The cat whirled, quick as lightning, and was gone.

The Maw took Thanos by the shoulders and steered him toward the exit. The Maw's doubts seemed to have fled. He was once again an assassin of the Black Order, a hard small voice in the night.

A faith we share, Thanos thought. A god who gives us meaning.

"Come," the Maw said. "Tomorrow is upon us."

The blood was already drying on Thanos's back. He sheathed his sword and followed the Maw into the market, into the stink and bustle of desperate souls. Side by side, like ancient gladiators, they strode through the first rays of the bloody sun.

ELEVEN

"**IN ORDER** there is security. In security there is faith. Those are the prime tenets, the unshakable foundation of our Church."

Thanos followed Proxima and the Maw down the center aisle of the sanctuary. At the front of the room, the priest stood before an altar so black, it seemed to absorb all light. Behind him hung a huge ankh carved of dark marble set into the arch-shape cut into the back wall.

"Please take your seats in an orderly manner," the priest continued. "There are many paths to enlightenment, many roads that lead to God. Your path, your road, has led you here today. For that, we of the Church bow our heads in gratitude and humility."

The priest's skin was a deep, weathered tan; his eyes were hard and commanding. He spread his arms wide, taking in the rows of recruits. Prospective Church members filed in: a medley of sizes, colors, and races, all dressed in the loose robes of Church acolytes. Forty or fifty in all, enough to fill about a third of the seats.

The Maw led Proxima into an empty row of pews,

halfway down the aisle. Thanos followed, pausing to gaze upward. Stone walls stretched up all sides of the room, leading to an intricate stained-glass window built into the roof of the Palace.

"The Church's enemies are many," the priest said, "and they delight in spreading lies about our rituals. We hope that by the time you complete this orientation, you will find your way to the light, and apprehend the true glory to be found within these hallowed walls."

Thanos settled into the hard wooden pew. Dull-red sunlight filtered down through the stained glass, casting odd shadows on his robes. An individual holo-tablet was fixed to the back of the pew in front of him, above a kneeling pad on the floor.

"You are about to begin your lives. Lives of holy devotion, of service and repentance. Of discipline. Above all..." The priest paused for effect. "Lives of purpose."

Proxima touched her ear. "Pip," she whispered. "Are you in position?"

The troll's tinny voice sounded in Thanos's subdermal earpiece. "Not quite," Pip said. "I kind of took a wrong turn."

Thanos shook his head. How many times had they gone over the Palace layout with Pip? Eight? Ten?

"Pip," Proxima whispered. "Where are you?"

"In the, uh, treasury room." A staticky whistle came over the earpiece. "This is an awful lot of gold."

"Now let me ask you to consult the holo-tablets before you," the priest said. "They contain the sum total of the Church's rituals and practices."

Proxima and the Maw reached for their tablets.

"Pip," Thanos hissed, *"don't touch anything.* Until you cut the power, everything's rigged with alarms."

"Ease up—I know where the junction room is. Just one more 'port and I'm there." Pip paused. "Too bad your hot lady friends bailed, Nil."

The Maw glanced over at Thanos. Again, for just a moment, Thanos saw the look of uncertainty the Maw had displayed over Avia's and Felina's bodies.

"In order to be considered a true acolyte of the Church, you must first shed the sins of your past." The priest held up his own tablet. "Click the holy name of the Magus to begin."

"Pip?" Thanos asked.

"Aw, damn it," Pip replied. "Missed again. Least now I know where the wine cellar is."

"YOU. Please click the Magus's holy name."

Thanos looked up. The priest was staring straight at him.

He mumbled an apology and scrambled to activate his tablet. A grim holographic visage rose up from the display: a scowling face, deep violet in color, with a shock of white hair.

"Blessed be the Magus," the priest said. "He who founded the Universal Church and pointed the way to salvation."

"Blessed be the Magus," Thanos repeated, along with the rest of the acolytes.

"Soon you will be asked to make a small monetary

contribution to the Church's good works. But first, we ask for a different sort of donation."

The priest held up a strange weapon, unfamiliar to Thanos. Its handle resembled the hasp of a sword—but where the blade should have been, a long metal cord snaked down onto the floor in front of the altar. The priest pressed a stud on the handle, and the cord flared to life. It whipped up through the air, buzzing and snapping with energy.

Proxima leaned over toward the Maw. "What is that?"

"A mnemonic flail," the Maw whispered back.

The priest gestured to the crowd. "All rise. Form a line, please."

The acolytes filed into the center aisle. Proxima placed a hand on Thanos's shoulder, holding him back. "We don't want to be first," she hissed.

He hung back, waiting until the acolytes almost filled the aisle. Then he walked out and took up position near the back of the hall, behind a smiling Zatoan girl. Proxima and the Maw followed.

"Pip?" Proxima asked.

"I'm in. Junction room, baby. Stand by."

At the front of the room, a large, muscular humanoid with pale skin knelt before the altar. The priest stood over him, the glowing flail held tight in one clenched fist.

"You came here for a reason," the priest said, fixing his deep-set eyes on the kneeling acolyte. "There is a pain inside you...a dark memory that drove you into the Church's arms."

The man looked up, tears in his eyes. "Yes," he said, his voice barely audible.

"The Church is mercy. But the Church is also discipline." The priest raised the flail. "What is your pain?"

"I-I-I killed my father. Ran over him with a groundcar, in a blinding storm. I didn't mean—"

The flail whipped through the air like lightning. When it struck the kneeling man on the back, a bright flash of electricity seized hold of him. He arched his spine and cried out in pain.

The crowd took a step back. No one looked away. Thanos felt frozen, almost mesmerized by the man's pain.

When the energy faded, the man's entire body shivered. His robe was untouched—not even singed.

The priest flicked his wrist, allowing the flail to come to rest on the floor. "What," he asked, "is your pain?"

"I killed my—"

Again the flail whipped down. The man fell to the floor, glowing bright. He gasped and rose back to his knees as the energy faded.

"What is your pain?"

The man looked up and blinked. He seemed puzzled, almost dazed.

"I don't know," he said.

The priest lowered his head, a solemn expression on his face. He placed a hand on the acolyte's head.

"Thank you for your contribution," he said, and gestured for the man to move aside.

The next acolyte in line, a thin Shi'ar woman

with a tattered mohawk, looked up at the priest. Her expression was a mixture of terror and anticipation.

"You came here for a reason," the priest said.

Thanos leaned over and whispered to the Maw. "What does that flail do?"

"It strips away memories, one by one," the Maw replied. "The first step in becoming a Church convert…they literally take a piece of you."

"They're not taking a piece of *me*," Proxima snarled. "Pip, tick tock?"

"I'm workin' on it," the troll said. "There're a lotta wires in this room."

Thanos listened as the acolytes confessed their sins. A Strontian had betrayed her fellows in battle, sacrificing them to save her own skin. A reptilian alien of some unfamiliar species had reverted to his ancient instincts and devoured his newly hatched children. A Skrull woman had disguised herself as a human to avoid fighting in a war against the Kree.

One by one, they felt the sting of the mnemonic flail. And each time, the flail lifted their memories, their sins, right out of their minds. One by one, they all staggered back to their pews, a dazed smile on whatever passed for their face.

"That flail channels a *huge* amount of energy," the Maw said, frowning. "The handle can't hold it all…. The Church must be transmitting power to this room from some hidden source."

Another acolyte staggered back. Thanos was only two people away from the altar now, with

Proxima and the Maw right behind him.

Proxima eyed the priest. "Pip," she whispered. "If you don't pull this off soon, I'm going to have to commit patricide."

"Couple more minutes."

A boy, barely out of his teens, rose to the altar and knelt down. Under his robes, he wore a tattered blue and gold Nova Corps uniform with no insignia of rank. Probably drummed out of the Corps for some offense. As the lash whipped down, his expression went blank.

As Thanos gazed at the flail, flashing and circling through the air, he realized he was tempted. He carried a full measure of pain around with him— several lifetimes' worth. How many memories would he be happy to lose? His defeat at the hands of his treacherous grandfather. His humiliation before Mistress Death. His mother, staring at her newborn child with a knife in her hand.

The glassy eyes of Avia and Felina, their blood leaking out onto the sand.

Is this my path? he wondered. *Not greatness, not humility—not even Death, but oblivion? The cold comfort of a debased religion?*

The Nova Corps boy stumbled aside. The priest turned to Thanos and lifted the flail. Thanos watched as its energy-trail whipped through the air, lighting up the dim room.

The lights went out.

The priest looked up sharply at his flail. It

flickered, sparked, and died in his hand, leaving him in near-total darkness.

"This way," the Maw said. He broke and ran, leaping as if weightless into the first row of pews. Proxima followed, pulling out her spear. She held it up; it began to glow with energy as it expanded to its full combat size.

The acolytes watched, squinting as emergency lights winked on along the walls. Some pointed at Proxima in alarm. Most just stared, smiling dully.

Thanos hesitated. He looked up as the priest staggered back against the altar. The man looked small, the giant ankh behind him outlined in the dim red light.

Thanos pulled out a small blaster and sited carefully, raising the weapon to avoid the rows of passive acolytes. He fired once, catching the priest in the heart. The priest flew back against the wall, staining the foot of the ankh with his blood.

That was enough to rouse the acolytes. They rushed out into the aisles, feeling their way past the rows of dark pews as they stampeded toward the exit. A few of them cast frightened glances backward at the priest and the mysterious stranger who had killed him.

Thanos smiled.

Proxima and the Maw set out on a diagonal path through the pews, running and leaping over frightened people. Thanos cast off his robes and followed. The acolytes scattered, clearing a path for him. By the time he caught up with Proxima, she and the Maw had also shed their robes, revealing their combat suits beneath.

"You see well in the dark," Proxima said.

They vaulted another row of pews and found themselves in a narrow aisle at the side of the room. Thanos turned to see the last of the acolytes rushing down the center aisle, pouring out the door.

The Maw placed both hands against the side wall. "Somewhere along here," he said.

"Secret passageways?" Proxima asked.

"The plans showed them on this wall," Thanos said, "One of them leads to the treasury room. The trick is finding which one."

"The *trick*," the Maw said, "is finding them at all."

He felt along a large inlaid panel the height of two men. Then he shook his head and moved along the wall.

A chill ran up Thanos's spine. He turned just as the panel made a clicking sound. It slid upward…

…to reveal a full squadron of the Church's Black Knights.

The Knights poured into the sanctuary, weapons drawn. About half of them were descended from the muscular green-skinned natives of Sacrosanct, the people the Magus had conquered centuries ago. The others represented virtually every race in the known universe: crimson Strontians, blue-skinned Kree, even a few Terrans. In their deep-violet, skintight armor, they resembled a single, unstoppable wall of humanity.

The huge room was empty now except for Thanos, Proxima, the Maw—and the Knights. Proxima stepped back to join Thanos, the two of them forming a right angle to protect the Maw.

"How many do you count?" she asked.

Thanos blinked. Was she testing him? "Twenty-five at least." He gestured at the dark passageway. "And more coming."

Proxima smiled and raised her spear.

The first Knight, a one-eyed creature with bright-pink skin, let out a cry. As the squadron charged, Thanos whipped out his blaster. He fired off three rapid shots; the one-eyed man and two others dropped.

A half-dozen Knights moved to surround Proxima, their weapons raised. She let out a war cry, surprising them, and stabbed her spear down into the floor so hard it splintered the marble tiles. The Knights stared at her as if she were mad.

The spear flared bright, then went completely black. Three beams of darkness split off from the point and flared out toward the Knights. When the beams made contact, the Knights opened their mouths to scream. But no sound escaped. The black light enveloped the Knights, sucking out their life-energy, absorbing all heat and light. The men crumpled to the ground.

"There," the Maw said, pointing.

Another group of Knights was advancing on them, activating portable energy-shield barriers. Thanos sheathed his blaster and reached for his sword. He swept it in a wide arc before him, grunting as he made contact with the lead Knight's shield. The blade sizzled and penetrated partway, knocking the Knight off balance. He dropped his shield and toppled into his fellow soldiers.

Thanos thrust again, tagging a Knight on the cheek. The Knight cried out, gloved hands scrabbling at his face. Thanos slapped him aside and fired the blaster with his other hand, shooting off quick bursts to pick off the advancing Knights.

He swept the sword wide, pressing the Knights back. As the blade passed before his eyes, an image of Avia rose to Thanos's mind. He shook his head, forcing it away.

He found himself backed up against the pews with Proxima by his side. The Knights pushed forward, tripping over the corpses of their fallen comrades. The air began to stink of blood.

Proxima let out a cry and charged down the aisle, spear raised. The Knights fell back, a group of them tumbling into the rows of pews. As she approached the main force, Proxima reached back and hurled the spear upward, then skidded to a halt.

The spear whipped through the air as if it were alive. It slowed and came to a rest above the aisle, hovering in place. Black light stabbed from its front and back tips, reaching out to engulf the Knights one by one. They screamed and fired their weapons wildly, at random.

The Maw crouched below the gunfire, on a kneeling pad at the base of a row of pews. He held a Black Knight's head in each hand, caressing their cheeks.

"There is no god," the Maw whispered. "No path to the light."

Their eyes went wide with terror. They seemed

paralyzed, held fast by his words.

"No *light* at all," he said.

Proxima held up her hand and twisted her wrist in the air. The spear responded, mirroring her movements. Black beams filled the room, rising up to hone in on each of their victims in turn.

"If there is a path," the Maw continued, "you have not found it. We have not found it, either."

Proxima's black-light beams began to fade. Bodies filled the aisle, sprawling out over the nearest pews. The few surviving Knights looked around in astonishment. Somehow three acolytes—one of them unarmed—had decimated an entire Church squadron.

"*I* have not found it," the Maw whispered.

His victims fell from his limp fingers. He sat watching, eyes hard and blank, for a long moment.

Without looking, Proxima held up her hand. The spear slid into her grip, halting in midair. "Maw?"

He looked up sharply, then moved to join Proxima. He cast one final glance down at the Knights he'd killed. Killed, as he had so many before, with the power of doubt.

His greatest weapon.

A lizard-faced Knight crouched behind a pew, speaking in a low voice into his shoulder-radio. The Maw whipped his head around to peer at the wall panel, still open to reveal the passageway entrance. Noises echoed from inside.

"More Knights are coming," he said. "This isn't over."

"Have you noticed something else?" Proxima asked

He looked around. The two of them were alone with a handful of frightened, bleeding Knights.

"Our *recruit,*" she hissed. "He's gone."

TWELVE

THANOS inched his way down the narrow conduit, wincing as his elbow brushed past an exposed electrical circuit. The crawlspace was dark, industrial, and barely large enough for him to fit through. Brown water dripped from a pipe above.

He paused, pulled out a memory module, and snapped it into a small holo-mount on his wrist. The Palace schematic rose up, bent and distorted to fit in the cramped space. He zoomed in until he found the crawlspace, branching out from one of the passageways off the large sanctuary. The tunnel ran for a short distance into the mountain, then seemed to dead-end into solid rock.

His heart quickened. I'm already past that point, he realized. I was right.

The crawlspace continued off the map, extending deep into the mountain. That meant there was something up ahead, something the Church had worked hard to keep off of any map. Something much more valuable than a room full of jewels.

He snapped off the holo, started forward again—

and froze. A slight metallic bumping noise, coming from up ahead. Faint, but growing louder.

Someone else was in the passageway.

He pulled out his gun, then holstered it again. Too much unshielded circuitry in here. An electromagnetic discharge could backfire—or worse, set the whole place ablaze. He unsheathed the sword instead and crawled forward.

Up ahead, the corridor divided. An even smaller tunnel branched off to the right, too narrow for Thanos to fit through, even in this body. He paused again, listening. The bumping was coming from the smaller conduit.

He twisted his body, positioning himself out of sight just past the branch in the passage. The bumping grew louder, became a metallic clanking. Another noise joined it: a strange, atonal humming.

Thanos frowned, puzzled. He raised his sword, flattening his back against the wall of the tunnel. If a squadron of Knights appeared, at least he'd have the advantage of surprise.

The humming grew louder, interspersed with words:

"Try to make me go to KREE-LAR I said no, no, no…"

Pip the Troll's head emerged from the tunnel. He looked around, spotted Thanos, and froze in mid-syllable. "Whoa!" he cried. "It's me! Don't shoot! Stab! Do not maim, is what I'm saying!"

Thanos grunted and sheathed the sword.

"Pip," he said, "What are you doing here?"

The troll shrugged. "I was about to 'port out of the junction room when I spotted this passageway. Guess I'm just naturally curious." He paused, frowning. "Wait a tic. What are you doing here? Looking for 'belief energy'?"

Thanos didn't answer. He gazed at the path ahead, wishing Pip would vanish.

"Something's hinky here." Pip craned his neck, peering down the tunnel in the direction Thanos had come. "What about Maw and Paw? Where are they?"

"When I left them, they were…" Thanos grimaced. "Occupied."

"By the Black Knights, I bet." Pip's eyes went wide. "Oh-ho! You double-crossed 'em, didn't you? Used them as a diversion, while you snuck in here."

"I presume they're on their way to the treasury room."

"That'll keep the Knights busy for a while. But sooner or later, they'll come after you, too."

Thanos looked around, frowning. Pip was right: Proxima and the Maw, he knew, could hold an entire army at bay—but not forever.

"And that leaves one big question, don't it?" Pip continued. "The two-thousand-pound Hulk in the room. What *exactly* are you lookin' for? What's hidden inside this mountain?"

"I don't think you want to see it," Thanos rumbled.

"Oh, I'm thinkin' I *do*."

"Pip," Thanos said, pointing back down the passageway, "there's a room full of jewels and a fully stocked wine cellar back that way. Why don't you just cut your losses and load up your little arms with as much loot as they can carry?"

"Under most circumstances, that'd be the offer of a lifetime." Pip smirked. "But you just pulled off a double-fakeout and risked pissing off two of the deadliest assassins in space—all to get to whatever lies at the end of this tunnel."

"It may be nothing."

"Yeah. Sure." Pip scurried forward, moving through the narrow crawlspace. "Whatever it is, I'm bettin' it's a lot more than just 'belief energy.'"

"Pip—"

"Sorry, Nil. *If* that's your name." Pip continued down the main tunnel, not looking back. "Like I said: naturally curious."

Thanos swore and moved to follow him.

They crawled at least a half-mile, around twists and turns, through spots almost too tight to squeeze through. Pip moved like a cat; Thanos had to struggle to keep up with him.

"Who let the Skrulls out? WHO? WHO?"

"No singing," Thanos growled.

The tunnel seemed to grow narrower. His limbs felt heavy. He began to tire of Pip's incessant chatter, the terrible off-key singing. The sight of his hairy little legs.

The dim light within the passageway slowly turned to a luminous blue. It's coming from up ahead, Thanos realized. It's here. It's really here.

His thoughts turned murderous. He didn't need Pip anymore; the troll had served his purpose. If he could sneak up and grab Pip's leg, he could run him through with the sword. He reached forward, slowly…

Pip whirled around. He caught a glimpse of the look in Thanos's eyes—and vanished in a burst of teleport energy.

"Sorry, Nil. I'm not as trusting as your lady friends. What happened to them, anyway?"

Thanos whirled around. Pip now sat in the passageway *behind* him, bathed in blue light.

"I'm not gonna stop you from heisting anything." Pip spread his arms. "Doubt I could. I just wanna come along for the ride."

"Why don't you teleport there ahead of me, then?"

"Because I don't know the way. This fakakta tunnel isn't on the maps."

Thanos crawled toward him. Pip vanished again, reappearing a few feet farther back.

"You can't catch me, so you might as well let me come." Pip gestured past Thanos, toward the source of the blue light. "Tell you what. *You* lead the way."

Thanos glared at him for a moment, then turned away. *Very well*, he thought. Pip's presence was an annoyance, but in the end it wouldn't change anything.

The passageway rounded a short bend and widened out into a massive open space. Thanos stopped short so quickly that Pip bumped into him from behind.

"Sorry," Pip said. "Oh. Oh wow."

Thanos took a step forward, looking around. The chamber's walls were unfinished rock, a jagged landscape of gray-and-blue slate; they stretched up several stories to a rocky ceiling. There was no floor that Thanos could see; the chamber seemed to extend deep into the bowels of the planet.

The tunnel gave way to a thin walkway with no railing, extending forward over the abyss. Around the sides of the chamber, four more identical walkways protruded from other holes in the wall. The walkways all ended at the same point: a large glowing sphere, 30 or 40 feet in diameter, floating in the exact center of the chamber. Blue energy roiled across the sphere's surface, casting ever-shifting patterns of light on the mountainous walls.

Pip stared at the sphere. "What in the name of brothels and opium is *that?*"

Thanos stepped forward onto the walkway. His pace was even, his voice calm. But inside he was screaming. This was the treasure he had hoped to find, the secret whispered by defrocked priests who had ventured deep inside the Church. By criminals who had bribed their way to the truth, hookers who'd heard whispers in the night. By the descendants of the first people of Sacrosanct, who'd worshipped its power.

It's real, he thought. *It's really here.*

"It's a Trans-Dimensional Nexus," he said.

"A Trans-Dimensional…" Pip paused. "Can you break that down for a brother?"

"It's been here for centuries. A past elder of the Church—possibly the Magus himself—found it buried deep inside the mountain."

As he approached the Nexus, images began to

appear in its swirling depths. Thanos, fighting for his life alongside a golden man with gladiator gauntlets and a glowing emerald gem on his forehead. The Infinity Gauntlet, gleaming with power on his fist. A scarecrow dressed in Thanos's clothes, a simple straw effigy guarding over a field of corn.

"It brings all worlds together." He spoke as if in a trance. "The past, other realities. Where we've been, and where we might have been, had things been different."

Another vision in the sphere: young Thanos on his homeworld of Titan. Playing in the fields with his handsome red-haired brother, while his loving mother and father watched in approval.

Pip peered around Thanos's legs. "I just see myself in a bunch of casinos and whorehouses."

Again the energy swirled. A tall, weathered building appeared against an unfamiliar gray sky, dozens of smaller buildings crowded up against it. The writing on its face was in a language Thanos couldn't quite place, but he thought he recognized one word: WAR.

"Even the future," he murmured.

The building wavered and vanished. In its place, a pair of strong, dark, feminine hands held a short, blunt wooden knife. The sight of those hands struck a chord deep inside Thanos, though both they and the knife were utterly unfamiliar.

Pip frowned. "So other than show bucket-list movies, what exactly does it—WHOA!"

Pip jumped back as the sphere flared bright. Thanos stood his ground, letting the blue energy flow through him. It gathered in the air, forming several distinct beams that shot outward. Metal receptor units mounted on the walls absorbed the energy.

"The Church hungers for power," Thanos explained. "The Nexus draws raw energy from all possible planes of existence."

As the sphere's energy died down, Thanos took another step forward. The other walkways, he noticed, were still empty. He half expected another version of himself to appear from one of the passageway entrances. Some Titan who had never abandoned his power—had not seen the things he'd seen, lived the life he'd lived among the beggars and thieves of Sacrosanct.

A Thanos who had not murdered his friends and then remarked: *It felt easy.*

Would that Thanos be more whole than he? Or less?

"Mistress." He held up a hand, felt the dance of electrons shimmering off the sphere. "Do you hear me?"

A faint crash sounded from above. Thanos ignored it. The face of the Nexus was a wall of static, taunting him.

"This is my last chance," he whispered, staring into the depths. "I thought maybe...this…I hoped it could show me the right path."

He felt vaguely foolish. A hollow, empty feeling came over him, just as it had in his room the previous night.

Another crashing sound, louder this time. "Uh," Pip said. "Nil?"

Thanos stared into the energy, studied the cerulean collisions of basic particles. His own words echoed in his mind: The Church hungers for power.

Is that why I'm here? he wondered. I told myself I wanted a guide, a signpost to point me to my true destiny. But in the end, am I really just drawn to power in all its forms?

A blue prominence flared out from the sphere. Thanos stood his ground. The Nexus held him in its sway, like a lover—a rival to Death herself. But now that he'd found the power, he had no idea what to do with it.

A movement caught his eye. He stepped back, squinting to peer around the bright-glowing sphere. At the mouth of one of the walkways, a dark figure stood watching. It raised skeletal hands to lower the dark green cloak from its face.

Mistress Death?

The third crash shook the chamber. Thanos stumbled on the walkway, struggling to regain his footing. Pip teetered on the edge, grabbed Thanos's leg, and pulled himself back up.

"Nil, buddy." Pip pointed up at the ceiling. "I don't know *what* the flark is going on up there, but I think we better get out before it arrives."

Thanos swatted him away. Pip let out a little cry and skidded back along the walkway, toward the rocky wall.

Thanos stared at the sphere. He gazed around it, craning his neck to see. But the other walkways were empty again, the entrances into the rock devoid of life. His Mistress was gone.

Rage washed over him. She had abandoned him. Again. Why?

He whirled around, fists clenched. Pip stood against the wall, staring upward...

The ceiling burst open with a thunderous crack, echoed and amplified by the stone walls. Boulders rained down, denting the walkways and tumbling down into the pit below. Thanos crouched low, shielding his face from the deadly barrage.

When the dust cleared, he looked up, already knowing what he would see. A muscular figure, green-skinned with blood-red tattoos, hovered before a jagged hole in the rock.

"Thanos," Drax the Destroyer proclaimed. *"I am your doom."*

THIRTEEN

"**I HAVE** *tracked you here, Thanos. Across the stars, through the unimaginable depths of space.*"

Drax hung in the air like an angel of vengeance. He stared down at the walkway, the Nexus painting him in shades of blue.

"Thanos," Pip repeated. "He said Thanos."

Thanos whirled around to see the troll staring up at Drax. Slowly, Pip lowered his eyes to the man he'd known as Nil.

"Oh," Pip breathed. He started backing up along the walkway, toward the wall. "Oh wow. Oh no. Oh holy flark, it's true."

"Pip." Thanos took a step toward him.

"No sir. Nonononono." The troll scrabbled backward, holding up a hand. "Stay back. Stay away from me."

Thanos stole a glance at Drax. The Destroyer still floated, perfectly still, before the Nexus.

"I'm out of here," Pip said, staring at Thanos. "Nothing's worth this. Not wine, not jewels, not even…" He gestured at the Nexus. "Hope you find what you're looking for, buddy. Wait, no. Knowing you, I hope you *don't.*"

A flash of yellow energy, a whiff of ozone, and Pip was gone.

Thanos stared at the space where Pip had stood. *I'm alone with the Destroyer,* he realized. *A creature shaped and equipped for one purpose: to end my life.*

He turned toward the Nexus, peering at the half-glimpsed images in its depths. He'd come here seeking answers, hoping the infinity of worlds within the sphere would point him to his true path. Failing that, perhaps he could harness the sphere's power—rebuild his shattered life through sheer brute force.

But now he knew there were no answers here. All the walkways, all the paths, led to a single point: the glowing ball of fire that hung before him. A dead end—with a living engine of destruction floating above it.

Thanos closed his eyes. In his defeat, he felt oddly at peace. Part of him hoped Drax would simply blast him to atoms, ending his long charade of a life.

But no attack came.

He opened his eyes and looked up at Drax. The Destroyer stared back, frowning. He seemed almost confused.

"Well?" Thanos asked.

Drax's eyes narrowed. *"I was born for this day, evil one,"* he said. *"And now at last it is arrived…"*

The Destroyer stopped in mid-sentence. Raising both arms, he wafted down to land before Thanos, his back to the Nexus. He raised a glowing energy-knife, holding it up in a menacing gesture.

This is it, Thanos thought. He braced for the blast that would end his life.

"You," Drax said. *"Where is Thanos?"*

Thanos blinked.

"His life energy hangs in the air," Drax continued. *"I know this. Where is he?"*

The sphere flared again, sending tongues of blue energy into the air.

He doesn't recognize me, Thanos realized. *He doesn't know who I am. All this stray energy…it must be interfering with his inborn tracking power!*

Within Thanos, the flame of ambition once again sparked to life. He raised thin green arms in a pose of surrender.

"I don't know," he said.

Drax sheathed his knife. He began to pace back and forth, in the small space between Thanos and the glowing Nexus.

"I have followed the evil one's energy signature," Drax said, *"down the cold light-years, across voids without measure. It has led me here, to this dusty speck of a world."* He rose up into the air, fists clenched. *"Where is he? WHERE IS THANOS?"*

Drax whipped out both knives and aimed them at the next walkway over. Energy leaped from the blades and stabbed down, blasting the walkway in half. It cracked and crumbled, loose pieces clattering noisily down into the void. Only a short stub remained affixed to the Nexus.

"THANOS!" he screamed. *"SHOW YOURSELF!"*

The chamber shook under the impact of Drax's assault. Thanos dropped to a crouch, gripping the side of the walkway beneath his feet—a walkway that, thankfully, was still intact. The Nexus seemed untouched, as well.

On a third walkway—the one on the *other* side of Thanos's perch—something appeared in the tunnel entrance. For a moment his heart jumped. Was it Death, returned once again? Had this been merely another test, another trial she'd concocted for him? Was she ready, at last, to welcome him back into her arms?

No—not Death. A squadron of Black Knights dashed out onto the platform, then stopped short. Their leader pointed up at the Destroyer and shouted orders.

Drax flailed about wildly, blasting in all directions.

The Knights opened fire. Thanos ducked down as the energy barrage sizzled over his head. He crawled rapidly toward the mouth of the tunnel, casting a regretful glance back at the glowing, shimmering majesty of the Nexus.

Before he reached the entrance, a slim blue arm encircled his neck in a grip like iron.

"So," Proxima Midnight hissed. "The secret of Nil is revealed."

For a moment, he thought: Does she know? But no. From the look on her face, Proxima was talking about the Nexus.

The Maw crept up next to them. He stared at the

glowing sphere. His fingers began to ripple open and closed in an odd, nervous motion.

"The hidden power," he said. "The engine that fuels the Church's holy works."

The Black Knights had assumed a formation on the adjacent platform, aiming their guns at Drax. The Destroyer whirled, returning fire. A chunk of the walkway beneath their feet gave way; three Knights tumbled, howling, into the depths.

"*Zealots!*" Drax yelled. "*Deluded fools! BRING ME THANOS!*"

A stray blast struck Thanos's walkway, not six inches from him. Proxima took a few steps back, maintaining her grip on his throat.

"We should…" he gasped, jerking his head toward the tunnel entrance.

She didn't move. "You deceived us," she said, turning blank eyes toward him. "You betrayed the Order."

"Knew you could…take care of yourself."

"True enough."

To his shock, she released him. Thanos stumbled away from her, toward the Nexus. Drax swooped low, firing just above his head; Thanos dropped, flattening himself against the walkway.

Drax's massive blast seared past, incinerating two of the Knights on the adjacent walkway. The structure beneath them creaked, cracked, and shattered. The rest of the Knights toppled and fell screaming into the endless depths.

He looked up. Proxima was staring down,

following the plummeting forms of the Knights. The Ebony Maw's eyes were still fixed on the Nexus, the roiling blue energies that dominated the chamber.

"The next squadron will have hover-packs," the Maw said, distracted. "They'll give your urban-primitive friend more of a challenge."

"*THANOS!*" Drax cried.

Proxima marched down the walkway, a dangerous smile on her face. She raised her spear. For the second time, Thanos thought: This is the end. She's going to kill me.

But instead of firing, she turned and used the spear to point at the entrance to one of the severed walkways. Another group of Knights had appeared at the mouth of the tunnel.

She lowered the spear, then crouched down and took Thanos's chin in her hand. "You were clever enough to get us in here," she said. "How do you suggest we leave?"

He blinked. "You're asking me?"

"You *are* a recruit to the Black Order, are you not?"

Thanos looked up as the new squadron of Knights took to the air. As the Maw had predicted, these wore personal flight units on their backs. Drax swooped and whipped through the air, picking them off with blasts from his knives.

A Knight paused, aimed, and squeezed off a careful shot. Drax howled as blood appeared on his chest.

Another of the Knights, tumbling in midair, fired wildly. His blast struck the mouth of the tunnel at the end of Thanos's walkway. Rock tumbled down, collapsing the entrance and blocking their escape.

Thanos closed his eyes, squeezed them tight. Bright patterns formed in his mind's eye, mirroring the energies of the Nexus. All at once, he saw everything: the path he had to take, the reason he'd come here in the first place.

The power *would* be his. Part of it, anyway.

"Come on," he said, and took off at a run— toward the Nexus.

The Maw followed immediately. Proxima hesitated, watching the blue energy sphere. A chunk of ceiling cracked loose under the heavy gunfire, plunging down to glance off the walkway. Proxima stumbled and grimaced, then turned to follow.

Ahead, the sphere glowed a thousand shades of blue. Teal and navy, sapphire and steel. The glimmer of pure atomic force, photons dancing to new tunes.

Thanos raised his arms and let it surround him.

The echoes of the Knights' blasters, the howl of Drax's cries, the crack and crumbling of the rocky chamber—all simply faded away. Images surrounded him: visions of the past and future, just as when he had first beheld the Nexus. But all of it closer, faster, more raw against his nerves. A trio of silver/gold/pink faces, flaring with power. The fields of Titan, bright with green life. The scarecrow. The tall building with WAR written on it.

And again, the blunt wooden knife. Held firm

in hands both soft and strong, hands that seemed to call out, without words, to the deepest part of him.

"Oh," Proxima said.

Thanos looked up. Once again he beheld the bands of hyperspace, stretching at multidimensional angles in all directions. He saw stars unborn, galaxies that lived only as probabilities. Worlds that lived only to worship dark gods.

He turned at a low chanting sound. The Ebony Maw stared off into the blue haze, mouthing quiet words. His speech was quick, his brow furrowed, as if he were solving some intricate puzzle.

Proxima frowned. "What does he see?

"I don't know," Thanos said.

He squinted and beheld, again, the edge of the universe. The distorted curve where shapes became surfaces, surfaces became lines. Where stars flattened into strings, and superstrings ended in knots of pure ether.

The energy beneath his feet, the air around him—all these were abstractions, creations of pure mathematics. He gazed into infinity—but not the false infinity of the Gems. This, truly, was the end.

The sphere shook with a great impact. The curve blurred and wavered; the stars faded to blue static. Drax, Thanos realized. He's turned toward the Nexus. He's firing at it—with us inside!

Thanos whirled around, searching for Proxima and the Maw. They sat crouched together in the blue haze, staring into each other's eyes. The Maw said something in an unfamiliar language, sharp and quick. It sounded like dolphins clicking.

Proxima bared her teeth in anger. Then she nodded to the Maw and stood up. As the Maw turned away, Thanos caught a quick glimpse of his grim, resolved face. His eyes locked onto Thanos's, and his mouth opened to form a wordless phrase:

All things must end.

Another blow shook the blue world. Through the curtain of energy, Thanos glimpsed Drax blasting off bolt after bolt into the sphere. The Knights surrounded him, firing wildly; some of their shots were striking the Nexus, too.

He almost jumped when Proxima touched his shoulder.

"The Maw has left the Order," she said.

Thanos blinked. He looked around, but the Ebony Maw was gone. Vanished into the endless sapphire depths.

"Our situation seems untenable," Proxima continued, wincing as power burst all around them. "Shall we make our exit?"

Thanos nodded. I know what to do, he realized. Despite all the failures, the disappointments, my path is clear.

"Just a step," he said.

He held out a hand, and she grasped it firmly. Around them, the energy screamed and roared.

Thanos drew in a deep breath and took a single step.

THERE was no transition, no sensation of movement. But in an instant, they were standing in the bright sun of the Sacrosanct spaceport. Ships rose up all around them, parked in open spaces: one-man stingers, small vessels, heavy cruisers. Across the paved field, a single large passenger liner was docked up against the administration terminal.

A medium-sized fighter ship, bristling with weapons pods, loomed above. Proxima gestured up at the hull, which bore the star-flecked, circle-in-a-square emblem of the Black Order.

"Right on target," she said.

Thanos blinked in the sunlight. Mechanics bustled around, spacemen donning helmets and trading sports scores. A stinger ship taxied past, heading for a small launch pad in the distance.

Proxima's wrist buzzed. "Hyper-comm message," she explained. "Recorded. It's being relayed from the ship now that we're in range."

She touched the comm-band on her wrist. A hologram rose up: a terrifying figure with sharp teeth and a pointed chin, draped in tattered black robes. He carried a long ornate weapon with multiple deadly blades jutting out at different angles. He seemed to be standing in some sort of industrial square, surrounded by large buildings.

Thanos knew this man. It was Proxima's husband: Corvus Glaive, cruelest and most fearsome of the Black Order.

"My love," Corvus's image hissed. "I have received your communiqué."

Proxima nodded, waiting.

"Events proceed rapidly here," Corvus continued. "I ask that you come swiftly."

Thanos stared at the image—but not at Corvus. In the background, blurred by the holographic transmission, a tall stone structure had caught his eye. A building he'd seen recently, within the Nexus. He squinted to read the sign:

KREE MINISTRY OF WAR

"If you believe this 'Nil' is one of us, bring him." Corvus paused. "I await the warmth of your touch."

The image vanished.

One of us, Thanos thought. The words echoed in his mind.

A hatch hissed open on the ship above, and a gangplank stairway dropped to the ground. Proxima stepped onto the lowest step, then turned back toward Thanos.

"Well?" she asked.

He hesitated. She smiled, as if reading his thoughts.

"We may overlook treachery," she said, "when coupled with initiative."

Thanos frowned. "What about Pip?"

She rolled her eyes.

"And you're okay with the Maw? Just leaving like that?"

"The Order is not compulsory."

"What did he say to you? Inside the Nexus?"

She paused, glaring. For a moment he thought he'd gone too far, asked one question too many.

"He seeks a more intellectual life. He said that what we do…the search for a god, the pursuit of slaughter…" She spat on the ground. "He said it felt too *easy.*"

A commotion rose up from the next ship over. A red, thick-bodied Strontian stood pleading with a trio of squidlike creatures in expensive business suits. "I told you, the minidrives were stolen," the Strontian said. "I—I can get 'em back. I just need time."

The squids shook their heads and advanced on the terrified man.

Thanos recalled the Strontian—and the ship, too. He thought of the last caper he'd pulled alongside the Shiv Sisters. Felina's pale visage flashed before his eyes. He could feel Avia's hand at his side, coaching him, guiding his sword hand.

He turned to gaze out over the long road, toward the bazaar visible in the distance. The scent of charred meat wafted down from the market, along with the distant shouts of merchants hawking their wares. Cook fires rose up from the low housing stretching out to either side—the "arms" of the great ankh.

Beyond the medina, past the taverns and slaughterhouses, the Palace stood tall and proud. No sign of the Nexus, of the battle fought within the mountain, showed on its golden, gleaming exterior.

The Church, he thought. It will be there tomorrow. It will be there when we are all dust.

"I've squeezed everything I can out of this pathetic world," Proxima said. "How about you?"

He turned left, scanning the low shacks and trailers of the western arm. He squinted, but couldn't make out his old house. It was too small, too far away.

Another cry from the ship next door. He turned to see the squid-men dragging the Strontian spacer away, ignoring his struggles. The Strontian's pleas went unanswered. In this place, everyone minded their own business.

Enough of this, Thanos thought. Enough petty thieving, enough living in poverty. Enough casting about for a path.

Enough of *friends*.

The Black Order meant power. Thanos thought of the image in the hologram: the tall, weathered building with MINISTRY OF WAR written on it.

Maybe, he thought, it really *has* all led to this.

He followed Proxima up the gangplank and into the ship. As the hatch hissed shut behind them, Thanos bade a silent, final farewell to Felina, Avia, and Sacrosanct.

THE PASSAGE

HIS QUARTERS aboard the Order ship were tiny—
even smaller than his room on Sacrosanct. He slid
the door open and half-tripped over a bare mattress.
When the lights came up, he gasped.

The Infinity Wardrobe.

Its mahogany bulk took up half the room. It
gleamed, polished to an almost impossibly perfect
shine. It seemed to call to him, beckoning him forward.

He didn't question, didn't even think to ask how
it could be here. He was already on his way to a new
world, a new beginning, a new affiliation with the
Black Order. What could be more appropriate than
a new body?

He stepped over the mattress and grasped both
doors, pulling them open.

As before, an array of figures fanned across the
roiling energies. Humans, Shi'ar, Skrulls. Multi-
segmented insectoids and glowing creatures of the sea,
long-extinct races and hyper-advanced species not yet
evolved into existence.

The images slowed. A single body settled into

place: a tall, muscular man in skintight military gear. Green boots and gloves; a high-finned helmet framing a pink face. White bodysuit with a proud ringed world emblazoned on the chest.

A Kree warrior.

Thanos smiled. Looking at the image, he felt newly energized. Ready to take on a world and bring it to its knees.

He stepped forward to embrace his new life.

BOOK THREE
HALA

In the annals of galactic history, the Kree Empire stands unmatched in power, size, and sheer longevity. This vast coalition began on the planet Hala, in the Greater Magellanic Cloud adjoining the larger Milky Way. Over the centuries, it has expanded to cover a thousand worlds in four galaxies.

Hala itself has grown to become the foremost "army town" in all of known space. More than two-thirds of its three billion inhabitants are employed, in some capacity, by the Kree military. The bulk of these are concentrated in Hala's unnamed central city, which sprawls out over the planet's largest continent.

In recent years, the Kree Empire has been challenged by the Skrulls, the Shi'ar, and several other warrior races. Though they have taken massive losses, the Kree have always emerged victorious. Despite rumors of Kree complacency, the threat has not yet appeared that could conceivably bring them down.

FOURTEEN

THE KREE Ministry of War rose high into a sky permanently stained gray with industrial smog. The Ministry had stood through centuries of invasions, budget cuts, Skrull infiltration, nuclear attacks, and assorted galactic storms. Its nearest neighbors were less than half its height.

On the 326th floor, in an office the size of a large closet, Corvus Glaive of the Black Order stared out the window. The city—the sprawling capital of the star-spanning Kree Empire—lay spread out before him. From this height, it resembled a field of metallic mushrooms, pocked and dented from countless enemy attacks.

"The planet is called Hemithea. A weak, hateful world ruled by women with gills who hide their people in colonies beneath the sea."

Corvus ignored the irritating voice. He glanced at his multi-bladed staff, propped up against the wall, then lowered his eyes to the row of skulls lining the shelf at the base of the window. One skull was sharp, with jagged bone projecting in all directions. Another was human-shaped, but larger than a basketball. A third, a spray-preserved jellyfish head, had no actual bones.

He smiled grimly. Not really a skull at all, that one.

"Hemithea has been on the Kree invasion roster for decades," the Kree officer continued. "It taunts us. Its very existence is an affront to the Empire."

Corvus picked up a skull and examined it. It was thick-boned, with sharp teeth and two curved tusks jutting out from its brittle cheeks.

"The SabreStar Armada stands ready. Fully fueled, and staffed with veteran officers and hot-blooded noncoms alike." A touch of anger entered the Kree's voice. "But no order comes. No battle cry rings out."

Corvus turned slowly. The officer inhaled a sharp breath. His name was Fal-Tar; he wore the green-and-white uniform of a mid-level Kree, with the traditional insignia—a large ringed world— emblazoned on his chest. The buttons on his shoulder showed that he'd risen about as far as a pink-skinned soldier could on this world.

The Kree prided themselves on their composure, on facing every situation with stoic calm. But Corvus had grown to know Fal-Tar quite well. There was no hiding the fear beneath the Kree's calm exterior.

"Sir?" Fal-Tar asked. "Should I, uh, continue?"

Corvus smiled. Even without his multi-bladed staff, he was an intimidating presence. Tattered black robes, steel gauntlets, metal-fringed boots, and, of course, his bone-white, deadly fanged visage. As first of the Black Order, he had presided over the conquest and devastation of a hundred worlds.

"His name was Augullox," Corvus said, holding up the skull in his hands.

Fal-Tar blinked.

"He, too, ruled a proud world," Corvus continued. "And he died, mewling, as my hands squeezed his windpipe to dust. His last word was…" He paused. "It might have been 'Never.' Or perhaps 'Mother.'"

"That makes a difference," Fal-Tar observed.

"And yet no one will ever know."

Corvus turned away, back toward the window. He enjoyed Fal-Tar's discomfort; it was one of the few pleasures he'd found on this dreary world. But the line of skulls reminded him of his glorious past, the rapture he'd felt in service to his former master.

To the Black Order, every world was a match waiting to be lit.

As Corvus bent to replace the skull on its shelf, a tingle of anticipation ran up his spine. *She's here,* he realized. *Soon, I will see her again.*

"The Council of Officers," Fal-Tar said. "They're just lackeys to the Supreme Intelligence. And the Intelligence refuses to authorize the invasion…"

He trailed off, then cast a nervous look up at the ceiling. The chamber of the Supreme Intelligence, ruler of the Empire, was on the top floor of the Ministry, 105 levels above. Or was it 106? Corvus couldn't recall.

"Midnight," Corvus said.

A look of confusion crossed Fal-Tar's face. He turned, following Corvus's gaze to the spare metal doorway. Proxima Midnight stood silhouetted, spear in hand, her battle collar rising jagged and wide from her dark cerulean face.

"My love," she said, eyes glowing white.

She stepped inside. Fal-Tar shifted aside, wedging himself awkwardly between the wall and the small desk. Proxima glanced around at the tiny office.

"Modest," she said.

"It belonged to the Civilian Adjunct to the War Ministry," Corvus replied. "His constituency was not large."

Proxima raised an eyebrow. "And where is this Adjunct now?"

"Oddly…" Corvus held up a humanoid skull. "…he has not been seen of late."

Proxima smiled.

"This is Fal-Tar," Corvus said. "He was just briefing me on a disagreement between the Kree command and many of the rank-and-file soldiers."

Proxima turned to study Fal-Tar. He grimaced and cleared his throat. "We believe," he began. "That is, I have assembled a coalition of brave warriors who believe our leaders, chiefly the Supreme Intelligence and his Warmaster Ronan, have grown soft. They have betrayed the ancient way of the Kree."

Proxima planted herself before Fal-Tar. He frowned and gazed up at her, meeting her eyes.

"You seek revolution," she said.

"Only if necessary." He glanced at Corvus. "We seek strong leadership."

"This world is known for its racial divides." She stared into his eyes. "Are most of these revolutionaries pink of skin? Like yourself?"

Fal-Tar gazed nervously at her blue face. "Both races are represented."

"But your *leaders*—the ones you accuse of betrayal—are almost exclusively blue."

"I serve alongside Kree of both colors," Fal-Tar said. "They have saved my life in battle, and I theirs."

Proxima turned away, ignoring his answer. She crossed to Corvus and touched him on the chest. Her fingers sent a jolt through him.

"Your breathing is rapid," she said.

He took hold of her arms, staring into her blank eyes. The familiar electricity, the passion they shared, seemed to fill the air. He wanted her badly—wanted to feel her body bend beneath his, to stop all this endless, pointless *talking*.

But there was the Order. First and always, there was the Order.

"Did you bring him?" Corvus asked.

"He waits in an anteroom, on this level. I wanted to brief you first." Proxima hissed in a small breath. "I wanted to see you."

Again, the electric charge in the air. She flashed him a hungry smile, so quick that only he could see it.

"It has been a long time," he breathed.

Fal-Tar cleared his throat. Proxima's mouth curled into a sneer. *Oh,* Corvus thought, *oh you poor little man. You shouldn't have done that.*

Proxima whirled back to Fal-Tar, gripping her spear tight. She reached out a dark finger to tweak a pair of tiny buttons shaped like ringed planets, pinned to his shoulder.

"What are these?" she asked.

"We call them chevs." He frowned, clearly resenting her touch.

"They denote your military status."

"Yes. Princepes Lieutenant, Homeland Division."

"Is that an *impressive* rank among your people?"

Anger flashed across his face. A spark of black energy flared atop Proxima's staff. Fal-Tar took a step back.

"Lieutenant," Corvus said. "Please fetch our recruit from the anteroom."

Fal-Tar glanced at Proxima, then back at Corvus Glaive. "You are a paid consultant to the Kree, sir. Not our master." He hesitated. "Remember that."

Corvus reached out for his staff. Quick as lightning, he raised it in the air and smashed down the large blade, cleaving his desk in two.

"Please fetch our recruit," he repeated.

Fal-Tar nodded quickly and hurried toward the door. Proxima watched him, a smirk spreading over her lips. As soon as he was gone, she raised her head and laughed.

"Stealth and negotiation," she said, gesturing at the splintered remains of the desk. "They do not come naturally to you."

"The Order was made for greater things," Corvus growled.

She didn't answer. Her eyes locked onto his, and as she stepped toward him, a burst of black light appeared on the tip of her spear.

All at once Corvus softened. "Midnight," he whispered. "Dear Midnight."

An answering plume of fire flared on the end of his staff.

"You've been lonely," she said. "These past months."

"Yes. A lone wolf on a world of preening dogs."

The tip of his blade glowed red-hot. As always in Proxima's presence, he felt powerful, almost intoxicated. The air between them seemed charged with invisible particles. Her presence, her scent in the air, was overwhelming. He wanted her more than ever before.

But again, there was the Order.

"Your first recruit," he said. "The troll?"

One look at Proxima's face settled that matter.

"The other, then. The one who waits outside." Corvus paused, remembering. "Nil?"

"That was the name he used on the Church world. He refuses to respond to it now."

"But you believe he has potential?"

"He betrayed us," Proxima said. "But not to the Church—for his own ends. That audacity impresses me."

Corvus stared at her. There was more, he knew.

She paused, frowning. "He is…changeable. Even his appearance seems to vary."

Corvus raised an eyebrow. "A shapeshifter?"

"I'm not certain. As we approached Hala, he adopted the pink skin and green-white uniform of the Kree." She paused, then began to pace across the small room. "He has both ambition and intellect. But sometimes his…perceptions…they don't seem to align with the consensus reality."

Corvus nodded, absorbing the information. A shapeshifter—or even a master of disguise, accomplishing the same ends through trickery— could prove useful.

"The truly great forge their own reality," he said.

"Perhaps."

Silence, then. Corvus found his thoughts growing dark, recalling the glory days of the Order's past.

"Supergiant," he said. "Black Dwarf."

Proxima nodded. "Gone. Fallen teammates, lost in the name of the cause."

"And the Maw?"

"A different sort of loss." She hesitated. "I received a message while in transit. He's arrived on Chakrus Prime, where he seeks to pursue the discipline of the Leyan monks."

"Meditation and learning." Corvus spat the words.

"He seeks a new purpose." She touched his chest again. "Just as we do."

He whirled away. Anger ran through him, hot and white. He wasn't sure why.

"Some of us know our path," she continued. "Others spend a lifetime seeking it. But almost all beings *have* one. Attempting to break from it…that usually leads to disaster." She paused. "The Maw sees beyond our reality, perceives the branching strings of the universe. It is his gift—and perhaps his curse, as well. Give him time."

"He always distrusted emotion," Corvus said. "He believed that our union, you and I, would prove the Order's downfall."

"He may be right." She grabbed his shoulder and twisted him to face her. "Or it may be our greatest strength."

The bond between them was as strong, as tangible, as ever. But his anger remained. He tore his gaze away and strode around the shattered desk to the window. The city, the thousand-year-old industrial metropolis, seemed to stare up at him with a million eyes. A Kree heavy cruiser, bristling with weapons, rose up from the distant spaceport and wove its way between the skyscrapers.

"We could conquer them." Corvus clenched a bony fist. "Rip out their throats, you and I together, until they broke. We could force the oldest and proudest warrior race in the galaxy to bend its knees in surrender."

Soft as velvet, her gloved hand encircled his chest from behind. Her voice in his ear was like fire.

"But to what end?"

"Yes." He whirled around, took her face in his hands. "In death, they would be the lucky ones."

She nodded, eyes wide.

"They would serve us," he continued, "but whom do *we* serve?"

"I miss him, too." Her voice was almost too quiet to hear. "I miss the master."

"We must find another."

"That is the true reason I traveled to Sacrosanct."

"Is it he? The one you've brought?"

"I don't know," she whispered.

"I can break men, I can burn worlds. I can even practice *stealth* and *negotiation.*" He pressed her against the wall, moving his face very close to hers. "But I no longer see the purpose of it all."

She grabbed his cheeks and pulled his lips to hers. He reached out, drawing her close, and felt her cold blackness against his heat. They rolled along the wall, still standing, past the window and out of the light.

"None," she whispered, clawing his neck. "No purpose."

She held up her spear, and he met it with his staff. Bright fire met black light, strobing and vanishing into darkness. He threw down the staff and grabbed for her, wanting her more desperately than ever before. She laughed and flung her spear into the wreckage of his desk.

Then there was nothing. No Kree, no doubts, no doomed worlds circling madly in the night. Just a cold-light woman and a man of fire, desperate to find some peace in the violence.

"Um."

Still clinging to each other, they whirled around.

Fal-Tar stood in the doorway, breathing hard.

"I…" he gasped. "I checked the anteroom. I checked the whole floor."

Their cheeks touching, Corvus Glaive and Proxima Midnight glared at him. Corvus raised an eyebrow.

"There's no one here," Fal-Tar said.

FIFTEEN

A SOLDIER brushed past, muttering apologies. Thanos whirled, eyes flaring in anger. He reached inside his coat and touched his dagger, taking care to keep the blade out of sight.

Then he stopped. The man was large, imposing—almost the right build. His skin was pink, like Thanos's, and he wore the same Kree uniform with the ringed planet on the breast. But he bore four of the little planets, the chevs, on his shoulder. That was too high a rank.

The man trudged by, head down, and disappeared into the crowd.

Thanos stood still, forcing his temper down. He had a specific mission; it wouldn't do to start killing people for minor slights. That would only expose him to premature scrutiny.

The masses of Hala surrounded him, rushing and bustling from place to place. Narrow channels of humanity, hemmed in by a maze of skyscrapers. Some of the buildings were old, made of veined stones that curved around to form archways and courtyards.

Others, constructed more recently, rose seamlessly upward, polished plasteel walls stretching to the sky.

Across the street, past a steady stream of hovercars, an area had been roped off. The roof of an old office building had collapsed. The Kree had spent centuries prioritizing military spending over all else; that had left Hala's rulers strong, but its infrastructure weak.

Fully half the people on the street wore some variation of the green-and-white Kree military uniform. Some were veterans, some active duty; most had pink skin, but a few blue officers mingled with the crowd. He studied them, mentally ticking off one possibility at a time. A tall pink man in a civilian jumpsuit—useless. Hunched blue man in heavy green cloak—too short. Mid-rank woman in a green helmet—too tough to pull off.

How different this place was from Sacrosanct. The Church world sprawled low under a hot sun, its denizens scrabbling for a few credits or a scrap of food. Here, the seeds of empire had sprouted into a high, sprawling metropolis. All the people seemed to have tasks; the soldiers buzzed about, each one a scurrying insect in the vast planetary hive.

There was poverty on Hala. But it was hidden, squirreled away in basements and shelters and soup kitchens, only spilling out occasionally onto the street. A beggar in a tattered veteran's uniform, crouched on a green blanket.

Sacrosanct, Thanos realized, had felt like a fresh start. This was something else. Already his killer instinct had returned, the rage-fueled focus that had almost made him conqueror of all known space.

Almost.

A whirring sound drew his attention. He looked up as a squadron of Accusers flew by on skycycles, dangerously low. The leader gave an imperious wave to the people below.

"Watch where you're going."

He looked down. He'd almost walked into a big pink-skinned man in active-duty uniform, with no helmet. The man stopped to glare at Thanos. "Idiot," he said.

Thanos ran his eyes up and down the man. Late 30s, medium build, a bit taller than average. Face that looked like it had been bashed up a few times and rebuilt via laser-filament surgery. And on his shoulder...

"I don't see any chevs on that uniform," the man said. "What the hell is your rank?"

"I have none." Thanos paused. "Yet."

"That's impersonating an officer. I could execute you right now for that."

"Or," Thanos said, "you could move out of my way."

"Maybe I'll blast a hole in your ugly face. Let you bleed out right here in the street."

The man touched a proton gun strapped to his waist. Most Kree carried sidearms, Thanos knew, even here on Hala. Pedestrians were beginning to circle around, avoiding the confrontation.

"I see *your* rank is captain." Thanos pointed at the man's shoulder, which bore three of the small planet-pins. "I knew a captain once. His name was Mar-Vell."

"Mar-Vell? He was some kind of hero, wasn't he?"

"He was a pompous fool. And yet, twice the man you are."

"You *worm.*" The man stepped forward, fists clenched. "I was twice decorated in the Kree-Skrull War."

"That was some time ago. How is it you haven't risen past the rank of captain?"

The man charged, his face a mask of fury. Thanos sidestepped easily and reached for the man's throat. He jabbed two fingers into the captain's windpipe, shattering a specific sequence of bones. The officer gasped and doubled forward.

"Kree anatomy," Thanos said, catching the man, "has its weak points. A byproduct of frozen evolution, perhaps."

He steered the captain firmly toward an alley between two tall buildings. "Traumatic Stress Syndrome," he explained to a curious civilian.

When they were out of sight, Thanos slammed the man up against the stone wall, keeping one hand clamped on his throat. The captain struggled to breathe.

"Who—are you?" the Kree gasped.

"No no. That's not the question." Thanos moved his face close to the captain, studying him. "Who are *you?*"

"T-Teren-Sas. Captain Teren-Sas, 18th Star Division."

"Teren-Sas. That's an ancient term, isn't it?"

"Y-yes. Means…to cut a swath across the land."

"Oh." Excitement washed over Thanos; he couldn't keep it off his face. "Oh, *that* will do."

He whipped out the dagger and thrust it into the man's heart. As Teren-Sas cried out, Thanos clamped a hand over his mouth and forced the dagger forward and up, pressing his victim against the stone wall.

"I apologize for the slow death," Thanos whispered. "But even on this warlike world, a proton blast would not go unanswered. Or a bullet."

He glanced back. People filed by on the street, lost in their own concerns. No one had noticed.

Teren-Sas let out a final gurgle and was still. The smell of death, of voided bowels and fresh blood, filled the narrow alley. Thanos wrenched the knife free and allowed the body to slump to the pavement.

For a moment he stood still, staring at the knife. A memory flashed in his mind: the last victim he'd killed with a blade. The stunned, shocked face of Avia Shiv.

He shook his head. That was then—another time, another life. As far away, now, as the glorious burning of the Infinity Gauntlet on his fist.

He tossed the blade aside, crouched down, and started rummaging through the Kree's belt. Located an ident-card with the captain's name, rank, and photo on it. He rolled the man on his side and unpinned one, two, three chevs from his shoulder.

Thanos was just pinning the last of the symbols onto his own uniform when a familiar voice said, "You haven't lost your skill with the blade."

He whirled around. Proxima Midnight stood,

tall and imposing, in the mouth of the alley. As she studied the Kree soldier's body, her mouth twisted into a cruel smile.

Thanos reached down to the ground, unhurried, and retrieved his blade.

"You once asked me to prove myself," he said.

She nodded.

Another figure loomed behind her: Corvus Glaive. Glaring, fearsome with his tattered black cloak and lethal staff. Every feature on his face was sharp, from his dark eyes to his deadly teeth to the bone at the tip of his chin. He stepped into the alley, studying Thanos.

"Your name," Corvus demanded.

Thanos handed him the ident-card. "Teren-Sas."

Corvus Glaive looked at the card. "Eighteenth Star Division," he read. He glanced at the soldier's body, then handed the card back to Thanos.

"I believe Captain Teren-Sas will require a transfer," Proxima said. "His fellow soldiers might ask the wrong questions."

"Fal-Tar can manage that," Corvus said. "Centuries of war have left the Kree's internal record-keeping in considerable disarray."

They stood side by side in the alley entrance. Good, Thanos thought. He'd been planning to confront them, to explain his plan. This would save time.

But they were blocking his exit. He felt a pang of fear. Corvus Glaive, he thought. The scourge of a dozen worlds. Once I was his master, but no more. Now I'm the same as anyone else to him: a potential victim. If he chooses, he can incinerate me on the spot.

And then Thanos remembered: Corvus Glaive is a killer, a warrior. There are only two options: gain his trust or become his prey.

Thanos drew himself up to his full height, glanced briefly at the planet-chevs on his shoulder, and turned to face Corvus. "What now?"

Corvus stared back, Proxima by his side. For a moment, Thanos felt the sheer horror that had swept across entire systems upon the arrival of the Black Order.

"You can kill," Corvus Glaive said. "Can you speak?"

SIXTEEN

THE PROUD Kree Empire. For centuries, it has spanned the stars, dominating the largest expanse of space ever united under one flag. It has withstood the attacks of gods and armies, sorcerers and Skrulls—resisted infiltration and invasion alike with a steely will and a force of arms unmatched in all the universe. No man, no alien, no otherdimensional entity has ever proven its equal."

Thanos paused.

"I am here to tell you: The Empire is doomed."

He raised his eyes from the marble lectern and gazed out across the vast hall. Two, maybe three hundred soldiers stared back at him. Every one of them wore some version of the green-and-white Kree military uniform.

The Hall of Battle stood on the outskirts of the city. It was one of the oldest structures on Hala, a relic of the Kree's ancient past. Rows of hand-carved stone benches ringed the main stage, rising up above it. Thanos had to stare up at his audience; he resented this, but he also recognized the justice of it.

The walls bore wide murals depicting ancient battles: Kree legions waging war against the Skrulls, against brightly feathered Shi'ar, against the sentient plants called the Cotati. Most of the Kree in the murals, Thanos noticed, had blue skin. Most of the soldiers in the room were pink.

Thanos himself wore the uniform and chevs of the dead captain, Teren-Sas. He had not donned the green-finned Kree battle helmet, with its opaque lenses. He wanted the crowd to see his eyes.

"The Empire is doomed," he repeated. "Not at the hands of our ancient shape-changing foes, nor by some Annihilation Wave from the Negative Zone. Our failure—the fatal flaw of the Kree—comes from within."

A low murmur rippled through the crowd. A group of hardened security officers paused in the act of polishing guns to look up at the podium. A cluster of old men, veterans of assorted wars, muttered knowingly among themselves. Medical officers, Operations, Security—each group paused, whispering, to consider Thanos's words. In the front row, a squadron of noncoms just listened, their eyes wide.

They're not sure, he thought. They don't know where I'm going with this yet. But they're intrigued.

He glanced to his right. Corvus Glaive and Proxima Midnight stood like a fearsome honor guard, allowing their representative to make his case. Corvus gazed around the hall, smiling a rictus grin. Proxima's blank eyes were fixed on the crowd; a flash of black energy played on the edge of her spear.

To Thanos's left, Fal-Tar hissed in a nervous breath. The Kree lieutenant had called this session in secret, assembling officers he knew and trusted. "Now he's turning it over to you," Corvus had said before the meeting. "A man he's never met. If this goes poorly, his life is forfeit."

"I'm surprised he agreed to that," Thanos had replied.

Corvus had bared his teeth. "'Agreed'?"

Thanos squared his shoulders and addressed the audience.

"A leader who does not respect his soldiers is no leader," he said. "A ruling body that betrays the ideals of its people cannot survive. The Kree stand for honor, for conquest, for the glory that lives in battle and sacrifice, and the victory won at the barrel of a gun…"

He pulled out his sword, aimed its thin blade at the domed ceiling high above.

"…or the point of a blade."

The ripple turned to applause. A few Kree banged on the seats in front of them. Most were nodding, turning to whisper to each other. But a few still sat with their arms crossed, frowning.

"The *Supreme Intelligence* " He spat the words, then paused, "…has failed us. This bloated creature feeds on the life-energy of our people, the millions who have died in service of the Empire. Yet the so-called 'Intelligence' is weak. Passive. Unworthy of your loyalty, your continued fealty."

A rumble ran through the crowd. Careful, Thanos

told himself. The Intelligence had indeed grown distant in recent years, withdrawing from contact with its subjects. But many of the Kree still worshiped it, almost as a deity.

He decided to shift tactics. "Consider the planet Hemithea," he said. "This filthy rock taunts the Empire, defies us with its so-called passive resistance. Its people have insulted us time and again, treated the mighty Kree as equals—no, as beings *lesser* than themselves."

"Filthy mountain goats," an older woman muttered.

A young officer with pink skin stood up. "I heard they took an *entire standard day* to respond to a demand for tribute."

Murmurs of agreement from around the room.

"And yet…" Thanos raised his voice over the rumbling. *"And yet,* these slights have not been countered. If ever a world begged for invasion, for subjugation at the barb of the whip, it is this one. Your peers, the women and men who serve in the field— all have called for swift action. The Chief-Techs, the Quantum Mechanics, and the Operations Specialists stand ready, prepared to guide the SabreStar Armada on this mission of vengeance. I see many representatives from those groups here in this room today.

"But what do we hear from the Intelligence? Silence."

More agreement, a few cheers. I've got them, he thought. They're on the hook. Time to reel them in.

"We have the Armada," he said, "the most fearsome battle fleet ever assembled. We wield the

Omni-Wave Projector, the weapon that has laid waste to dozens of worlds. And most of all: We have *you*. The most disciplined, highly trained corps of officers and soldiers the universe has ever known. To deny you your birthright, your pursuit of conquest, is not merely wrong. It is an offense against *nature*."

The cheers grew louder. Even Fal-Tar was nodding now.

"Join me," Thanos continued. "Let me lead you to victory over Hemithea, over all who spit on the word *Kree*. In the crucible of fiery battle, we will return the Empire to its lost glory."

A flurry of applause filled the room.

"Excuse me. Sir?"

Thanos searched the audience. A brawny young man stood up, a troubled expression on his face. A woman with very similar pink features sat at his side; a single planet-shaped chev adorned each of their uniforms.

"Many of us agree with you," the man said. "Including my sister and me. You say what we have been thinking, but have been afraid to speak aloud."

"That," Thanos replied, "is precisely what I hope to correct."

"But what exactly are you proposing we *do?*" the woman asked. "Storm the Supreme Intelligence's chambers? Wage civil war across Hala?"

"We must launch the Armada," Thanos said. "We must be true to ourselves."

"But what of the Accusers?" the young man asked.

"They report directly to Warmaster Ronan, and he is right hand to the Intelligence. They will not allow us to defy its direct orders."

"The Accusers will fall in line," Thanos replied.

"They are blue skins," an old officer snarled. "They care nothing for us."

"Defy the Intelligence?" a woman muttered. "Madness. It's blasphemy."

The crowd began to fracture into small groups, speaking in low, troubled voices. Thanos frowned, choosing his words carefully.

"The Kree are feared throughout known space," he said. "The approach of our ships, the flare of the Omni-Wave, the sight of green-and-white legions marching across an arena of conquest…these are harbingers of doom, omens to chill the blood of lesser beings from the Magellanic Clouds to the farthest reaches of Andromeda.

"But there is another side to the Kree, one we choose *not* to show to outsiders. A warm, nurturing side. No people in the universe care more deeply for their families, their friends, the officers they fight beside. None have a stronger sense of spirituality, a more vital connection to their own world and the stars beyond."

The crowd grew quiet. Most of them were nodding. Corvus and Proxima watched Thanos carefully, as if grading his performance.

"And that spirituality," Thanos continued, "that warmth, that knowledge of connection—all of it stems from our inner core. It is born of, nurtured by, and utterly dependent on our warrior spirit."

Fal-Tar gazed straight out at the crowd, a curious expression on his face. Was that a tear in his eye?

"*This* is what the Supreme Intelligence has lost track of. *This* is the reason we must seize control. Even if it means blood is shed on the tar of the spaceport before the Armada can reach hyperspace and the prize that waits at the starbow's end."

A mural on the far wall caught Thanos's eye: a bald pink man in ragged clothes, raising his staff to lead his people into battle.

"Centuries ago, Morag—first leader of the Kree—stood in this very spot, urging his people on to glory against the Skrulls. He began a legacy of honor and conquest, a tradition of pride that has fueled our people for centuries. Now history calls, and we must rise to the challenge of our ancestors.

"To do otherwise is to sacrifice our souls."

The noncoms stood first, yelling and pumping their fists in the air. The veterans glanced at them, then rose to their feet, wincing with the effort, and joined in. One by one, the other groups began to clap and cheer.

Corvus Glaive stepped up to hiss into Thanos's ear. "My Midnight chose you well."

Thanos smiled.

"Teren-Sas."

The voice cut through the cheering. A thin man, seated in the back row. He wore a dark green uniform with three chevs on his shoulder—the same rank as Thanos's assumed identity.

"That is your name, is it not?" The man leaned forward. A jagged scar bisected his face from the upper-left down to the lower-right corner of his chin.

"It is," Thanos said.

"I find it curious," the man continued, "that no others from your division are present here today."

Fal-Tar stepped forward. "The 18th Star Division was ordered offworld yesterday. Another arbitrary decision by the Warmaster."

Or, Thanos thought, a computer error orchestrated by Fal-Tar himself.

The man didn't seem satisfied. As the crowd grew quiet, he stood up. A few other officers sat near him, including two of the few blue-skinned men in the room.

"There are stories about Teren-Sas," the scarred man said. "It is said you drugged a fellow officer, a young Tech named Sere-Nah, while on a mission to a hostile planetoid. After you bedded her, she scorned you and refused your advances. So you left her to die on that barren world."

Murmurs rose up among the crowd.

"When the contact officer, a man named Char-Nak, attempted to rescue her, you fired the ship's main engines. Char-Nak was conveniently caught in the reactor chamber as eight million ergs of transpatial energy erupted all around him. The resulting burns left him two-thirds blind and unable to speak."

Thanos reached down to touch the hilt of his sword. For the first time, he wished he'd learned more about the man whose identity he'd adopted.

Looks of suspicion from the crowd, now. The security officers had stopped polishing their guns and sat staring at Thanos with naked suspicion.

"And now you stand before us," the man continued, "urging us to rebel against our leaders, abandon traditions and institutions that have stood for thousands of years. Why should we trust you?"

"Enough." Fal-Tar pulled out a proton gun.

The scarred man took a step down, toward the stage. He fixed his eyes on Fal-Tar.

"I know you," he said. "You are a man of honor, though some doubt your courage." The man cast his gaze over to Thanos, and then to the Black Order. "But I do not know *him*. And I certainly don't know these offworlders who stand with him today."

Fal-Tar blinked. His gun hand wavered.

Thanos looked out over the crowd, over rows of suspicious eyes. Only a moment ago, they'd been ready to follow him across the galaxy. Now…

Options flashed through his mind. Whatever sins the real Teren-Sas had committed, clearly he'd been exonerated. Command had accepted that the woman was stranded by necessity; the contact officer's injuries had been ruled a tragic accident. Otherwise, Teren-Sas would not have remained an active officer.

I could bluff this out, Thanos thought. I could deny responsibility, challenge the group to consult the official records. That, he suspected, was what the late Teren-Sas would have done.

It was what Thanos would have done, too.

He removed his hand from his weapon and stepped out from behind the podium. "You are correct," he said, looking the scarred man in the eye.

The man blinked.

"You do not know me," Thanos continued. "And I have indeed made mistakes in my life. The warrior's path is brutal, and at times it hardens our hearts. Everyone in this room knows that pain."

A few mutters of assent.

"I have sinned," Thanos admitted. "But that was a different time. *This* time, this moment, does not allow me that luxury. The stakes are too high. We face a crisis of faith, of leadership—a threat to the Empire itself.

"This much I know, in my heart: The Kree need a leader. A soldier who has fought in the trenches and along the spaceways, who has known both the glory and the price of war. Not a pompous Accuser who speeds his skycycle high above the crowd. Not a disembodied head in a tank.

"I did not choose this time, but it has chosen me. And so I have become a good man. I *must* be a good man, a good leader. Because the alternative is unthinkable."

The soldiers watched him carefully now. About half seemed convinced, nodding their heads and whispering to each other. Others still frowned, suspicious.

"Will you join me?" Thanos reached out a hand to the challenger. "Will you trust a fellow soldier, a man who has fallen low enough to understand your struggles?

Will you grant me the privilege of leading you?"

The man stared at Thanos's hand. He took a step back, as if threatened by the gesture.

"I'd—*hakkk*—like to say something."

An old bald man struggled to his feet. He wore a heavy, solid-green uniform of a type not used for many years. As he tottered against his walking staff, a few other veterans rushed to support him.

"My name is Zy-Ro," the man said. "I was a Chief-Tech before most of these babies took up arms to fight for a bottle of synth-milk. I fought the Skrulls, the Shi'ar. Even visited *Earth,* that wretched ball of mud. Should have burned the Omni-Wave across that whole cursed place, scorched it from pole to pole."

"I agree." Thanos gestured for the man to continue.

"We planted the flag on a dozen worlds. Hundreds." Zy-Ro paused for breath. "And now we won't even send a regiment to this Hemi, Hemo, whatever? I hear it's just a desert planet full of nomads."

"I hear they breathe methane," an old woman said. "I mean, methane?"

"The Kree used to keep order," Zy-Ro continued. "Move in, teach the locals who's boss, then leave behind a couple of Sentries. They were a living reminder of who was in charge."

Another veteran laughed. "The Sentries aren't living, Zy. They're robots!"

"Shut up, you old coot!" Zy-Ro brushed pridefully at his uniform. "The Sentries were a *constant* reminder. But at some point, they were deemed 'not worth the fuel required for transport.' Now they just stand there, towering over the Hala spaceport, rusting on their feet."

Thanos raised an eyebrow. He'd seen the Sentries—giant robots built to resemble soldiers—lined up, unmoving, in rows along the edge of the spaceport. Relics of the Kree's imperialist past.

"And what about the ships?" Zy-Ro looked around, apparently disoriented. "They're not…I mean, they're falling to…"

A large woman crossed to Zy-Ro and steadied him. She had heavy silver cables plugged into her skull, reaching around her torso and into her uniform. A Quantum Mechanic, Thanos realized. This class of officers was relatively new; with their ability to interface directly with starship computer systems, they had effectively replaced the Techs. It was said they could control the Omni-Wave weapons telepathically.

Thanos strode off the stage and up the steps, into the audience. When he reached Zy-Ro, the woman was settling him down into his seat. A mixed group of soldiers, mostly veterans and Quantum Mechs, had gathered around them.

Thanos reached out and touched Zy-Ro on the shoulder. "Thank you for your service."

The old man looked away, as if embarrassed at his own fragility.

"I promise you," Thanos continued, "we will restore the Empire to its glory. The blood you shed, the sacrifices your comrades made in times past, will not be in vain."

A tear appeared in Zy-Ro's eye.

Thanos turned to the woman. "You represent the Mechanics?"

She nodded. "Captain Al-Bar."

"Your support is crucial." He gestured at Zy-Ro. "The venerable Chief-Tech spoke true. The ships *have* been allowed to decay. No invasion can succeed without your expertise and constant repair work."

"That is true," she said.

"The key is power." Thanos whirled, speaking to the crowd all around him. "All empire, all sense of self, is based on power. We must seize it. Nothing else matters."

"That's the first honest thing you've said today, Teren-Sas."

Thanos turned. The challenger from before, the man with the scarred face, stood at the base of the aisle. His officer friends had gathered around him, blocking Thanos's path back to the stage.

"If you seek power," the man continued, "you should know that the Kree respect deeds over words."

One of the other officers, a woman, handed the man a heavy, thick-bladed sword. That officer had pink skin, but the others with them were blue. Thanos wondered whether one or more of them was a plant, sent by the Supreme Intelligence to disrupt the meeting.

"You compare yourself to Morag," the scarred man sneered. "This is how he dealt with challengers. Not with words—nor a bloodless firearm."

The man pressed a stud on the sword's hilt. A deadly electric charge sparked along the length of the blade.

"You look like a Kree," the man continued. "But you talk like a *Skrull*."

Thanos felt the crowd hush around him. A *Skrull*, he thought—the ultimate insult. It didn't matter anymore whether the challenge was sincere or calculated. Either way, Thanos had to respond.

Fal-Tar watched nervously. Proxima and Corvus moved to either end of the stage, assuming defensive positions. They eyed Thanos, waiting for a signal—or for the first sign of violence.

Thanos locked eyes briefly with Corvus and cocked his head. Corvus reached behind the podium and tossed Thanos's sword across the room, over the startled challenger's head. Thanos held up a hand and snatched it out of the air.

He shifted his hand, testing the sword. The ordinary sword, with its thin blade. The sword he'd acquired on Sacrosanct, from a woman whose face he could now barely recall.

The scarred man waved his own sword in the air, leaving an electrical after-image in its wake. "The traditional weapons are ion blades. You place yourself at a disadvantage."

Thanos smiled. "This will do." He stepped forward, holding his sword up before him.

In the next aisle, Proxima Midnight slammed her spear down onto the floor. Waves of black-light energy rose up from it. The crowd let out murmurs of surprise.

"No one is to interfere," she said.

Thanos was impressed. He hadn't even seen her leave the stage.

One by one, the Kree nodded. They began to edge away from Thanos and his opponent, leaving the wide aisle open for the duel. The Quantum Mechanics helped Zy-Ro to his feet; the young noncoms scurried out of their seats in clumps, smiling at the prospect of a fight.

One of the blue officers shrugged and clapped the scarred man on his shoulder, then retreated to the side.

Thanos took another step toward his opponent. "What is your name?"

The man frowned. "What?"

"Your name."

"Ray-Mar." The man's sword wavered. "Why do you ask?"

"I would honor you after your death."

As Thanos closed in, Ray-Mar thrust forward. His sword cleaved the air, flaring with electricity. A bold stroke, Thanos thought, intended to intimidate one's opponent. Against the real Teren-Sas, it might have won the day.

Thanos parried it easily. As the blades touched, several hundred volts jolted through his sword, surging into his hand. With an effort, he maintained his grip.

At just the right moment, he leapt back and whirled around in a full circle. His blade struck his surprised opponent in the shoulder, drawing blood. Ray-Mar cried out in surprise.

On the stage, Corvus Glaive let out a delighted

hiss. Fal-Tar seemed terrified. His eyes followed Thanos's every move.

Ray-Mar jabbed wildly. Thanos ducked low, and his opponent's sword struck a stone column, knocking the man off-balance. Ray-Mar fell to the floor and rolled away in retreat.

Thanos strode down the aisle, the sword gripped tight in his fist. He realized, to his surprise, that the skills he'd picked up on Sacrosanct had given him the upper hand. Perhaps that life wasn't so distant as he'd thought.

He stomped a boot down on Ray-Mar's hand. Ray-Mar cried out and lost his grip on his sword. It skittered across the floor, sparking harmlessly.

The old man, Zy-Ro, rose to his feet. "FINISH HIM!"

A hush fell over the Kree. Weapons Officers, Security, Navigators, and Ops Specialists all watched, waiting. An aisle away, Proxima Midnight smiled in anticipation.

On the floor, Ray-Mar winced, flexing his hand in pain. Thanos slashed and split the man's uniform down the middle, carving a shallow vertical wound into his chest. Ray-Mar's chevs burst free of his shoulder, clattering to the floor.

Thanos stood above him, twirling his sword and drinking in the man's fear. For the first time in as long as he could remember, he could feel his Mistress's presence. Death hovered just out of sight, waiting to claim her victim.

Ray-Mar clutched his chest, then held up a hand

coated with a thin sheen of blood. "Well?" he hissed.

Thanos smiled. He looked down at his enemy, watched Ray-Mar's expression turn from defiance to confusion. Thanos maintained eye contact long enough to let Ray-Mar know: *I am your master now.*

Thanos sheathed his sword. He reached down and scooped up the three small planet-shaped pins from the floor, then held them out to his dazed opponent.

"You'll be needing these," he said.

Stunned, Ray-Mar took hold of his recovered chevs. Thanos held out a hand, and Ray-Mar reached out to grasp it. He allowed Thanos to lift him to his feet.

"The rebellion," Thanos said, "needs every soldier."

Ray-Mar nodded.

Thanos felt all eyes on him. The Kree were nodding, beginning to accept the outcome. Proxima and Corvus eyed Thanos, their weapons grasped firmly.

On the stage, Fal-Tar slumped in relief. Thanos almost laughed at the Kree's expression. *Little man,* he thought, *you're welcome. I've Just saved your life.*

Thanos raised his voice, turning slowly to address all occupants of the room in turn. "In four days," he boomed, "the ships will launch. No one will stop us: not Ronan, not the Intelligence, not the gods themselves. *Hemithea will fall.*"

For a moment, time stood still. Then the room exploded into applause, louder and more fervent than before. The Kree shook their fists in the air, chanting "Hemithea! Hemithea!" The old man, Zy-Ro, banged his staff against the floor. Captain Al-Bar, the

Quantum Mechanic, met Thanos's eyes and mouthed the words: *We are with you.*

Ray-Mar's friends were bandaging his chest. He turned to Thanos, smiled, and pumped his wounded fist in the air.

"Hemithea!" he cried.

As the Order approached, Thanos felt a twinge of doubt. In sparing Ray-Mar, he had failed Death; he no longer felt her presence. But for now, the plan must trump his instincts. Thanos had been challenged—not merely his will, but his reputation, as well. Saving Ray-Mar had allowed him to redeem his new identity, to prove himself a fair and honorable leader.

Ray-Mar had been right about one thing: *The Kree respect deeds over words.*

Death would have her day. The Mistress would drink in thousands, millions of souls. Soon the Kree army would usher in a new era of slaughter, wash whole galaxies in blood…

…under the firm hand of Captain Teren-Sas.

The Kree milled out of the hall, talking excitedly among themselves. A few of them paused to clap Thanos on the back.

Corvus Glaive and Proxima Midnight approached Thanos. Proxima's smile was as unnerving as ever.

"Well played," she said.

Fal-Tar approached, swiping madly at a comm-tablet. "Word of your speech has already spread."

Corvus raised an eyebrow. "The Supreme Intelligence?"

"He'll have to negotiate soon. This is growing too big, too fast, for him to ignore."

Proxima's eyes were still fixed on Thanos. "And what will you tell him?"

Thanos's gaze strayed to another of the murals lining the stone walls: a symbolic depiction of a pink Kree in full battle gear and helmet. He sat astride a sleek hyperspace vessel, urging his armada forward against the twisted battleships of the Skrull. Ba-Tarr—that was his name. The first Kree commander to wear the now-familiar green and white, and the first to take the war to his ancient enemies' homeworld.

"Whatever I must," Thanos said.

SEVENTEEN

"**HEY, DO** whatever you want. I'm just telling you: If you continue with this pathetic plan, you'll be squashed flatter than a baby Skrull under a mass driver."

Gamora leaned back and took a long drink from her glass. Tiny explosions popped in the liquid as it flowed into her mouth.

Thanos fought to keep his panic in check. Why? he thought. Why is *she* here?

Corvus and Proxima said nothing. They sat rigid on their stools, waiting for Thanos to reply.

They were gathered around a high table in the Raptor, a military bar just outside the spaceport. It was old, but clean, a place for spacers to grab a quick drink before resuming their duties. A sharp contrast to the dirty, lazy public houses of Sacrosanct. Soldiers bustled back and forth, saluting each other and snapping out drink orders.

Thanos's head was spinning. When the Supreme Intelligence had announced he was sending a representative, Fal-Tar had suggested the Raptor as a safe place to meet. But now Thanos felt trapped, as if he'd been snared in an invisible web.

Gamora? Of all people in the universe?

Corvus Glaive frowned at Thanos, then shifted his staff. Fire flared at its tip. Grinning, he leaned forward over the table until his bony countenance hung inches from Gamora's face.

"Is that a threat?" he asked.

"I'm not being paid to make threats." She shrugged at the staff, then turned to stare Corvus in the eye. "Just to deliver a message."

"The Order," Proxima said slowly, "does not respond well to threats."

"Or messages," Corvus added.

Thanos studied Gamora's olive-green face, her dark emerald robes, gloves, and cape. Possibly the deadliest woman in the universe—and he knew her very, very well. Thanos had adopted Gamora as a child, raised her, taught her the assassin's arts. Now she sat across from him, on the last world where he would ever have expected to find her.

Does she know? he wondered. *Is she really here for* me?

And what of the rest of her team? Were the Guardians of the Galaxy on Hala, too?

Gamora drained her glass and banged it on the table. A waiter rushed up with a fresh drink. It sparked and bubbled even more violently than the first.

"The Kree crave battle," Thanos said. "They are determined to invade Hemithea. Your masters cannot stop it."

"There's so many things wrong with that statement, I don't know where to start." Gamora began ticking off items on her long green fingers. "First off, have you been to this Hemithea they're babbling about?"

Corvus and Proxima stared blankly.

"It's a barren rock," Gamora continued. "Something like 50 people live there, and 48 of them are starving. I could conquer it with a hot-air balloon and an X-Acto knife."

Thanos nodded. He'd already realized the Kree soldiers knew nothing about their invasion target.

"*That's* why the Supreme Intelligence hasn't ordered an invasion." Gamora took another drink. "He knows he can wait five years, and the Hemitheans will just die out on their own. Three if there's a bad storm."

She paused, waiting for a challenge.

"Second," Gamora continued, "I have no *masters*. I'm just a freelancer, delivering a message from the Supreme Intelligence."

Corvus raised an eyebrow. "Does the Intelligence not have Kree to do his bidding?"

"I don't see a lot of Kree speaking for *your* side." She laughed. "The Kree power structure is not prepared to engage your little rebellion in formal negotiations. That would be seen as a display of weakness."

"So they sent a member of a *lesser* race to deliver their message."

She grinned. "You got it, bony."

"And this does not insult you?"

"Forty thousand credits soothes a lot of hurt feelings. Besides, the drinks are comped." She drained her glass. "Mine, not yours."

Thanos felt Corvus and Proxima's eyes upon him. I have to say something, he realized. They're deferring to me; they expect me to take point. If I don't pull this off, I'll lose their support.

"We were not deceived by the agitators sent to disrupt our meeting," he said, leaning forward toward Gamora. "A clumsy move on the Intelligence's part."

"Don't know about that. Don't care." She stretched out her gloved arms and mimed an elaborate yawn. "Kree politics bores the hell out of me."

"The rebellion *will* go forward."

"Again," she replied, "don't care."

"The ships will launch. I couldn't stop them now if I tried."

She turned sharply toward him, her eyes dark and probing. A memory flashed through his mind: Gamora at age 10, asking some question about the fusion reactions within a star. The same searching, suspicious expression on her face, alert for deception or an ill-conceived bluff.

"When the Accusers mow your guys down, I'll be watching the vid-feed with a tub of popcorn in my lap." Her voice was careful, measured. "That's an Earth tradition."

"I'm familiar."

"I think perhaps you are."

Again, a stab of panic. Did she know?

"I've done my homework on you, *Teren-Sas.*" Her merciless eyes stayed on him. "You've left a trail of broken lives in your wake. Did that officer on the Terran mission ever recover from the psych-probe you left her in?"

Panic gave way to relief: Gamora didn't seem to know his true identity after all. On the other hand, he found himself wishing again that he'd investigated Teren-Sas's history more thoroughly.

"My enemies rarely recover," he said.

"That's cute. Put it on a bumper sticker—another Earth custom." Gamora held up her empty glass, frowning. "Should I have one more? I did mention they're comped, didn't I?"

Thanos felt his temper rising. So arrogant, he thought. She'd always been that way, even as a child.

"What do you want?" he growled.

"I have what I want. Forty thousand credits." She rose from the bar stool. "And I've delivered my message. Like I said, you can do what you want."

"There will be blood," Corvus Glaive hissed.

"Cool." She swept her cape around her and turned to leave. "Have fun with that."

As she strode through the crowd, a few Kree turned to watch. Gamora's flowing garb stood out in the blur of uniforms. She paused to hiss in a startled soldier's face, then swept through the door and was gone.

The buzz of the Raptor filled Thanos's ears. People laughed, flirted, whispered confidences. A waitress with a full tray nudged past him, murmuring apologies.

Thanos realized he was shaking. *Gamora,* he thought. *Was* she on to him? Was she playing with him, setting some sadistic trap? The Guardians could be lying in wait just outside the bar. The Destroyer might be polishing his knives, salivating at the thought of revenge against his longtime foe.

"Teren-Sas?" Corvus asked.

Thanos drew in a deep breath. Forced his doubts and his fears to recede. There was no time for second thoughts—not now.

"Tomorrow," he said, feeling his confidence build. "Tomorrow it begins."

"You realize," Corvus said, "the Intelligence will attempt to put down the rebellion."

"I'm counting on it." Thanos smiled. "In fact, I'm more concerned that he won't."

"What do you mean?" Proxima asked.

"The Supreme Intelligence keeps his people on a leash. But that leash is long. He may allow them to launch the ships after all."

Corvus leaned forward, his head snaking back and forth in an unnerving fashion. "And you *don't* want that?"

"No more *questions!*"

Thanos slammed his fist down, splintering the table. Wooden legs cracked; drinks spilled in all directions. Corvus and Proxima jumped to their feet as the table collapsed.

I didn't feel it, he realized. I didn't feel the blow. He stared down at his hand, unclenching and unclenching his fist. It was thick, rocky, gray.

The fist of Thanos.

Reality seemed to waver. For a moment, the walls of Death's castle surrounded him, high and claustrophobic. Thick, green-tinged stones, smelling of decay.

He blinked, and the bar returned. A waiter stood nearby with a trash bag, eyeing the wreckage of the table. Patrons had risen to their feet, watching.

Corvus and Proxima knelt before him—eyes downcast, their weapons clutched loosely at their sides.

"Master," Corvus Glaive said. "Forgive us."

Stunned, Thanos glanced down at his fist. It was Kree-sized again, and bore the green glove of Captain Teren-Sas.

He turned back to Proxima and Corvus. Had they seen? Had they beheld the true face of Thanos, returned to them?

Proxima winced as a bit of broken glass bit into her knee. She glanced at her husband, then turned blank eyes to gaze up at Thanos.

"What is your bidding?"

Thanos studied them. Two of the most powerful beings in the universe, capable of ravaging worlds. And yet, above all else, they craved a master. Their power, their iron will, even the *love* Corvus and Proxima shared—all of it rested on that simple power dynamic. The Order played at dominance, but their lives were submission.

Just like the Kree.

Thanos smiled. He gestured, broadly, for the duo to rise.

"Let's get some sleep," he said. "After all, we're only mortal."

○————————————○

PROXIMA MIDNIGHT led her husband away from the Raptor, into the depths of the city. Beggars lined the streets; trash blew across the gutters. Long-shuttered storefronts bore faded signs promising discount cosmetics and cash for precious metals.

Corvus Glaive was silent.

When she was sure they were alone, Proxima pressed him up against a flickering streetlamp. She stared into his eyes.

"It's him," she said. "I'm sure of it."

Corvus let out a strange moan.

"He will lead us," Proxima said. "Again."

Corvus collapsed in her arms, sobbing. She held him, rocking him slowly in the dim light.

"Thank the gods," he gasped.

EIGHTEEN

FAL-TAR, Princepes Lieutenant in the Homeland Division of the Exalted Kree Army, gazed up at the smog-clouded sky. All around him, across the vast expanse of the spaceport, the chant rose up: "In-vade. In-vade. IN-VADE."

Proxima Midnight favored him with a mocking grin. "Your revolution is here."

Fal-Tar turned away. The outworlder was right; this should have been a moment of triumph. But all Fal-Tar could think was: I don't belong here.

They stood with Corvus Glaive just outside the thick circular structure of the central command building. Its tower rose up into the sky, filled with command posts serving as traffic control for the enormous number of ships coming and going from Hala. Satellite dishes provided constant contact with the Kree's orbital stations and outposts elsewhere in Hala's system.

Barracks stretched out along the pavement on either side of the tower, low warehouse-style military quarters covering a quarter-mile of land.

Kree soldiers, hundreds of them, stood outside the barracks, pumping fists in the air and chanting their demands. Officers and noncoms, Techs and Security and Navigators and Quantum Mechanics. All waiting for the command to board their ships.

But not all the Kree were united in this cause. A coterie of high-ranking generals stood clustered together just outside the door of the command tower. They whispered angrily among themselves, casting glares at the assembled soldiers. Every one of them had blue skin.

The air seemed charged with ozone. Thick and moist, mixed with soot from the industrial plants in the distance.

Fal-Tar checked his chronometer. Four minutes. Four minutes to the deadline they'd given the Supreme Intelligence, the ultimatum to invade Hemithea—or face open rebellion.

"Soon," Corvus Glaive said. "Soon we will learn what your people are made of."

Fal-Tar grimaced back. He'd been leery of Corvus from the beginning. Stories of the Black Order had circulated around Hala, tales of slaughter and genocide. Fal-Tar knew his wife would have warned against this alliance. She'd have told him to smile, walk away, and live to fight another day.

But Ji-Ann wasn't here. She was stationed somewhere in Shi'ar space, doing her duty for the Empire. In her absence, their daughter Ki-Ta had been placed in a state-run communal school, a facility for military orphans. There she would be judged and classified for future service, as per Kree tradition.

Fal-Tar almost never saw Ki-Ta. He was afraid of her. At age five, she had her mother's steely, intimidating glare and unshakable will. She was already more of a true Kree than Fal-Tar would ever be.

That realization, that fear, was what had brought him to this point. From a young age, Fal-Tar had known he was no warrior. His life since then had been a series of humiliations and compromises, hard-won promotions followed by unexplained losses of status and income. No one—not even Ji-Ann, beautiful, sharp-edged Ji-Ann—truly respected him. And respect was what he craved, more than anything else in the world.

So he'd chosen a career with the Homeland Division. He'd risen within the nooks and crannies of the Kree hierarchy, developing contacts among the various classes of officers and enlisted men. He'd taken a seat briefly on the Council of Officers before deciding it was a sham, a powerless body designed to trick the rank-and-file into believing they had a voice in policy.

And then Corvus Glaive had approached him with an offer. All Fal-Tar's instincts had screamed: This is wrong, this is dangerous, this creature cannot be trusted. This venture will end in blood and death.

By that time, however, he'd grown accustomed to ignoring his instincts. And he couldn't resist a chance for power. So he struck the deal.

Corvus Glaive was frightening enough. But then

Proxima Midnight had arrived—with that mysterious Kree Captain who seemed to hold some power over the Black Order. For some reason, Teren-Sas frightened Fal-Tar more than the other two combined.

But it was too late. He'd made his choice.

Perhaps there's hope, Fal-Tar thought. Maybe this rebellion will succeed. Then will you respect me, Ji-Ann? Will you return home to me, acknowledge me as a leader of our people?

He gazed up at the sky. He wondered where her squadron was, what she was doing at this exact moment. Wherever it was, he was sure—from bitter experience—that she was not being faithful to him.

And yet, he knew, he would love her forever. Her beautiful blue face would live in his mind until the day he died.

"Look," Proxima Midnight said, pointing with her black-light spear.

Fal-Tar gazed out over the spaceport. A paved road called Heroes' Way ran through the center of the port, serving as both a parade processional and a runway for the older airships. Sentries lined the sides of the road—ancient robots many times the size of a man. They'd been built as support for invasion forces, but they'd become statues over the centuries, ceremonial figures symbolically watching over the glorious Kree army.

And past the Sentries, beyond Heroes' Way, were the ships. To the left, along the tarmac, hundreds of starships stood in neat rows: disks and teardrops and fusion-spheres, modern liquid-circuitry craft alongside ancient cruisers made of bolted metal. To the right, past the maintenance hangar, a smaller group of short-range ships sat in a more casual arrangement. Sharp-pointed rockets, blocky sublight cruisers, a few single-man stingers. Every ship, large and small, that wasn't already out on maneuvers elsewhere in the four galaxies.

A full quarter of the Kree armada, assembled together on the crowded field. All aimed at the stars.

Fal-Tar's breath caught in his throat. Despite his shortcomings, he was of the Kree. The sight of the armada made his chest ache with pride.

But Proxima wasn't pointing at the ships. Above, in the sky, a swarm of single-rider skycycles approached. Accusers, the elite attack force of the Supreme Intelligence. Their cycles buzzed like hornets; they flew imperious in their dark-green uniforms, black masks hiding their eyes.

Over by the barracks, a rumbling rose up from the soldiers. As they turned toward the Accusers, some of them set their faces in masks of defiance. Others looked unsure.

"This," Corvus Glaive said, "should be interesting."

"IN-VADE," the soldiers chanted, growing louder. "*IN-VADE.*"

One of them threw a rock in the air. An Accuser veered sideways on her cycle, narrowly avoiding the projectile.

Fal-Tar glanced at his chronometer. Two minutes to go.

One skycycle surged forward, ahead of the rest. Fal-Tar recognized the rider: Ronan, the Warmaster. First of the Accusers, right hand to the Intelligence. He raised up his hammer, the ceremonial weapon of his rank. His amplified voice boomed out over the spaceport.

"Disperse," Ronan said. *"Return to the barracks. The Intelligence commands it."*

The soldiers broke into groups, murmuring frantically. They cast nervous glances upward, pointing at Ronan and his crew.

Fal-Tar felt a sudden rush of panic. "Where is he?" he demanded, turning to Corvus and Proxima. "Where's your precious Captain Teren-Sas?"

Corvus just smiled his bony, inhuman smile. Proxima's eyes were wide with anticipation.

"He's supposed to be here," Fal-Tar continued. "He said the Accusers would fall into line!"

Corvus slapped him across the face, incredibly fast. Fal-tar toppled backward and fell to the ground.

"He is our master," Corvus Glaive hissed, looking down at him.

Fal-Tar touched his stinging cheek. He could feel the eyes of the soldiers, watching the confrontation from a distance. The buzzing of the Accusers' cycles seemed to echo inside his head.

He rose to his feet, struggling to retain his composure. "You must take his place," he said, gesturing to Corvus. "You must talk to the Accusers."

Corvus smiled, even wider than before. "The Accusers will only speak to a Kree."

"You sought power," Proxima taunted. "Did you not?"

Fal-Tar looked around. The soldiers had paused in their chanting, watching him from the barracks on either side of the central tower. The whole field seemed to hesitate.

Fal-Tar closed his eyes, marshaling his courage. Then he turned to look upward, toward the Accusers.

"WARMASTER!" he yelled.

Ronan hesitated, his cycle pivoting in the air. He held up his hammer, allowing energy to surge visibly through it. Then he began a slow, expert decline to the base of the control tower.

The Black Order stepped back. Fal-Tar stood alone, watching the skycycle approach. Time seemed to slow; he felt as if he were slogging through mud, swimming against an onrushing tide. Once there had been promise in his life: youthful excitement, the prospect of advancement, a beautiful woman with laughing blue lips.

Now all that was behind him. Once again he thought: I don't belong here.

He stared at Ronan's glowing hammer. If he killed me now, Fal-Tar wondered, would they be better off? Ji-Ann and little Ki-Ta, whose face he barely knew?

Ronan braked to a stop, hovering barely a foot above the ground. *"You,"* he boomed, pointing his energy-hammer down at Fal-Tar. *"You are responsible for this disturbance?"*

Fal-Tar winced at the piercing voice. He felt a

surge of anger. Ronan, he realized, had left his voice-amplifier on in order to intimidate the soldiers.

"I am," Fal-Tar said.

Ronan glared at him for a long moment. Then the Accuser turned to gesture at the fleet of ships parked across Heroes' Way. The Sentries stood unmoving, silent witnesses to this moment in Kree history.

"Against all orders, the ships are primed for takeoff." Ronan turned to sweep his hammer before the uneven line of soldiers. *"The men and women of Hala gather—again, against their masters' orders. Whom, then, do they obey?"*

Fal-Tar forced himself to meet the Warmaster's steady, unforgiving gaze. He tried to speak, but his mouth was dry.

"You?" Ronan laughed. *"A small man who has somehow managed to avoid being drummed out of the officer corps? An accidental soldier?"*

Two more Accusers wafted down to hover just above Ronan. They grinned at Fal-Tar, amused by their leader's taunts.

"You're no leader." Sneering, Ronan held up his hammer. *"You are barely Kree."*

A blast of energy leapt from the hammer. It struck the ground barely an inch from Fal-Tar's feet. He jumped, let out a noise, and lost his balance.

The Accusers burst into laughter.

Fal-Tar struck the ground and whirled in anger. The Accusers grinned down at him, buzzing and capering in the sky. Corvus and Proxima had moved away, toward the cold stone of the control tower. She seemed amused; he looked grim.

The soldiers had moved closer. Some gazed defiantly at the ships; others watched Fal-Tar and the Accusers.

A beeping noise rose from Fal-Tar's wrist. The chronometer read ZERO.

Time's up, he thought.

Slowly, possessed by some spirit he could not explain, Fal-Tar rose to his feet. Ignoring the Accusers, he turned to face his people, the assembled soldiers. When he spoke, the words seemed torn from his lungs.

"March," he cried. "TO YOUR SHIPS!"

The soldiers let out a primal battle cry. They started forward, thrusting their fists into the air. "IN-VADE," they chanted. "IN-VADE. *TO THE SHIPS!*"

Ronan glared down at Fal-Tar, then gestured upward. His skycycle shot up above the crowd, the other two Accusers following behind.

The soldiers closed in on Fal-Tar like a wave. They swept him forward, ushering him onto Heroes' Way. He cast a quick glance back at the control tower to see Corvus and Proxima still watching. They hadn't moved.

Two young soldiers, the brother and sister who'd spoken at the meeting, took up position on either side of Fal-Tar. "Well spoken," the woman said, and clapped him on the back. Her face was grim with purpose.

Again, Fal-Tar allowed himself to hope. Maybe there *was* a path forward for him. Maybe Ronan was wrong; maybe Fal-Tar could redeem himself, lead his people to a new life. A new purpose.

Maybe he was Kree after all.

As the tide of soldiers surged across the Way, he glanced up. The Accusers circled above, keeping pace with the crowd. This was the real test of the revolt: Would they turn on their own people? Would they open fire to prevent the launch?

Ahead, past the Sentry robots lining the road, stood the starships. A few of them, the newer ones, already pulsed and smoked with power. The Quantum Mechs had activated the drives mentally, from a distance.

A blast lanced down from one of the skycycles. The beam struck the ground, narrowly missing a clutch of Security officers. They skittered sideways, stumbled, and shook their fists upward.

A warning shot, Fal-Tar realized. The line still hadn't been crossed. Even the Supreme Intelligence would not order Kree to kill Kree. Not over an issue like this—a military operation, an invasion in the name of the Kree Empire itself.

"IN-VADE! IN-VADE! IN-VADE!"

Fal-Tar smiled, pumping his fist in time with the others. Soon, the fleet would descend upon the helpless world that had defied the Kree. He couldn't remember its name right now.

"IN-VADE!" he cried. "IN-VADE! IN-V—"

Something odd caught his eye—a flash of red light. He turned in alarm, thinking it was another Accuser weapon. But no—the angle was wrong. The

Accusers had risen higher, keeping their distance.

Another red flash. With a shock, he realized what it was: the eye of a Sentry.

A second Sentry—the nearest one, at the edge of the road—swiveled its head toward him.

Impossible. The robots had been dormant for decades—maybe centuries.

"Look out!" he yelled.

The Sentry's eye-blast incinerated three old Techs who'd been lagging behind the main force. The noncoms nearest them cried out and ran, sprinting across the road toward the ships. They collided with a group of Quantum Mechanics, and together they looked up with mounting dread.

The Sentries were moving. They walked stiffly toward the soldiers, encircling the group. Trapping them on Heroes' Way.

Fal-Tar surveyed the scene. The robots towered above the crowd, lurching and whirring, their long-disused metallic joints straining to carry out some new programming. Their eyes glowed red, deadly optic beams surging and recharging after each energy blast.

The next assault killed eight Medical officers. Their death-screams rose up into the thick air.

Fal-Tar struggled to understand. Why would the Intelligence activate the Sentries? The Accusers were heavily armed—if the Intelligence gave the kill order, the Accusers could easily carry it out. Yet Ronan and his force had risen even higher, tilting their cycles to watch the carnage. They looked...confused.

Panic began to spread among the soldiers. A Quantum Mechanic—Captain Al-Bar—took off at a run for the ships, metal implant-cables trailing in the air behind her. A Sentry turned, locked on with glowing eyes, and vaporized her.

We're trapped, Fal-Tar realized. They're picking off anyone who strays from the road. We'll never reach the ships.

Was this the offworlders' doing? He couldn't see Corvus and Proxima anymore. The control tower was too far away, blocked from sight by the Sentries' massive legs.

More blasts rained down. A noncom drew her gun, yelling for her companions to attack one of the Sentries. They crouched down and fired small-gauge proton pistols, focusing on a single spot on the Sentry's foot. Beams sizzled against the tough plasteel covering—but the Sentry barely seemed to notice. It lurched forward and swept its hand across the road, smashing the lead attacker's skull. The others scattered.

A tall, scarred man grabbed Fal-Tar's arm. Ray-Mar, he remembered. The soldier who had challenged the rebellion at the meeting, and escaped—barely—with his life.

"He has done it," Ray-Mar said. He seemed calm, almost resigned. "Teren-Sas has betrayed you."

A shadow fell over Fal-Tar. He shoved Ray-Mar away, to safety. Then he turned to look up at his attacker.

Oddly, Fal-Tar didn't think of his wife. He tried

to picture his daughter, but he couldn't remember her face. Past collided with future, and all he saw in his last lingering moment was the brutal now: the Sentry's massive boot, dropping out of the sky to end his fearful, compromised life.

NINETEEN

"WOW," Gamora said. "That's what I call a *mess.*"

Crouched down in his hiding place among a tangle of cables and machinery, Thanos smiled. He lifted his head and risked a look out into the room.

The chamber of the Supreme Intelligence was as vast as a courtyard. Beside Thanos's nook, the preserved bodies of dead Kree stood in rows of individual cylinders, stacked all the way up to the high ceiling. Those minds—the life-energies of the Kree—nourished the Intelligence, providing it with a constant source of power. Technicians, mostly pink skinned, moved around the base of the cylinders, monitoring readouts and adjusting cryo-suspension machinery.

The Intelligence itself lived in a huge tank built into the wall, just past the bodies of its citizens. Its gelatinous emerald face was 30 feet high and studded with organic feeding tubes that moved like living things. It rarely spoke.

In the main chamber, Gamora stood before the Intelligence along with Phae-Dor, a blue-skinned member of the Kree Science Council. He wore the violet tunic and vest of a civilian scientist, and he seemed very unhappy. His attention was divided between a small comm-tablet and a huge holo-stage filling most of the room. The hologram displayed a scene of silent chaos: The long-dormant Kree Sentries had come to life, trapping a large group of soldiers in a small area of the spaceport. Accusers swooped and hovered above on their skycycles, pointing down as they exchanged urgent radio communications.

"Ronan reports…one moment…" Phae-Dor touched his earpiece. "They are receiving no signals to or from the Sentries. No idea who's behind this."

The huge yellow eyes of the Intelligence bulged wide, but it made no sound.

"You." Phae-Dor lowered the tablet and turned to Gamora. "This is your doing. You'll pay for this."

"No, you'll pay *me.*" Gamora seemed utterly unconcerned. "You hired me to deliver a message. I delivered it."

"And this is the result!"

Again, Thanos smiled. *Phae-Dor,* he thought, *you unutterable fool. You've picked the wrong woman to antagonize.*

In the hologram, a Sentry leaned down to target a small group of Kree Techs. Deadly beams flashed out from the robot's eyes.

"Like I said, *you've* got a mess on your hands." Gamora laughed. "Your people, your robots. Your problem."

Thanos felt a surge of excitement. *This is it,* he

realized. Everything was coming together. Soon he would depose the Intelligence and seize control of the Kree Empire. Then he would wield an army to shake the stars.

But everything depended on the next few minutes. At that thought, a paralyzing doubt took hold of him. He realized he was challenging—or at least manipulating—the Supreme Intelligence, the Accusers, the Black Order, the entire Kree army, Gamora…perhaps even the Guardians of the Galaxy. And he had no ships of his own, no Infinity Gems, not even the Titan powers he'd been born with.

Events had moved fast on Hala. There'd been no opportunity to reflect, no time to consider the possibility of failure. Suddenly the whole venture seemed like madness.

Well, he thought, I've been called mad before.

In the hologram, a trio of Kree weapons specialists crouched back-to-back, firing heavy-grade particle rifles. One beam grazed a Sentry, sizzling against its metal hide. Another shot came within inches of striking down a hovering Accuser.

"Sire," Phae-Dor said, turning to face the Supreme Intelligence. "The Accusers are asking permission to defend themselves."

"That's a tough one." Gamora smiled. "If they start picking off soldiers, your little *rebellion* is likely to break out into open warfare."

Phae-Dor whirled back to her. "You will be held accountable. You and your band of galactic outlaws."

"I'm just enjoying the show."

"Lying witch. *Someone* has activated the Sentries!"

Thanos didn't even see her move. By the time he heard Phae-Dor's strangled cry, Gamora had slammed the Kree scientist up against the glass of the Intelligence's tank, a sharp knife pressed to his throat.

"I don't lie, little man." Her voice was smooth, even. "I *do* kill. Sometimes with very little provocation."

Phae-Dor struggled to breathe. Behind him, on the other side of the glass, the gigantic eyes of the Supreme Intelligence stared down at the drama.

Thanos glanced at the holo. At the spaceport, the situation was deteriorating. The Kree soldiers had gathered together in small groups, keeping low. They fired in concentrated bursts, but their weapons were no match for the Sentries. The robots moved slowly, their joints rusty from disuse. But with their sheer bulk and the power of their eye-beams, they seemed unstoppable.

"S-sire." Phae-Dor twisted his head, appealing to the Intelligence. "We must tell the Accusers—how to—"

"Tell them only one man can stop this," Thanos said.

As he stepped out of his hiding place, all eyes turned in his direction: Phae-Dor, Gamora, the Techs, and, lastly, the slow blank orbs of the Intelligence.

"Oh," Gamora said, studying Thanos. *"Oh."* She loosed her grip on Phae-Dor, almost absent-mindedly. "Didn't see that coming."

Phae-Dor stumbled away, rubbing his throat.

"These chambers—" He coughed and cast a nervous glance back at Gamora, who smirked in response. Then he straightened and turned to glare at Thanos. "These chambers are supposed to be secure."

"All security is enforced by the common people. I've become friendly with a lot of them lately." Thanos turned to face the Supreme Intelligence. "Some of them aren't too happy with your administration, *sire.*"

The Kree ruler's yellow eyes glared down at him.

"Who are you?" Phae-Dor asked.

"Teren-Sas," Thanos replied. "Captain, recently of the 18th Star Division. Now at large."

Phae-Dor tapped at his comm-tablet. He was an irritant, a bureaucrat whose dignity had been challenged. It was Gamora's cocked head and knowing glare that worried Thanos.

"Your military file has been partly redacted." Phae-Dor lowered the tablet. "No photo."

"Looks like a lot of things are falling apart around here." Thanos gestured at the hologram. "I can fix that."

On the spaceport road, a group of Mechanics had rigged up a makeshift proton cannon. They fired it at a Sentry, striking it point-blank in the eye-projectors. The robot lurched, swatted blindly with one enormous hand—and connected with a low-flying Accuser. The Accuser cried out and toppled from his cycle, plunging to the ground.

"Captain Teren-Sas," Gamora said, "is one of the architects of the current rebellion."

"You give me too much credit, lady. I merely

fanned the flames. However…" He paused for effect. "I *did* manage to activate the Sentries."

"The Sentries at the spaceport have been dormant for decades," Phae-Dor said. "How did you do this? *Why* did you do it?"

"I'll take 'how' first." Thanos gestured at the hologram. "In the course of planning this operation, I befriended an old Tech named Zy-Ro. One of the few people left alive who held the Sentry codes."

Phae-Dor began to speak into his earpiece in low, urgent tones. Thanos raised a hand to cut him off.

"Don't bother trying to find Zy-Ro," Thanos said. "You won't."

"You turned the Kree's ancient weapons against them." A flicker of doubt crossed Gamora's face. "Brutal. But slick."

On the hologram, a female Accuser dipped low, yelling out to the crowd. A young noncom leapt up and grabbed the bottom of her cycle, wrenching her off balance. The Accuser fired her rockets. The soldier screamed as the jets seared his arm.

"The Kree are already divided internally," Thanos said. "Out of such struggles, new patterns are born." He smiled. "Like the roiling fusion energies at the heart of a star."

Gamora seemed to bolt upright. She cast a quick glance at Thanos, then at the Supreme Intelligence. Then she started for the door. Phae-Dor made a protesting noise, but stopped short as Gamora whirled toward him.

"Don't worry. I'm not bouncing off this planet without my cash." She turned to the Intelligence and gave a mocking salute. "I'll check in tomorrow, Big Head. Assuming you're still in charge."

As she strode out of the chamber, a thunderous crash sounded from the hologram. The Kree soldiers had managed to topple a Sentry. They swarmed over it, blasting it at close range, tearing off pieces of metal plating.

Phae-Dor turned to Thanos, gesturing at the screen in exasperation. "Is *this* part of your plan?"

"Absolutely. Here's how it works." Thanos began to pace back and forth before the hologram. "Several factions of Kree soldiers were eager for…well, *some sort* of revolt. They didn't really know how to proceed. Their leader, Fal-Tar, wasn't exactly an inspiring figure." He searched the chaotic hologram. "I suspect we may have lost him already."

A Sentry's hand reached down and plucked up a Kree soldier from the ground. The man twisted and fired, catching the Sentry square in the chest. The Sentry staggered, then vaporized the man with an eye-beam that seared off two of its own fingers.

"I took that discontent," Thanos continued, "and focused it into the rebellion you see before you. The key was to set a deadline, a time for the ships to launch. A starting point for the glorious invasion of Hemithea."

"Hemithea is a worthless rock," Phae-Dor scoffed. "The Intelligence has ruled its subjugation unnecessary."

"Irrelevant. The point is not the destination, but the journey." Thanos gestured, again, at the spaceport images. "Nothing energizes a mob like a good crusade."

"And then?"

"I hoped the Accusers would attack the crowd," Thanos said. "That would have ignited a civil war. But I suspected they would hesitate to open fire on their own people. So I prepared a backup plan."

"The Sentries," Phae-Dor said.

"The Sentries."

Thanos turned toward the holo. Three Accusers had fallen from their skycycles; they gathered together on the road, penned in along with the soldiers. The Sentries stood above them in a circle, punching holes in the tarmac with their deadly eyebeams.

"I've lost track of the casualties," Thanos continued. "But I estimate a few dozen soldiers so far, along with two or three Accusers. And the Sentries will continue their attack until they are brought down... or until I order them to stop." He smiled. "No one else holds the codes."

The Intelligence moved for the first time. Its entire head shook, sending bubbles roiling through its enormous tank. The feeder tubes on its face pulsed and surged. As its huge yellow eyes turned to focus on Thanos, a booming, echoing voice rang out.

"WHAT," the Intelligence asked, **"IS YOUR PRICE?"**

Thanos smiled.

"Absolute control over the Kree military.

Warmaster is too modest a title. Perhaps Warlord Supreme?" He stared, grim and defiant, at the Intelligence. "You may remain as a figurehead. Pun somewhat intended."

The hologram pulled back to a wide view. A second swarm of Accusers was approaching, small figures against the gray sky. Below, the Sentries had the soldiers contained. A few security officers panicked and ran; a giant metal boot rose up almost casually and crushed them like insects.

"The Kree are many and powerful," Phae-Dor said. "Several divisions are currently offworld. We *will* destroy the Sentries."

"Eventually. But how many will die before then?" Thanos gestured at the images. "And unless I tell them otherwise, the soldiers will blame the Accusers for the Sentry attack. The authority of Ronan—and of the Supreme Intelligence—will be forever tainted."

The soldiers had sighted the second group of Accusers now. A few noncoms squeezed off shots into the air.

"Consider it," Thanos said. "But decide quickly. Already the soldiers are taking aim at your Accusers."

The Intelligence said nothing, but its feeder tubes pulsed again. In the outer chamber, machinery hummed and whirred, electrical impulses flashing among the hundreds of preserved Kree bodies.

Thanos turned his back and strode off, straight through the hologram. He walked unflinching through a screaming Kree soldier who had been burned beyond recognition. By Sentries or Accusers? It scarcely mattered, now.

When he reached the far wall, Thanos pulled out a small remote-control device and pressed a button. A stone wall slid back, opening the chamber to the outside.

"You should let air in more often, sire," he said, not looking back. "A ruler must be in touch with his people."

He strode out onto the balcony, breathing in the thick, industrial smog. Hala lay spread out a half-mile below, like an enormous weapon waiting to be fired. He couldn't see much of the spaceport from this vantage, but a cloud of smoke rose up beyond the high control tower.

I've won, he thought. I've got them. Their precious Empire hangs by a thread, and only I—only *Captain Teren-Sas*—can preserve it.

Then he remembered: Gamora. He still distrusted her—there had to be a hidden reason for her presence. Thanos's plan was solid, but he was alone. One mistake, one overlooked enemy, could bring everything crashing down.

But no. Even the assassin he had raised from a child could not stop him now. Soon he would have a world, an army. An empire.

He felt a rush of excitement. Mistress, he thought, I've done it. I've rebuilt myself, become the man—the conqueror—that you wanted me to be. I have the power—

"Teren-Sas?"

Phae-Dor stood just inside the chamber,

beyond the stone-rimmed wall. He suddenly seemed confident—almost smug.

"You might want to see this," he said.

Thanos stepped inside. The hologram showed a single figure on a skycycle: Ronan the Accuser, his expression grim, but confident. The image dollied back to show him hovering just above the crowd, calling down to a group of gathered Kree soldiers. In the background, the Sentries' eyebeams continued to decimate the ground force.

Phae-Dor manipulated an audio control on his tablet. Ronan's amplified voice rose up, filling the chamber. Thanos moved closer, a sinking feeling in his stomach.

"Proud warriors of the Kree," Ronan began. *"Hear my words…"*

" **…THE ACCUSERS** *are not your enemies,"* Ronan continued. *"This is the work of some unknown foe. Perhaps the Skrulls."*

Proxima Midnight held up a rimless magnifying lens, watching the drama from the base of the control tower. The Sentries still had most of the soldiers hemmed in, restricting them to a small segment of Heroes' Way. The second group of Accusers were just swooping down to join the fray, keeping out of reach of the towering robots.

Beyond lay the ships. Several hundred rumbling, surging vessels poised to rise up and seize the stars.

The throbbing, grinding pulse of the Empire.

Proxima turned to her left. Near the door to the tower, a group of Kree generals had gathered in a circle, whispering. She couldn't hear what they were saying, but they seemed to be engaged in an intense debate.

On her other side, Corvus Glaive stood watching the Sentries. His teeth ground together in a strange, low sound; his staff was clutched firmly in his hand. To anyone else, his expression would have seemed cruel, sadistic. Only Proxima could tell: He was suffering.

"My love," she said. "This is the plan."

He said nothing. Ground his teeth again, a bit louder.

"Divide the enemy," she continued. "Allow others to soften them up, then move in. We've used shock troops ourselves, for similar purposes." She shrugged. "We have been the shock troops. In service of the master."

At the word *master*, Corvus hissed in a sharp breath. When he turned to Proxima, she saw the same desperate look he'd give her the night before under the lamppost. A look of terrible, bone-deep doubt.

Proxima Midnight felt a crushing weight, a burden placed on her shoulders. She loved this man, more than anything else in the universe. This should have been his moment of triumph: the hour of the Black Order's rebirth. And yet he seemed terrified.

"It is his plan," she said. "He is returned, to lead us."

Corvus stared at her. "Is he?"

She looked away, troubled by his gaze.

Out on the road, the battle had split into two fronts. One group of soldiers sat hunkered down behind a fallen Sentry, squeezing off scattered shots at the remaining five robots. Another group—mostly Techs and the cybernetic Quantum Mechanics—argued with Ronan, who swooped up and down in the air.

"The Accusers stand with you," Ronan insisted.

A Mechanic shook her fist at him. "You stand above us!"

"Brun-Stad." Ronan swooped low, indicating a young male Mechanic. *"You and I fought together, at the battle of Scherezade Segunda. You know my loyalties."*

The young Mechanic, Brun-Stad, gestured at the Sentries. "I thought I did."

Ronan whirled to see the Sentries closing in on their prey, squeezing off eyebeams in rapid succession. Deadly bolts of force slashed into the tarmac, melting pavement and ending Kree lives. Two dozen bodies lay scattered across Heroes' Way, some still sizzling from the beams that had brought them down.

Ronan's eyes narrowed. He nodded grimly, squeezed his skycycle's handle, and began to rise into the air. As he soared up above the other Accusers, he called out to them and pointed at the Sentry.

"For Hala!" he cried.

"FOR HALA!"

The Accusers pivoted and, like a swarm of bees, began a deadly, pointed descent. As they approached the first Sentry, a barrage of energy-beams blasted forth from their hammers and cycle-mounted rifles.

The huge robot pivoted—too slowly. Before it could fire off a single eyebeam, four Accusers had slammed into its neck, knocking it off-balance.

The soldiers watched the aerial combat, unsure who to trust. As the Sentry began to topple, they scattered out of the way. The enormous robot landed with a crash, shaking the ground.

Smiling, Ronan swung his cycle down in an arc toward the fallen Sentry. Without slowing, he leapt off and landed on its neck with a loud clanging noise. He swung back his hammer and smashed the Sentry's eye-lens, then reached inside. He wrenched out the mangled frame of the Sentry's beam-projector and held it up in the air.

The soldiers cheered.

The tide began to turn. Accusers fanned out through the air, shielding the ground-based soldiers from the Sentries' assault. At Ronan's direction, the noncoms provided covering fire while the Quantum Mechanics aimed disruptors at sensitive systems on the robots' faces and joints.

But the Sentries continued firing, and they didn't fall easily. Eight soldiers and two Accusers died bringing the next one down. The battle began to spill out past the road, onto the shipyard. A Sentry stumbled backward into a disk-shaped starship, sending cracks spreading across the vessel's outer hull.

Beside Corvus and Proxima, the generals let out a howl. Holding proton rifles above their heads, they charged toward the road. Proxima raised the magnifying lens to follow their progress

The soldiers on the road cleared a path. With practiced ease, the generals dropped to the ground and blasted a Sentry. One shot to the eyebeams, another to the knee joints. Two more to the head, one to the midsection.

The Sentry fell.

With a sinking feeling, Proxima realized: The Kree were all coming together, forming a united front. Officers, Accusers, noncoms, and generals—all allied against the Sentries.

"The plan," she said softly.

"It fails." Corvus shook his head, a cold look in his eyes. "He has failed us."

He. Teren-Sas. Not the master after all—just an upstart Kree with big plans, a glib tongue, and a talent for disguise.

"I would kill him," Corvus continued. "Slowly, with great pleasure. But he seems to have run off with his tail between his legs."

"I think our *ship* is gone, too." She peered through the lens. "A Sentry just fell on it."

She glanced at the battle. The Kree had the Sentries on the defensive, backing them up toward the hangar at the center of the shipyard. The Accusers maintained an aerial barrage while the soldiers and generals advanced steadily on the ground.

"Sometimes I wonder," Corvus whispered. "Is this all an illusion? The dream of a madman? Has the world already burned to ions and ash?"

Proxima turned to him. In battle, she thought, he's the strongest warrior I've ever known. But without a master, he is weak. It's up to me: I must be his strength. I must bear the burden.

"This," she said, gripping his hand tight. "This is real. *We* are real."

He looked at their clasped hands. Stared at them, as if he'd never seen them before.

"I failed," she continued. "It was I who recruited this…Nil, this Teren-Sas. I believed him to be our salvation. I failed you."

His eyes went wide. He looked up at her in surprise, shaking his head.

"No," he said. "Never."

An empty skycycle crashed to the ground, not three feet away. Proxima turned toward it, watching calmly as it burst into flames.

"Come," she said, and swept an arm forward.

She started off toward the road, still gripping Corvus's hand. His stride was hesitant at first, halting; she had to pull him along.

They had only traveled a few feet when Proxima's commlink buzzed: a text-only message, relayed from the damaged ship's hyper-comm system. She read it and laughed.

"The Ebony Maw," she said, "is on Battleworld. He believes he may have found us a new recruit."

Corvus paused. A smile spread slowly across his brittle face.

"So much for *new paths,*" he said.

As they approached the battle, Corvus's pace grew steadier. The look on his face turned to determination, then rage. When they stepped onto Heroes' Way, a soldier strayed across their path. Corvus reached out, snapped his neck, and tossed him aside.

"The Order," Corvus said. "The Order prevails."

Proxima didn't even break stride. She led him on an elliptical path around the battle, which had spilled off the road into an area of now-toppled starships. The Sentries had rallied again, forcing the soldiers back against a maintenance hangar.

It didn't matter, she knew. It wouldn't be enough.

"My Midnight." Corvus drew up even with her. "Have you another ship?"

She stopped. Ignoring the cries of battle, she swept her spear across the gathered vessels, sending a trail of black light shimmering though the air. Ahead lay every manner of spacecraft: tall ships, short, cubes and spheres, compact hypercylinders and massive generation starships.

Proxima Midnight turned to her husband and smiled.

"Pick one," she said.

TWENTY

RONAN the Accuser swooped low over the troops, roaring like a lion. At his command, a dozen Kree soldiers formed a line up against the maintenance hangar. They marched steadily toward the Sentry, firing off proton guns. Five Accusers followed Ronan on skycycles, their weapons blazing through the air.

Phae-Dor placed a hand on Thanos's shoulder. "Not quite what you expected?"

Thanos stared at the hologram. The Sentry's eyebeams swept through the air, blasting one Accuser out of the air. But the rest kept coming, concentrating their fire on the robot's midsection. Bit by bit, they drilled a hole in its stomach. Cables and circuits sparked, catching fire.

The Sentry staggered.

"The proud Kree," Phae-Dor continued. "No people in the universe care more deeply for the officers they fight beside. Your words, no?"

Thanos resisted the urge to strike him.

Beyond the hologram, the large wall-panel still gaped open. The smell of burning metal, carried on the air from the spaceport, swept through the chamber.

"Perhaps you have underestimated your pawns." Phae-Dor turned away in contempt and began tapping at his comm-tablet.

In the holo, the Sentry toppled and fell. Soldiers swarmed over it like ants, cheering and battering at it.

Thanos turned to face the Intelligence. The fluid in its tank seemed calmer now; its gigantic eyes stared steadily down at him.

"There's still time to stop this," Thanos said. "Give me what I want, and I will end the Sentries' rampage."

"It will end soon," Phae-Dor said. "The Intelligence has determined: Your actions are irrelevant."

Phae-Dor pinched the screen on his tablet. The holo zoomed out to show the entire battlefield: Only two Sentries were left standing. The others lay among their victims, machine guts strewn across the pavement. The severed nose cone of an old rocket-style starship lay atop one of the robots.

"This changes nothing," Thanos replied. "The invasion—the people will still demand it. And even if you agree to attack Hemithea—"

"IF AND WHEN I AGREE, THEY WILL OBEY."

The voice was like a jolt of electricity. Thanos fought to keep his face calm.

"THEY WILL CHARGE INTO BATTLE," the Intelligence continued. **"AND THEN THERE WILL BE ANOTHER BATTLE. AND ANOTHER."**

Phae-Dor looked up with a condescending smile.

"Did you think you were the first fool to try to seize power in a coup?"

"THE KREE NEVER GIVE UP. THEY NEVER STOP, NEVER SURRENDER. THIS I KNOW."

With a grinding noise, the stone wall began to close. Slowly the panel slid back into place, shutting out the sunlight.

"FOR I *AM* THE KREE."

It's true, Thanos realized. He'd overplayed his hand. The Kree soldiers had been so angry with their superiors, so ripe for revolution. The Sentries had seemed like the perfect spark to set off a civil war.

Instead, they had brought the Kree together.

"You knew," he whispered, turning to stare up at the Intelligence. "You planned everything."

Inside the tank, the fluids churned.

"You *played* me." Thanos shook his head. "Her, too. Gamora."

He glanced at the hologram. A single Sentry still stood, blasting eyebeams in all directions. It was clearly damaged, lurching and staggering down the road. The Kree moved to surround it, both on the ground and in the air.

Thanos pulled himself up to his full height, glared briefly at the smirking Phae-Dor, and started toward the door.

"You will regret this," he said. "One day you will fall."

"THAT IS THE NATURE OF POWER."

The walk to the exit seemed endless. Half of him feared the remote-control device in his hand would fail to open the door. The other half expected a proton beam to slice his head off.

He reached the exit. The door opened. Quickening his pace slightly, he strode through it. The last thing he heard was the Supreme Intelligence's voice.

"ESTABLISH A LINK WITH THE SPACEPORT. I WOULD ADDRESS MY PEOPLE."

The door hissed shut behind him. A pair of blue-skinned guards stood in the narrow hallway. Their eyes followed him as he squeezed past and stumbled into a waiting elevator.

Thankfully, it was empty. Most of the Kree forces were occupied at the spaceport. He stabbed the down button, and the car began to drop.

Thanos slumped against the wall, his thoughts whirling madly. The Kree had already turned against him; Fal-Tar was probably dead. Even the Order, he knew, would abandon him. *I've miscalculated*, he thought. *I tried to reach too far, too fast. Now it's all gone.*

Pain stabbed through his chest. He clutched at his uniform, bunching the fabric decorated with the green ringed-planet design. With a shock, he remembered: *I'm mortal now. Mortals have...what do they call them? Heart attacks?*

The elevator slowed. Its doors slid open, and a disabled man in the dark-green uniform of a veteran staggered inside.

Thanos barely noticed. He squeezed his eyes shut,

willing the pain to recede. I am Thanos, he thought. I am still Thanos. I wield control over my mind and my body. I will not be brought down like this!

Slowly the pain faded. He massaged his chest, felt the knot begin to smooth out. Not a heart attack after all. Just a muscle spasm. Nerves.

His head began to clear, survival instincts kicking in. The trick, he realized, was to get off this planet alive. The Supreme Intelligence had declined to stop him from leaving, but it might still send an assassin to quietly end his life. He couldn't count on the Order—and whatever happened, he had to avoid Gamora.

Still, he thought, I can do this. All I need is a ship. A ship and a new start.

The veteran lurched forward. Thanos glared at him. The man's legs were useless; he walked on hinged crutches fixed to his forearms. Cables, like the ones the Quantum Mechanics used, dangled from his neck. An artificial vocalizer was implanted in his throat.

"Get away," Thanos said. "I have no coins for you."

The man lunged, landing with all his weight on one crutch. With the other hand, he reached out and grabbed Thanos by the neck, twisting him around. The second crutch twisted and bent on its hinge, clamping tight around Thanos's throat.

The man's mechanical voice hissed in Thanos's ear. "Teren-Sas," he said.

Thanos struggled, but couldn't break free. The man's cybernetic cables pressed cold against the back of his neck. He made a strangled noise.

"You don't recognize me? *Char-Nak.*" The man paused. "I have looked prettier."

"I…" Thanos gasped. "I don't…"

Then he remembered. Char-Nak. The soldier, the contact officer, whom Teren-Sas—the *real* Teren-Sas—had tried to kill during an offworld mission.

"You've made quite a name for yourself," Char-Nak rasped.

"Not…not Teren-Sas."

"No. Of *course* not."

"You…served with him." Thanos tried to twist his head around to face his attacker. "Can't you see?"

The crutch around Thanos's neck loosened slightly. He turned to stare into Char-Nak's face, and his heart sank. Char-Nak's eyes were filmy and unfocused, sunken in a field of red scar tissue that covered most of his face.

He was completely blind.

Thanos felt a cold object jab against his stomach. He looked down and saw a proton gun gripped firmly in one of the cables dangling from his attacker's neck. Char-Nak's mechanical voice was chillingly even.

"See how it feels when radiation lights up *your* insides."

Panic raged through Thanos. He squirmed, twisted, struggled. But it was no use. Char-Nak had planned this too well.

"This is for Sere-Nah."

The world exploded in pain. Thanos registered

a bright flash, a falling sensation, and that hideous, scarred face. Then nothing.

Nothing at all.

o———————o

THANOS, *I am your doom. I have tracked you here, across the stars, through the unimaginable—"*

"Dude!" Rocket Raccoon exclaimed. "Who are you talking to?"

Drax the Destroyer paused, embarrassed. He glanced at the streetlamp above him as it winked on for the night. Then he looked down at his diminutive teammate.

"Just practicing," he said.

"You'll get your chance," Gamora said. "Soon."

She stared at the large wooden door—the side entrance to the War Ministry. The elevators leading to the Supreme Intelligence's chamber had deposited her here. Now all she had to do was wait.

Darkness was falling over the stone-and-metal city. Just down the street, the Guardian called Groot crouched before a homeless veteran, gesturing expressively with his wooden tree-limbs. They seemed to be engaged in an intense conversation, but given Groot's limited vocabulary, Gamora couldn't imagine what that might involve.

"Pretty quiet out here," Peter Quill said. He sat on the pavement next to the Ministry door, fiddling with a primitive-looking mechanical device perched on his lap. He looked almost obtrusively human in his red jacket.

"Guess all the Kree are busy at the big throwdown."

"Good thing," Rocket said, raising a rifle bigger than his own mutated body. "Gam, you *sure* that's Thanos up there?"

"I'm sure. I'd know him anywhere." She paused, turned to look down. "Quill, what are you *doing?*"

"Trying to tune in the spaceport," he said. He unfolded a pair of metal rods from the top of his device and arranged them into a V shape, pointing upward.

Gamora cast another glance at the door, then knelt down to look over Quill's shoulder. As he moved the metal rods back and forth in the air, a blurry 2D image flickered into view on a tiny black-and-white screen. A clutch of soldiers stood posing atop the last of the Sentry robots. One woman held up its severed hand in triumph.

Gamora gestured at the machine. "Another Earth communications device?"

"Used to watch *Doctor Who* on it in my bedroom."

He adjusted the rods—antennae, Gamora realized—and the image sharpened. The soldiers turned as a hologram of the Supreme Intelligence appeared on the spaceport field.

"WARRIORS OF THE KREE." The Intelligence's voice was twice filtered—through the hologram and then through Quill's primitive video receiver—but it was unmistakable. **"WE STAND UNITED ON THIS PROUD DAY…"**

Quill turned down the volume. "Looks like the Kree solved their little rebellion," he said.

Rocket scurried over to join them, hefting his gun. "I still say we shoulda been down there kickin' ass."

"We're not here to get involved in local problems," Gamora said. "We're here for Thanos. That's all."

"Then let's get *in* there," Rocket replied. "Take 'im by surprise."

"And set off a dozen alarms?" Gamora shook her head. "I don't want Thanos slipping out in the confusion. He doesn't know I'm on to him—he'll come out soon enough."

Groot was hunched over now, concentrating hard on something. The homeless man watched him, eyes half-focused.

The Destroyer approached, studying the door to the Ministry. He seemed uncharacteristically troubled. Gamora rose to her feet.

"Drax?" she asked.

"I tracked him to this world," Drax began.

"Sure," Quill said. "That's why we arranged for Gamora to get that job with the Face of Boe."

They stared at him, baffled.

"Doctor Who!" He shook his head, placed his device on the ground, and stood up. "Am I the only fanboy on this team?"

"I tracked him," Drax repeated, still staring at the door. *"However…"*

"What?" Gamora asked.

"I no longer sense Thanos."

She blinked. "He's *in* there," she said, pointing to the door. "Upstairs. I saw him."

"His energy signature is gone."

Gamora blinked. She stared at the door, waiting. But nothing moved.

"HEED ME," said the Supreme Intelligence, tinny tones emanating from the machine on the ground. **"I AM PLEASED TO ORDER THE IMMEDIATE INVASION OF THE HATED WORLD HEMITHEA. TOO LONG HAVE ITS LUSH FLOATING CITIES DEFIED OUR EMPIRE…"**

As the Kree erupted in cheers, Quill scooped up the device and switched it off.

"Hey," Rocket said, "what's Groot up to?"

Groot's tree-bark face was scrunched up in intense concentration. As Gamora and the others approached, a bright-red fruit blossomed at the end of his hand. He plucked it off and handed it to the homeless man.

The veteran accepted the gift. He stared at it for a moment, then took a hefty bite.

Rocket clapped the tree-man on the back. "Mission accomplished."

"I am Groot," Groot said.

"Some things never change."

The two of them started off down the empty street. Quill moved to join them, followed by Drax. The Destroyer seemed to have forgotten about Thanos already.

The homeless man smiled, juices dripping down his chin.

Gamora lagged behind. She stared at the Kree

Ministry of War, its stone walls rising high into the darkening sky.

"It was him," she whispered. "I know it."

She grimaced, shook her head, and turned away. Took a final glance back, then hurried down the street to join her team.

THE LIGHT

THERE was a hole in his stomach. Blood poured out of it, sticky and wet against his fingers. He grabbed tight, tried to cover the hole, to keep the life from bleeding out. But it was no use.

A bright glare began to shine from his wound, seeping up and around his clutching fingers. Light, pure and white, spreading everywhere. Rising up to surround him, wrapping him in its embrace. It burned white-hot and radiant, like the inside of a star. That reminded him of something, but he couldn't remember what.

It's inside me, he thought. It's inside me, and now it's leaking out. Somehow, through his fog of dream-logic, he knew what that meant.

Thanos, the Mad Titan, was dying at last.

He looked up to see a figure silhouetted dark against the blinding glare. Black hair, slim body. A warm excitement rose inside him. Was it her? Death, come to meet him at last?

He struggled to rise, reaching out his arms. Why hadn't he thought of it before? The one sure way to belong to Death was simply…to die.

"So," the figure said. "Come crawling back to mommy?"

His heart sank. As his eyes adjusted, the figure resolved into a small humanoid form with large, accusing eyes. The mother-shade.

"Another failure," she said.

He looked away. He couldn't bear to see that face.

"You thought she'd welcome you," the shade taunted.

"She will." He held up his hands, warm and sticky with blood. "I am dying. Soon I will be with Death."

"Not as her lover. You'll be a thrall, nothing more." The shade gestured at her own, frail form. "A wraith like me, crawling in the mud of her realm."

"I served her." He clenched his fists. "On Sacrosanct, and on Hala, too. I sowed havoc, wrought chaos. I brought her souls!"

"A few dozen. Barely a twitch of the cosmic scythe."

"I would have done more. I would have brought the Kree Empire to its knees."

"You've done nothing. You've *learned* nothing. Followed the same twisted paths, the same tired patterns. Made the same mistakes, all over again."

"I was brought down before my time," he protested. "The man who…my assassin…he was trying to kill another man entirely!"

"A man whose sins *you* assumed," the shade replied. "Had you not enough sins of your own?"

He turned away, wincing at the pain in his stomach. She mocks me, he thought. Here I lie, unable to rise, my life's blood leaking away. In this, my lowest moment, she seeks to humiliate me.

"Mother," he hissed, "I only wish it were truly you here before me now. I would rip out your heart all over again and feast on it."

A slow, terrible smile spread over the mother-shade's face. "Thank you," she said.

"For what?"

"For vindicating my judgment."

She began to fade, becoming immaterial. The light burned through, washing her away.

Panic seized him, a sharp pain. "Wait," he protested.

The light grew brighter, blotting out all else. The shade was barely visible now, a pencil-sketch outline against a world of white.

"No!" he cried. "No, wait. I don't want this."

"What?" The voice seemed to come from a long distance away. "What don't you want?"

"I don't want to die!"

He felt a strange sense of interruption, of disconnect—as if a switch had been flipped, a phonograph needle scratched to a halt. The light narrowed, irising into a tight circle focused on his helpless, wounded body.

The mother-shade stood above him, clear and sharp, an accusing, contemptuous glare on her face. Behind her loomed the wooden form of the Infinity Wardrobe, its mahogany doors open wide.

"You mean," she said, "you don't want to die *alone.*"

He blinked. Within the Wardrobe's swirling

depths, figures flashed past, side to side. Human, Kree, Shi'ar. Some of them looked familiar, as if they were lives he'd lived and forgotten, long ago.

"I can do it," he said. "I can rebuild. I *will* prove myself worthy."

The shade turned her back on him, contemplating the Wardrobe's depths. Bodies flashed by faster, becoming a blur of eyes, torsos, legs. Too many forms, too fast to make out. Too many lives.

"Give me another chance," he pleaded. "One last chance."

The images began to slow. At last, the display came to rest on a single form: a tan-skinned humanoid man of medium height. His eyes were brown, his hair short-cropped. There was nothing striking about him.

"Yes," Thanos said. "Yes, I accept."

The mother-shade turned again, facing him. Her body seemed to waver, fading almost to mist.

"How little..." she said, shaking her head. "How little you know yourself."

"Tell me," he replied. "Help me. Please."

She gestured dismissively. He found himself flying past her, *through* her—into the Wardrobe. The new body wrapped itself around him, transforming his essence. His stomach wound seemed to shrivel up, healing in the blink of an eye.

As he stretched and changed, the mother-shade's faint voice came to him. "You don't fear Death," it said. "You never have."

Once again, the past receded into the distance.

The future beckoned. He felt an odd, familiar sense of hope.

"What, then?" he asked. "What do I fear?"

But there was no answer. No hint, no trace of the mother-shade remained. And before Thanos could repeat the question, he too was gone.

BOOK FOUR

THE VELT

It was said that when the Mad Titan came to the Velt, for the first time in his life he knew peace.

UNKNOWN

TWENTY-ONE

THERE was a runner, a woman in shorts and a T-shirt, legs pumping along a rubberized track. There was a virus, a swarm of cells too tiny to see. There was a runner, panting and sweating, grabbing at the skin of her cheeks. There was a runner screaming, collapsing, flesh melting from her face.

There were people, a succession of them, held by the throat at arm's length. There were gasps, pleas, eyes bulging and glassy. There were snapping noises. There were no people.

There was a plane—gray steel, no markings. There was a bomb, a tube with fins, dropping from a hole in the plane. There was a city. There was a roar, a flash, a column of smoke. There was no city.

There was a man with a hole in his chest. There was a heart pumping, straining, veins and arteries snapping and bursting. There was a heart in a hand, blood vessels spurting and dying. There was a man toppling backward. There was a man with no heart.

There were ships: massive engines of destruction powered by fusion and antimatter. There were rips

in space, in hyperspace, up and down the bands—
holes and gashes left by the ships. There were worlds
at the ends of the rips: blue globes with white clouds.
There were people on the worlds. There were bombs
dropping from the ships. There were viruses. There
were columns of smoke. There was flesh melting from
faces. There were people held by their throats. There
were people with holes in their chests, their stomachs,
their heads and necks. There were worlds, brown and
smoking. There were hearts in hands. There were
people. There were no people.

"You're twitching, mister."

Thanos opened his eyes and saw the girl. She
was Earth-human, maybe 10 years old, freckled with
blue eyes. Her frame was thin, her clothes ragged. She
smiled, showing several gaps in her teeth.

"Father!" the little girl called, turning toward the
door. "He's awake!"

Thanos struggled to rise, banishing dream-
images of dying men, dying worlds. He lay in a
small bed, a plain metal frame with a thin mattress
and no headboard. The room had metal walls and a
low ceiling. He leaned his head against a small pillow
propped up against the wall.

The girl turned to him with a serious look. "Life
and water to you, mister."

"What is this place?" he asked.

She frowned. "You're supposed to say 'And to you.'"

He stared at her. She had the solemnity, the
determination to follow rules, of the very young.

"And to you," he said.

"Father!" she yelled.

Thanos sat up, the bed frame creaking under his weight. He examined his light-brown hands, his wiry legs. He wore a robe that had once been white.

"Who are you?" he asked.

The girl smiled. "I am Lorak."

"I mean..." Thanos glanced at the door. The girl's father had not appeared. "I mean, who are... all of you?"

"We are the People."

"What people?"

"Just the People." She frowned, as if she were dealing with an idiot.

"And this place?"

"It's the Velt, of course." She turned again. "FATHER!"

Thanos lurched to his feet, flexing his arms. His muscles felt sore—presumably because he'd been bedridden for some time. And his new form was lighter, less muscular than the Kree body. But everything seemed to be working.

The girl watched his every move. She seemed interested, but not afraid.

"You want to go find him?" she asked, pointing at the door.

Thanos nodded. He followed her out into a narrow corridor with the same metal walls as the room. A logo of some kind—an inverted triangle—was imprinted on the wall. He tried to trace it with his fingers, but it was too faded to make out clearly.

"Come on," Lorak said.

They picked their way past an assortment of farming equipment: shovels, clippers with chipped blades, a rusted hoe—all propped up against the walls. At the end of the hallway, a door led out into sunlight. He stepped through and shrank from the bright light.

His eyes cleared quickly. A small settlement lay spread out before him, built of a mixture of woven- and thatched-grass tents. Some were one-person dwellings; others were as large as small houses. Campfires dotted the grass, which grew thick and uniform and yellow all around.

A few people turned to look. They wore worn tunics and robes, and they were all very thin. A couple of them smiled.

"This is the Velt?" Thanos asked.

"Part of it." Lorak smiled. "The good part!"

Thanos looked up. The sun shone down brighter than he was used to. It seemed to dominate the sky— as if it were lower, closer, than a star should be. Clouds gathered at its edges, along with a few odd, rectangular black shapes.

"We weren't sure what to do with you," Lorak continued, "so we put you in the Machine Shed."

He looked back at the building: a flat metal warehouse with a low, arched roof. It was the only permanent structure in the settlement.

He studied the encampment. A short distance away, a group of men and women bent down in the grass, clipping it and gathering it into a wicker basket. In front of a large tent, two women were frying some of the grass over a fire. It smelled vaguely like pine nuts.

There was a slight metallic smell in the air, too. But no meat, Thanos realized. They were vegetarians.

"FA! THER!"

A thin blond man appeared from one of the tent flaps, smiling as he spotted Thanos and the girl. "Stranger! I am Morak." He held out his hand in greeting. "Life and water to you."

Before he shook Morak's hand, before he even returned the greeting, Thanos knew: If I have to spend any time at all among the People, I'm going to wind up slaughtering every one of them and skinning them down to the bone.

○————————○

THE people were indeed vegetarians. Worse, they were pacifists. They grew a small range of crops—corn, wheat, a bit of miller—on a haphazard patch of farmland just outside the settlement. When Thanos saw it, he was appalled. Yellow wheat plants grew in diagonal rows that intersected and interfered with the taller cornstalks. The whole thing looked like a middle-school agriculture project gone wrong.

Another tribe, the Apaga, lived some distance away. Their technology, Thanos gathered, was slightly more advanced. Most of the People's clothing had been obtained from them on rare trading expeditions.

"Have you considered attacking them?" Thanos asked, one night. "Conquering them, seizing their dwellings, making them your slaves?"

The little girl, Lorak, froze in horror and turned to her father. A look of panic crossed Morak's face. He approached the campfire where his wife, Azak, crouched tending a pan.

"Perhaps you would like a crust-stalk," Morak said, holding out a fried nightmare wrapped in some sort of cornmeal.

Thanos accepted it in silence. It tasted like burnt grass.

He looked up at the sky. The sun was obscured now, hidden by one of the dark plates. They seemed to move back and forth in the sky, creating an artificial day/night cycle. But the sun hadn't set; its light still bled down from behind the plate, casting a slight glow on the ubiquitous yellow grass.

"This world is tidally locked," he muttered. "One side of it faces the sun at all times. This side."

Morak looked uncomfortable. But little Lorak stared at Thanos, waiting to see what came next.

"Someone must have engineered those orbiting screens." He pointed up at the dark plates. "To make the surface habitable. Otherwise this grass would have burned off eons ago, and all life with it."

Azak rushed to her little girl, concerned. But Lorak seemed fascinated.

"Have you ever tried to get off this planet?" Thanos asked.

Morak and Azak exchanged puzzled looks. "Planet?" Azak asked.

"Velt. Off of Velt." Exasperated, Thanos pointed up at the sky. "Up there!"

The three of them stared at him for a moment. Then Lorak burst out laughing.

"He's funny!" she said.

Thanos turned away and took another bite of his crust-stalk. He grimaced.

"The Apaga eat meat," Lorak said.

He paused mid-bite and raised an eyebrow.

HE DECIDED to leave the next day. The People had no vehicles, so his journey would have to be made on foot. Worse, they had little concept of distance or geography. They tried to draw maps in the dirt, strange swoops and arcs of lines that went nowhere. The results were incomprehensible.

They couldn't even tell him how far it was to the Apaga's settlement. "Two days' walk," Morak said.

"Maybe three," said Lurman, the local potter.

The tribe, all hundred or so of them, gathered together and loaded Thanos up with a pack full of tasteless vegetable-based foods. He was restless, eager to get started.

After some debate, Morak disappeared into the Machine Shed and emerged with a large bottle full of water. "We have only four of these left," he said. "I hope you will return it someday."

"Thank you." Thanos accepted the bottle and crammed it into his backpack. He pointed at a rusty scythe blade, discarded in the grass. "May I take that as well?"

"Ah," said Hubak, a tall farmer. "I had planned to sharpen that and re-fix it to a hand thresher."

Thanos stood perfectly still, his face stoic.

"But of course you may have it," Morak said.

Thanos allowed himself a small smile as he scooped up the blade. He wasn't sure if the People were more disturbed at Thanos raiding their meager resources, or at the possibility that the blade might be used for violent purposes. Either way, he had a feeling that they'd be as relieved as he was to have him on his way.

"You'll want to avoid Ranium City," Lurman said. "To set foot in it means doom."

"And the Canyon of Shadows." Azak stood with a protective hand on little Lorak's shoulder. "Ghosts dwell there."

I'm *sure* they do, Thanos thought. But a part of him wondered. This was a new world, after all. A new life.

"And whatever you do, avoid the chimeras' caves. They're over…" Morak waved an arm off into the distance. "…that way."

"I can draw you a dirt map," Lurman said.

Before Thanos could protest, Morak touched Lurman on the shoulder and shook his head.

Thanos shouldered the pack and started off, tromping through the grass.

"Life and water to you, stranger," Morak said.

Thanos turned and muttered the response. The tribe stood before their pathetic tent dwellings, the same dull smile pasted on all their faces.

All but little Lorak. "Bye, mister!" she cried, jumping up and down. "I hope you find lots of meat to eat and slaves to conquer."

TWENTY-TWO

THERE was no road, no footpath to follow. The yellow grass became green, then yellow again, and then brown. All the grass, regardless of its color, came to exactly 18 inches in height. That was odd.

He passed a grove of pine trees, then picked his way through a cluster of palms. Both varieties, he recalled, were native to Earth. But on that world, they rarely appeared in the same area. .

Another mystery.

The sun beat down steadily, raising sweat on his brow. The Velt seemed to have few clouds; on that day, nothing passed between the grassland and the orb in the sky except for those odd, rectangular plates. They seemed to rotate in sync with the sun, creating an artificial night that fell all at once, without transition.

The pack was heavy on his shoulders. But the gravity was a bit less than he was used to. He forged on.

A few hours out, he caught sight of a rocky cliffside rising off to the right. If he'd understood the People's muddled warnings, that was the fastest route to the home of the Apaga tribe. But some sort of cave-dwelling predator called the chimera—a mixture of bear, lion, and tiger—lived there. Thanos suspected the People of exaggerating the chimera's ferocity, but he was only lightly armed and unused to the capabilities of his new body. He decided to avoid the caves.

He veered left. The cliffs receded, leaving only brown grass. There were no distractions, no cosmic entities or annoying vegetarians chattering in his ear. For the first time he could remember, Thanos was alone with his thoughts.

He felt empty, hollowed out. Only the vaguest goals remained in his mind: find the Apaga tribe; escape this planet. Every time he tried to focus on an objective, it was as if his mind upended and the thoughts spilled out across the grass.

Oddly, it wasn't a bad feeling. He felt like a piece of dough baking in the sun. Becoming something new.

A rabbit darted by, zigzagging in the grass. He'd seen several of them, along with squirrels and a few raccoons. Was this an Earth colony? Or some sort of zoo, a preserve, the property of some cosmic being? The Collector, perhaps?

He caught sight of a metallic glint in the distance. Ranium City, the first landmark the People had mentioned. He squinted, estimating it at three, maybe four miles off. Oddly, it seemed to reflect the sun's rays straight at him, as if it were elevated. Was it mounted on a rise or cliff of some kind?

He glanced back. Behind him, the closest dark plate was beginning its passage across the sun. A shadow covered the land, creeping over a scattering of oak trees. The zone of darkness followed his path, gaining steadily on him.

He'd covered perhaps 30 miles since leaving the People's settlement. How much farther, he wondered, to the home of the Apaga? Thirty more miles? Three hundred? A thousand?

How big is the world?

<hr>

RANIUM CITY wasn't a city, but a half-dozen low metal buildings clustered together. They resembled the "Machine Shed" of the People's settlement—except that each of these structures was burned out, blasted, and abandoned. The roofs had alternately caved in and exploded outward, scattering rubble across the grass.

He picked his way between two buildings. The grass was patchy, broken up to reveal areas of bare, dry ground. The metallic odor he'd noticed at the People's camp was stronger here; it smelled like burnt solder mixed with industrial solvents.

He peered inside a building. The interior was a mass of collapsed walls and smashed machinery. An ash shadow on the floor might have been the last trace of a long-decomposed human being.

A rabbit bounded out through the doorway and vanished around the side of the building.

He remembered the People's caution: *To set foot there means doom.* Some sort of accident had occurred here, probably flooding the area with radioactivity.

But from the look of things, that had been long ago. Centuries—perhaps millennia. Surely the radiation had died down by now.

Besides, the rabbit seemed healthy enough.

The interior wall of the building bore an etched symbol—the same one he'd seen inside the Machine Shed. Here he could see it clearly: a stylized "V." One side of the letter was rendered in multiple brushed-metal strokes.

V. For Velt?

He stepped back outside. The building's rusty door hung loose on a single hinge. It bore a triangle-in-circle radiation symbol and several warnings: DO NOT ENTER. DANGER: RADIATION. MASKS AND BADGES MUST BE WORN. All in English.

He paused, shading his eyes to squint up at the sun. *If I stare long enough,* he wondered, *will I see the eye of the Collector? Are you up there, my old nemesis? Gazing down on a poor, humbled Titan, laughing at his fallen state?*

Nothing stared back. No answer.

No god in the sky.

Without warning, darkness fell. The plate slid overhead, masking the sun from view. Night came to Ranium City, leaving Thanos alone in a field of broken grass and shattered steel.

Alone, he realized, and very tired.

He located a building with a partly intact roof. He barely managed to pull out his bedroll and curl up in a corner before he fell into a deep sleep.

IN THE MORNING, the Velt's mysteries seemed no clearer. If anything, the world looked stranger, its paradoxes defined in sharp relief.

He explored each building in turn. One had a large loading bay with a balcony overlooking it. Another was crammed with smashed, broken computers. A third was a warren of small offices, filled with tiny desks that smelled of rotten wood.

A fourth building was intact but barren, completely cleared of walls and furniture; only a few support beams broke up the space. A strange noise, a sort of atonal humming, seemed to rise up from the floor. When he knelt down and placed his ear to the floorboard, the sound seemed to vibrate through his bones.

There were no starships in Ranium City. No shuttles, heavy cruisers, or one-man stingers. Not so much as an orbital-range rocket. If the Velt's architects had once had interstellar capability, there were only two possibilities: Either that technology had crumbled to dust long ago, or they'd taken it with them when they fled.

Everything was labeled in English—doors, tables, faded signs. AUTHORIZED PERSONNEL ONLY. WHEELCHAIR ACCESS VIA RAMP. COMMISSARY. MEDICAL WING. WAITING ROOM—PLEASE CHECK IN AT DESK.

This *had* to be a preserve of some kind. Or else some sort of colony. But the people of Earth had barely begun to venture off their own planet—they were at least a century away from colonizing other worlds. Unless more time had passed than he knew while he lay dying on Hala? Had the Wardrobe transported him into the future?

And if this was an Earth settlement, what about that word *Velt*? It wasn't English. Could it be a corruption of *veldt,* which meant grassland? Or *welt,* the German word for world?

One thing was sure: *Someone* had engineered this place and seeded it with plant and animal life from Earth. Some advanced race, human or otherwise, had constructed the technology that surrounded him. And some accident had blasted their city to pieces, leaving the Velt's survivors to fall into a primitive, ignorant state.

The People had completely forgotten the history of their world. Perhaps the Apaga would know more.

He packed up his things, took a short drink from his dwindling supply of water. Then he paused to look back at Ranium City.

He frowned, staring at the collection of buildings. None of them rose higher than three times his own height. How, then, had they appeared to be elevated before, when he'd beheld the city from a distance?

He turned to look out over the grass, which shone bright yellow under the newly exposed sun. He squinted, struggling to make out the farthest landmarks. The horizon seemed to blur into the sky, partially obscured by distant clouds. He'd noticed the distortion subliminally, but hadn't paid attention until now. Was it some heat-diffusion effect, a trick of the atmosphere? Or something else?

So many mysteries. He shouldered his pack and started off.

By midday, he'd exhausted his supply of vegetable snacks. He gazed hungrily at the rabbits; they taunted him, darting back and forth in the grass. He pulled out his scythe blade and stabbed it in the air a few times. Then he stood perfectly still, his eyes focused in the distance. When a rabbit passed by, he whipped the blade down and speared the creature through the heart.

The lessons of Sacrosanct. He skinned the rabbit and ate it raw with his bare hands.

By the time he reached the Canyon of Shadows, his water was gone. The sun seemed even hotter than before. He licked dry lips, wondering: *Does it ever rain on this world?*

For the first time, the earth sloped downward. The grass thinned out, soft soil giving way to hard, jagged rock. Odd-shaped stone formations rose up all around. Taller than a man, they cast eerie shadows on the bare ground.

The air seemed to shimmer with heat. Thanos forced himself forward.

The metallic smell hit him all at once, stronger than before. He looked down and spied something lodged in the rock: a steel grate with several thin compartments built into it. He dropped to his knees and swept away some loose dirt, revealing a simple air vent.

When he moved close, the smell became almost overpowering. In the corner of the vent was etched that familiar, stylized "V."

A shadow fell over him: thin, curved. A woman? He felt a rush of fury, of rage and fear. He whirled around, whipping out the scythe blade.

No woman. Just one of the rock formations, looming red above him.

He knelt there for a long time, in the deepest hollow of the Canyon of Shadows. Panting, gasping, he felt his rage and fear pour out of him onto the rock, soaking into the dry earth to be absorbed by hidden engines. Ancient spirits, ghosts of the Velt's mysterious architects, seemed to gaze down on him, judging his progress.

Night came, hard and sharp as a curtain falling onstage. Then day. Perhaps another night.

There were more ghosts. Ghosts that seemed to seep in through his pores, probing and poking at his deepest secrets. They left as quickly as they came, taking bits of him with them and vanishing back into the red rock walls.

When he emerged from the Canyon, he wasn't sure quite who he was. His past, his journeys, even his name seemed elusive, like a set of keys he'd left in another room. He was not of this place, not yet. But he wasn't what he had been, either.

And a different sort of wisdom had come over him, a self-knowledge he'd never possessed before. This confusion was nothing new. A lack of identity was, ironically, an unique part of his identity itself.

I've *never* known who I am, he realized.

○──────────────○

AT FIRST he thought the lake was an illusion—a mirage, a hallucination born of thirst. His legs could barely carry him, his eyes were filmed and dry. Better, perhaps, to drop to the ground and die in the hot grass.

He ran to the water. Knelt down and plunged a hand in—and it was cool, wonderful. He splashed it on his face, his chest. He threw off his pack and crawled in, scrabbling like a crab that had forgotten how to walk on land.

Later, he would notice that the lake was perfectly oval-shaped. Too regular to be a natural formation.

Invigorated, he resumed his march. Soon, he began to notice signs of habitation. The grass stopped abruptly, giving way to farms with perfectly straight borders. Stalks of corn grew in neat high rows. The next farm was filled with smaller plants, red blossoms on short green stalks. Sorghum? He wasn't sure.

Past the farm sat a low, makeshift shack. In the distance he could see a collection of small houses. Then more farms. Farther off, almost lost against the strangely curved horizon, was the hint of a second village. All neatly arranged in a grid pattern—a sharp contrast to the seemingly random farmlands of the People.

There were cows. They stared at him from behind a hand-fitted wooden fence. He walked up to the edge of the fence, glaring at the nearest one—at its dull, lowing face. He thought about cracking its back, splitting it open, and eating its bloody meat raw.

A half-mile later, he saw the angel.

She stood before a large boulder, just outside one of the fenced-off crop farms. She was dark and light at once, a glittering figure with vast, shimmering wings. Strong, powerful, with a halo of stars and bright-glowing eyes. She leaned forward, her dark muscular arms gripping a long sword planted in the ground.

She was the most beautiful thing he had ever seen.

The angel turned, her eyes locking onto his. Then she turned back to the sword and let out a long, shuddering sigh. He had the strange feeling she was letting go of something, some inner agony.

Again, he felt the fear.

When she turned to look at him again, she was human. Dark skin, large features, and probing, searching eyes. The wings had vanished; the sword in her hands was now a common gardening hoe.

"You're beautiful," he said. "Still."

A look of amusement crossed her face. Then something else: not fear, but a sort of weighing of the risks. She tossed away the hoe and pulled out a small object: a blunt knife made of wood.

At the sight of the knife, he felt mesmerized. Helpless, moved by something larger and more powerful than himself. He had seen the knife before, in a vision or a dream. But as with so many parts of his past, the details were lost.

She smiled. Tossed the knife up in the air and caught it by the handle.

Thanos gestured at the houses less than half a mile away. "Is that home?"

She turned without a word and started off. Tossing the knife up and down, she gestured for him to follow. An outline of wings seemed to ripple in the air, as if they still clung to her back. Invisible, out of reach, but always with her.

"Let's find out," she said.

TWENTY-THREE

HER NAME was Masika. She said it meant "born during a storm." That told him there were storms on the Velt.

As they drew closer to her village, they came upon more people out working the farms. He saw golden wheat and leafy green plants—potatoes, probably. When they passed the shack he'd seen, a high-pitched squawk filled the air.

"Slaughterhouse," Masika explained.

When she asked him his name, he paused, then confessed that he didn't remember. He expected a verbal jab or at least a raised eyebrow in response, but she just pushed out her lip, looked down, and nodded.

"Sometimes I'm not sure either," she said.

She led him down the narrow walkways running through her village. The Apaga's homes were wood-framed huts with thatched roofs—much more permanent than the flimsy tents the People inhabited. The Apaga themselves seemed healthier, too, and wore fitted clothing.

A woman walked by wearing a lightweight fur

hat. "Is that made of rabbit?" Thanos asked.

"We believe in using every part of the animal," Masika replied. "Unless the animal pisses you off. Then half of it goes in the trash."

He stopped, blinked, and then laughed.

The village, she explained, was one of several comprising the larger Apaga settlement. Each small village had a grid of farmland around it. The layout was flexible; farms belonging to one village often butted up against another's property.

"We trade off crops," she explained. "If one group has a bad year, the others help out."

"Are there ever disputes?" he asked.

"Not really. The land…it's all pretty much the same." She paused outside a large hut. "Even the grass always grows to the same height."

"I've noticed that. How is it possible?"

"What?"

"How can that be? About the grass?"

She looked at him, frowning. "It just is."

He followed her inside. The outer room was large, furnished with imperfect handmade furniture. Charcoal portraits adorned the unfinished wood walls. Thanos stopped to study a sketch of Masika herself, a simple head shot.

"It captures your eyes," he said.

"My father's work."

"He knows you well."

"He did."

He followed her into a series of smaller rooms:

a sitting room, a bedroom, a pantry. One room was filled with an enormous, eight-foot loom. A half-finished rug spilled out of its wooden frame.

"My mother's last project," she said. "I haven't had the heart to remove it."

Thanos frowned. "She died?"

"My father, too. And his parents. All within the last two years."

He searched his mind. "I'm sorry?" he offered. "Are those the words?"

She smiled slightly, peering at him out of the corner of her eyes. "They'll do."

There was an awkward silence. Masika led him back to the outer room and plopped herself down in a wicker armchair. He unshouldered his pack, happy to be rid of the burden.

"House is a bit empty. And I had to take over all the farming." She stretched her arms, wincing, "Not too many women do it alone. I don't mind, though."

He studied her arms. "It looks good on you."

She nodded, dismissing the compliment. "You came from the People's settlement, right?"

He nodded.

"I spent some time with them," she said. "When I was a teenager."

"Oh?"

"I went through...I guess you'd call it a 'rebellious period.' My parents thought a dose of pacifist philosophy might calm me down." She smiled. "Kind of had the opposite effect."

He smiled back. "The People are very, uh…"

"…boring. Stupefying is a good word."

Her laugh was quiet but warm. He drank it in, eager and hungry. He felt like a newborn baby, absorbing every scrap of information he could.

"I stayed with a nice couple," she continued. "But I don't know how that tribe even survives on the Velt. They wouldn't last two minutes on a chimera hunt."

Thanos looked at her. "Your people hunt the chimera?"

"Once every 17 years. It's a ritual thing…good for morale, but it always exacts a price." She raised an eyebrow. "You a hunter?"

A vague memory of blood rose to his mind. "I've stalked prey."

"Well, there's a hunt coming up in a couple weeks." She smirked. "Maybe you can show us a few moves."

He paused, studying her. She had hard eyes; dark, wide features; and short-cropped, jet-black hair. Her arms and legs were strong, muscles well developed from working in the fields. She was shorter than Thanos but taller than most of her people. She could have been as young as 25 or as old as 40—he couldn't tell.

No wings, though. Maybe he'd imagined that. Maybe he imagined a lot of things.

"Oh! Hello."

Thanos whirled toward the doorway. The speaker was a muscular man in his 30s; he carried one of the wooden knives clasped in his fist. He stared at Thanos, then turned to Masika with a questioning look.

"Who is this?" he asked.

Thanos tensed. The man's words weren't unfriendly, and that blunt knife certainly wasn't a threat. But something in the air had changed.

"He was given no name," Masika said lightly. "Or he's chosen to forget it." She gestured at the newcomer. "Stranger, this is Basi."

Basi walked straight up to Thanos and held out a hand. His lips seemed to twitch, a hesitant motion. Then a broad smile spread over his face.

"Welcome," he said.

Surprised, Thanos took the hand. Basi shook it with vigor, stealing little glances at Masika.

He likes her, Thanos thought. Perhaps he even loves her—and he senses that I could be a threat to him. Yet I sense no deceit in his welcome, no hidden agenda.

Basi disengaged and turned to Masika. "The clan is practicing in a few minutes," he said, balancing his knife on the edge of his finger. "Want to get in some sparring practice?"

She made a sour face. "Damn chickens have to be brought in before dark. But maybe our new friend would be interested."

Basi hesitated for only a moment. He flipped the knife up into the air; in the low gravity, it spun slowly for a second. He whipped his other hand around and snatched it out of the air.

Masika smiled. Her dark eyes flitted from one man to the other.

"Sure," Basi said. "Why not?"

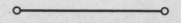

THE NIGHT-PLATE was still a ways off from the sun, but the Apaga farmers seemed to keep their own schedule. They marched into town from the fields, their backs stooped. Yet they seemed cheerful, stopping to pet dogs and smile at their neighbors.

Chattering nervously, Basi led Thanos through the maze of huts. "You're not from here," the young man said. "What part of the Velt do you come from?"

Thanos didn't answer.

"Are you from Earth?"

He turned sharply. "What do you know of Earth?"

"My grandfather says we lived there once. But I'm not even sure what Earth is."

Scattered memories flashed through Thanos's mind: a blue globe bristling with orbital weaponry, a metal man in red and gold with a glowing circle on his chest.

"You're not missing much," he said.

A man with a grass-cutter stopped to smile at Thanos. He frowned back, puzzled. The man shrugged and moved on.

"So you came here," Thanos continued, "some generations ago. Are there any remnants of that technology among your people?"

For a moment, he pictured a small hyperspace ship lying forgotten in a barn somewhere.

"I'm afraid not." Basi gave him an apologetic smile. "All that science, that power...it never led anywhere good."

"So there's nothing at all?"

"A few records from the ancient times. But we don't consult them very often."

The Velt was definitely an Earth colony—Basi's words confirmed that. But his phrasing stuck in Thanos's mind: *ancient times*. Again he wondered: Have I traveled into the future?

"Who holds these records?" he asked.

"I think Poto has 'em in her house. But good luck talking to *her*."

A rabbit scurried by underfoot. Thanos stumbled to avoid it.

Basi's face brightened. "Look, we're here."

The houses thinned out into a large town square, shaded by a variety of elm and oak trees. Again, the effect was jarring. On Earth, thatched huts and oak trees rarely coexisted.

A small crowd of men and women, along with a few children, stood watching as a man and a woman squared off under the hot sun. They danced in a circle, jabbing and feinting with those wooden knives.

"That's Pagan," Basi said, moving forward to point at the man in the square. "His family is well respected. The woman is Rina."

The young man, Pagan, lunged forward, stabbing straight out at his opponent. She leaped away, tossing her knife up into the air. The combat stopped for a moment as the knife hovered briefly in the low gravity. Both Pagan and Rina stared up as it dropped, lazily, back into her hand.

A murmur of approval rose from the crowd.

Thanos frowned. "Is this combat?"

"We don't think of it as such," Basi replied. "More like meditation."

Thanos watched the exercise, puzzled. Pagan and Rina alternately thrust and threw the knives, which behaved oddly in flight. The gravity was part of the reason, but he realized there must also be some odd aerodynamic component to their design. Every time the combatants or their weapons came close to touching, one fighter danced out of the way. It seemed to be part of the exercise.

Rina flicked her wrist and flung her knife past Pagan. The knife executed a full arc in the air, whirling around his head and circling back toward her. He responded, throwing his own knife upward at an angle. The two weapons passed in midair, avoiding contact by no more than half an inch. The combatants snatched the knives out of the air and turned, sharply, to bow to the crowd.

As the spectators applauded, Pagan strode over to Thanos and Basi. He clapped a sweaty hand against Basi's back.

"Nice work," Basi said.

"All in the wrist." Pagan turned to Thanos. "Who's this?"

"Friend of Masika's. He doesn't have a name."

Pagan stared at Thanos, a challenging look in his eye. This one, Thanos thought, is an alpha. Of all the people in this village, he's the dangerous one.

Thanos felt a flame ignite inside him. An old fire, a challenge he couldn't ignore. "You're good with that thing," he said, pointing at Pagan's knife.

Pagan smiled. He tossed the knife into the air, whirled around, and caught it behind his back.

"Not much of a weapon, though," Thanos continued. He allowed a hint of menace to creep into his tone.

Pagan's eyes narrowed. Basi eyed his friend.

"Oh?" Pagan asked.

"I prefer something sharper."

"Why would you want that, stranger?"

"Pagan," Basi cautioned.

"In case something needs skinning."

He stared Pagan in the eye. People were gathering now, watching the confrontation. The sun blazed down.

Pagan stepped toward him. Thanos tensed. Pagan dropped to one knee, whipping the knife around in his hand, and lunged. He sliced down, thrusting the knife toward the ground beside Thanos's legs.

The rabbit dropped silently to the ground. Blood leaked from the wound in its head.

Thanos blinked, startled. He hadn't even seen the rabbit approach.

Pagan reached down and lifted the beast by the ears. He held it up before Thanos. As the crowd watched, the rabbit twitched once, let out a high wail, and was still.

"Skin this," Pagan said.

The crowd smiled and murmured its appreciation. Basi grimaced and turned to whisper in his friend's ear.

Pagan laughed and tossed the rabbit away.

Thanos turned and stalked off. He wasn't sure where he belonged; he still didn't know whether there was a way off this world. But he knew one thing: If he decided to stay with the Apaga, sooner or later he'd have to deal with Pagan.

HE STOOD alone, leaning on the wooden fence. Behind him, the farm belonging to Masika's family stretched for a solid mile before giving way to the village. Ahead, yellow grass extended to the horizon, broken up by a few farms leading to other settlements.

When he squinted, he could just make out the gray rise of the chimeras' caves, 50 miles or more in the distance. That was odd. A world with this level of gravity and atmosphere should have a shorter horizon than that.

Again he wondered: How big is the world?

And was there a place in it for him?

"My father used to stand out here for hours," Masika said.

He didn't turn around. She moved up next to him.

"He had all kinds of cobbled-together measuring equipment," she continued. "It's still cluttering up the damn house. Used it to keep track of the humidity, rainfall, crop output…"

"…the grass?"

She nodded. "You're right. We don't cut the grass— even in the farmlands. It just doesn't grow there."

"But everywhere else, it's the same height." He smiled. "Divine intervention?"

"I believe in hidden powers." She leaned forward on the fence. "But I don't believe in gods."

They stood in silence for several minutes. Above, the Velt's night-plate moved closer to the sun.

"It's the horizon that puzzles me," he said. "See how the grass seems to merge with the sky?"

She shook her head. "What else should it look like?"

He studied her. She had an appealing physicality about her, a way of dominating the space she inhabited. He liked the way her body bobbed back and forth as she leaned against the fence.

"Who's Poto?" he asked.

"Crazy old woman." Masika laughed. "Did Basi mention her name? He's terrified of her."

"Yes." Thanos frowned. "He likes you, you know."

She didn't answer. Leaned forward again, peering out across the grass.

"Were your parents happy?" she asked.

The question jarred him. "With each other? Yes."

"I *think* mine were. But it's hard to…" She shook her head. "If they'd had longer, who knows?"

He nodded. "Not many couplings can last a lifetime."

"I don't think I want to marry." She glanced sidelong at him. "It sounds dull. Even worse than living with the People."

He laughed.

"Do you want to marry?" She didn't look at him. "Someday?"

"I don't..." He paused. "I had someone once. Not a person you'd marry. I think...I think she's finally lost to me."

The sun slid behind its screen. Darkness fell; a chill descended on the air.

"You're afraid of something." Her voice was a whisper in the dark. "What is it?"

He edged closer to her. Reached out a hand and swept it across the darkened countryside.

"How big is the world?"

She met his eyes for just a second and nodded. Then she leaned sideways and rested her head on his shoulder.

They stood together for a long time, staring at the dark grass. Her body was warm, the breeze cool as it swept off the farmland. And for one night, all the questions seemed just a little smaller, a bit less important than before.

TWENTY-FOUR

"LET'S TRY another tack," Thanos said. "I've heard the word Earth mentioned by some of your people. Do you know anything about that?"

The old woman turned her drawn, almost emaciated face to him. She took a step back toward the wall and touched the metal device in her ear. Her eyes flitted quickly from side to side, as if she were listening to some alien transmission.

"The study of thinking machines teaches us more about the brain than we can learn by introspective methods," she said.

Thanos shook his head, baffled. He sat back in the overstuffed chair and raised a hand to his brow.

The air in Poto's house was stuffy. The hut was crammed with things: furniture, chipped plates, animal bones, piles of clothing. In the corner, a parrot shuffled nervously in its cage. It seemed to have no voice.

Thanos had noticed a few pieces of old technology scattered around the house: a USB cord holding an old photo up on the wall, a planter that might have been an oscilloscope, now holding a small tree. All too old to provide many clues to the Apaga's past. And all too primitive, too low-tech, to have been scavenged from a starship.

Except, perhaps, for that earpiece. Poto fingered it, her lips moving silently. It was smaller than a beetle and studded with tiny switches. Was she really receiving something through it?

"The ability to solve mazes is strongly correlated to analyses of our daily problems," she said.

Poto wore a long, loose robe. The only bit of color on her was a thick, decorative choker made of bright beads, encircling her wrinkled neck. Another remnant, possibly, of the Apaga's past on Earth.

He'd been listening to the old woman for a solid hour—an hour of evasions, non sequiturs, and awkward pauses. His mind was whirling, but something kept him from walking away. Poto's ramblings bore a strange internal logic, and they were peppered with Earth references: mazes, schizophrenics. Either she was in real-time contact with someone from beyond the Velt, or she was listening to recorded archives stretching back before her people's arrival.

Or maybe she was just crazy.

Thanos knew he couldn't give up. He'd developed a terrible suspicion about this world, and he sensed the answers were here.

"I've been studying the horizon," he said. "Did your people notice anything odd about the atmosphere, the diffraction patterns? Are there notes anywhere, from the landing?"

Again, she touched her ear.

"In the old days, before communication was subjected to rigid scientific analysis, a variety of haphazard systems existed." She shook her head. "Very crude, very unscientific."

"Okay, wait." He pointed at her ear. "Are you repeating something you're hearing, right now? Some sort of transmission?"

She backed away from him, clutching her ear.

"Their brain-pan is larger, proportionally, than a dolphin." She stared at him, her voice a low hiss. "They can bite through a human thorax without stopping for breath."

He held up his hands in a gesture of surrender. "I'm only asking questions."

"Sparrows had reached 20 kilos in weight, with straight swordlike beaks." Her eyes went glassy. "Now and then one went mad and attacked people."

"Fine. I give up." He rose to his feet. "Just one more thing."

"I can still be shocked," she said, looking away. "But more in wonderment than in fear."

"The boy, Basl. He said you might have records from the ancient times."

She glanced over, seemed to focus on him for the first time.

"I'm assuming the computers stopped working a long time ago," he continued. "Are there any sort of storage devices? Hard drives, liquid crystal? Organic memory pods?"

Poto touched her choker and nodded, a quick birdlike motion. Then she crossed over to the bird's cage. It turned to acknowledge her presence, but still it made no sound.

Thanos frowned. What was she doing?

The old woman touched the bird's head—a quick, light motion. Then her fingers dropped to the bottom of the cage. She grabbed up a handful of shredded paper and carried it over to Thanos.

He accepted it, wincing as a parrot turd fell off onto the floor. The paper was old and brown, so brittle it almost fell apart in his hands, and it had been sliced into thin strips. But he could make out individual numbers, the occasional word. LOG, COMMAND, VECTOR. CONTROL.

He turned to stare up at the old woman. "The records?"

"There is entwined seven-tentacled lightning." She smirked at him. "It is fire-masses, it is sheets, it is arms!"

"You old fool. Give me that!"

He lunged at her, reaching for her earpiece. She screamed and swiped out with a sharp-fingered hand, clawing him across the face. He cried out and grabbed her by the throat, squeezing the beaded choker against her neck.

They stood locked together for a moment. Her eyes bulged out, but not with fear—with pure hatred. A sense-memory came to him. He'd held a woman by the throat before, snapped her neck with a twitch of his wrist. His mother?

He reached up and plucked the earpiece out of her ear. She wriggled free of his grip and stumbled back into a small chair. He released her, raising the earpiece to listen.

Static, faint but constant. No words.

There was fear in her eyes, now. Her fingers moved along her throat, re-ordering the beads around her neck.

Disgusted, he tossed the earpiece away. Poto's eyes followed its path as it rolled along the floor. When it was close enough, she lunged down to snatch it up.

"You know nothing," he spat. "You've thrown it all away."

She raised the earpiece to her ear. Shook it once, in the air. Then she seemed to grow distant again, listening.

"There were the gentlemen-suicides back on Earth," she said.

He felt a wetness on his cheek. Reached a hand up; it came away bloody. She'd tagged him better than he'd realized.

"There were girls who fell in love with such men," Poto muttered. "However stark and dreadful their personal fates might be."

He cast a final glare at her. He felt furious, consumed by rage. He knew the feeling was irrational, and yet on another level it seemed utterly normal. As if he'd returned to his natural state of being.

"The sky is stripped," she said. "I am too weak to write much. But I still hear them walking in the trees…"

He turned and strode out the door, allowing her voice to recede behind him.

○————————————○

WHEN he reached Masika's house, his rage hadn't subsided. He stopped at her well, pulling up just enough water to wash off his stinging face. Then he stalked inside.

Thankfully, she wasn't home. He crossed through the large outer room, past the tiny side room where he slept, to her bedroom. The bed was neatly made, undisturbed; a small freestanding closet stood against one wall. An image rose, almost reluctantly, to his conscious mind: the Infinity Wardrobe.

He flung open the closet doors. An array of old tools hung from nails, arranged in neat rows. Some he recognized: a handheld particle counter, a soil-sample tool with sharp coring point. All, he was certain, of Earth origin.

He loaded up his pack with as many implements as he could carry and walked back outside. A few villagers smiled at him, tried to engage him in conversation. He just brushed past, grunting, hauling his burden.

When he reached the field, he unpacked the tools and dropped them in a big pile. He crouched down and picked up a pair of ordinary shears, then grabbed hold of a single blade of grass.

"Eighteen inches," he growled.

He snipped off half of the grass stalk and threw away the top section. He leaned in and stared at the grass, waiting for something to happen.

The sun burned down. A mild breeze blew up, rustling the field of grass.

With a snarl, he turned away. He picked up a laser rangefinder and aimed it into the distance. Its display stayed dark; the battery was exhausted. He thrust the coring tool into the dirt, but it too was empty of power.

He picked up a small telescope, aimed it at the sun, and swore as the light burned into his eyes. When his vision cleared, he turned the telescope toward one of the night-plates, off in the distance. He could see its edge through the lens, forming a perfectly straight line against the sky.

When he looked down, the truncated blade of grass was gone. He scrabbled around, ran his hands through the surrounding blades. Had it vanished? Or had it grown back to full size and mixed in with the others in the minutes he'd been distracted?

"Can't be," he muttered. "Can't be real."

Hands trembling, he aimed the telescope at the horizon. Grass covered the ground, a carpet of yellow-brown stretching as far as he could see. And then, at the limits of his vision, it curved upward.

Panic washed over him, mixed with anger. He cracked the telescope over his knee, breaking it in half, and flung the two sections away. Lens fragments rained down on the grass.

He clenched his fists, squeezed his eyes shut. Vaguely, he recalled: Once, I had cosmic awareness.

I could jaunt from world to world in a heartbeat; I could even exist on several planets at once. Now…

…now I'm trapped.

"I was four years old, you know."

He opened his eyes. Masika stood before him, her eyes hard. She held up the shattered end of the telescope.

"When my father first showed it to me." She shook the telescope at him, dislodging the last few shards of glass. "He pointed it at the chimera's cave. I saw something move, and ran off to hide in my room. Wouldn't look through the telescope again for two years."

He stared at her. He knew he should back down, explain himself. But the rage still held him in its grip. He felt like a wounded beast scratching madly at the bars of its cage.

He gestured at the telescope fragment. "Perhaps it's time you put away childish things."

"Perhaps that's not your decision."

She took a step back and looked at the ground. "What are you doing with all this?" She stared at the shears, the soil sampler, the useless rangefinder and particle counter. "What are you trying to learn?"

"This world. It's so…small." His tone was almost pleading. "Don't you want more? Don't you want something better?"

"I was hoping I'd found something."

Before he could interpret her meaning, there was a rustle in the grass. He turned to see Basi and Pagan approaching, along with a few other young villagers.

"I'm talking about the world." Suddenly he had to make her see. "I think I've figured it out. All of it."

He grabbed her by the shoulders. She frowned, but didn't move.

"This world," he said. "It's not a world. Not really."

"Masika?" Basi asked.

Masika waved him away. She stared into Thanos's eyes. "Go on."

"The horizon. It curves up, not down."

She shrugged, baffled.

More villagers began to gather, attracted by the disturbance. Pagan stood at the front with Basi, motioning the others to stay back.

"Don't you understand?" Thanos stared at Masika. "We're not on a planet at all. This isn't the ground, the outside of a world." He let her go, made a wild gesture up at the sky. "It's the inside!"

As soon as he spoke the words aloud, the spell seemed to break. He looked around at the gathered Apaga…30, maybe 40 of them now. They were lab rats, experimental animals. Prisoners in an invisible cage.

Masika twisted free and took a step back. Basi moved up next to her, but again she motioned him away.

"I'm sorry." Thanos held up his hands. "I didn't mean to frighten you."

"I'm not frightened," she said. He could tell she wasn't.

"I just…can't you see?" Panic began to rise in him again. "The Velt is a fake, an artifice. It's run by machines—they control the weather, the days and nights. The grass." He paused. "It's a trap!"

She shrugged helplessly. "The Velt is the Velt."

"All this…" He gestured around. "This is the inside of a sphere. The sun—it's not up in the sky, not really. It's held in the center of the hollow sphere. Somehow."

They stared at him as if he were a madman.

"And there's—there's so much more in the universe." He stepped back against the fence, addressing the group. "Don't you want to see it? Don't you want to know what's out there?"

Basi looked around. "Out where?"

"We could do it. All of us, together. First we will conquer the People. With your greater technological knowledge—"

"Conquer the People?" Pagan asked.

"Yes." Thanos stepped right up to him. "You understand. I know you—I know what kind of leader you are. You could spearhead the attack, force them into submission."

Pagan watched Thanos come, his eyes hard. Then he spread his arms and shook his head.

"The People have done nothing to us," he said. "Why would we want to attack them?"

A murmur of agreement ran through the crowd. Masika moved up to Thanos and reached out to touch him on the shoulder, but he turned angrily away.

"You're not human at all," he hissed. "You're sheep. Sheep in a pen."

Poto's cackling laugh rang through the air. The

crowd parted and she approached, hand held up to her ubiquitous earpiece.

"The creatures outside looked from pig to man," she said, "and from man to pig, and from pig to man again. But already it was impossible to say which was which."

People began to laugh. Even Masika risked a smile. Thanos stood perfectly still, his fists clenched.

"Stranger." Basi walked up to him, holding up one of the blunt knives. "Perhaps a round of meditation?"

Thanos looked from Basi over to Masika, who watched them both with a sympathetic grimace. Pagan stood with the rest of the people, eyeing the scene with distaste.

Thanos turned to Basi again. A condescending smile tickled the young Apaga's lips.

Thanos punched him in the stomach, a powerful roundhouse blow. Basi cried out and doubled over; the knife went flying. The villagers backed off, startled.

"No!" Masika cried. But Thanos's glare stopped her in her tracks.

Basi started to climb to his feet. Thanos grabbed him by his vest and wrenched him up.

"You think you're a man?" Thanos growled. "You think you could satisfy her?"

Basi sputtered something. Thanos backhanded him across the face.

"You're a boy," Thanos continued. "A sheep. A nothing."

Basi held up both hands in a ritual combat motion. Thanos slammed the flats of his palms against

Basi's hands, forcing him to the ground.

"You'll die here. All of you." Thanos was lost in the blood-fever now. "You deserve to die. Mewling little worms, caught in a trap. You can't even imagine a way out!"

His fist came down again, despite his victim's cries. His light-brown fist, clenched tight, knuckles hard and skinned. Up and down on Basi's skull, his chest, his stomach. The brown fist, up and down. The brown fist.

The gray, rocky fist.

He lost track of the blows, of time passing, of the harsh sunlight on his neck. The crowd vanished; the grassland receded. All he knew, all he could see and feel, was flesh and bone cracking, bending, breaking beneath his relentless assault.

A hand on his shoulder. He whirled, fist raised. Pagan stood facing him, eyes wide.

Thanos smiled and rose to his feet. At last, a worthy enemy. The first he'd met on this world—

"Stop," Masika said. "You have to stop."

She loomed behind Pagan, her eyes hard. In those eyes he saw urgent knowledge.

"You'll kill him," she said, gesturing down at Basi,

Thanos glanced at his fist, still raised to strike. It was light brown, the joints speckled with blood. His knuckles ached.

Basi let out a little cry. He clutched his ribs and rolled a short ways across the ground. Thanos looked down at his broken, bloody face.

"Well?" Masika asked. Her voice was gentle. Despite all he'd just done, the dark self he'd just revealed, she seemed to understand.

He looked around at the gathered Apaga—a hundred of them now, in a semicircle. Maybe 200. They watched in silent judgment, their faces wide with disapproval.

Rats, he thought. Rats in a cage.

"No," he said. "No no no."

He lurched away from Masika, ignoring her outstretched hand. Grabbing up his pack, he vaulted the fence and sprinted off into the grass.

"Let him go," Pagan said.

How big is the world? Now he knew.

"Not big enough," he murmured. "Never enough."

He ran, not looking back. He didn't want to see the villagers' dull faces, the farms and huts receding behind him. But most of all, he didn't want to see Masika—beautiful, knowing Masika—reach down to take Basi's bruised and bloody hand.

TWENTY-FIVE

THERE was only one way to be sure.

They rose up into the sky, trunks twisted into helix shapes, rough bark giving way to flat green leaves against the sun. Chestnut trees, he realized. Four of them, stooped and leaning, yet still tall and proud. They looked like old gods looming over some empty domain.

He looked back. The Apaga village was barely visible over an endless sea of grass. He nodded. The trees formed a distinctive landmark, the only notable feature for miles around. They would do.

The trunk of the oldest tree formed a sort of hollow, just big enough for a man. He sat down and opened his pack. Some strips of dried meat that Masika had given him, a washcloth from the People's settlement. A few crude items from the collection belonging to Masika's father: a sextant, a wrench, a magnifying monocle designed to fit directly over one eye. He hadn't stopped to return those.

He pulled everything out, then repacked only the items he would need. Finally he stood up and surveyed the world that was his prison.

There was only one way to be sure.

He began to walk. He chose a path leading away from the Apaga village, because he didn't want to see them again. He tacked to the left of the chimeras' caves, giving them plenty of distance. Above all, he wanted to keep his path as straight as possible.

As the night-plate approached overhead, he heard a distant chattering of voices. The People, he realized. He could just barely see the edge of their settlement, past the jigsaw puzzle of fields they used for farming.

When darkness fell, he bedded down under a fir tree and was quickly asleep.

For the rest of the trip, he saw no people, no settlements, no ruined cities or shadow canyons. Just grassland, green and yellow and brown by turns. He walked for days—three, maybe four. It was hard to tell. Night seemed to fall at less regular intervals.

He realized he was walking at an angle to the night-plates. They moved in their own rhythm, unsynchronized with his. From his perspective as a moving object, a day would last six hours, sometimes less, then drop all at once into a long night. The next day might be 14 or 15 hours in length.

And all around, nothing but grass.

He wondered whether he'd lost his way. It was imperative that he continue in a straight line, correcting rapidly for any necessary detours. He had always had an innate sense of direction; he hoped he could trust it now.

He killed rabbits, drank from the rare stream. By

the end of the fifth day—or was it the sixth?—he was parched, exhausted, and reeking.

Then he saw the trees. The beautiful, elegant chestnuts rising up out of the green grass.

"It's true." He staggered up to the old tree, collapsed into its hollow opening. "It's true."

The world was round.

His feeling of triumph was short-lived. If this was true—if, as he'd come to believe, the Velt was a small artificial world, completely enclosed—then he was no closer to escaping than before. He'd seen no new technology during his journey, no further clue to the fate of the people who'd built this cage.

Again. He would have to do it again.

He started off directly opposite from the chimeras' cave this time, into unknown territory. For two days he saw nothing: no people, no settlements. Even the landscape was flatter, more nondescript than usual. The grass seemed more brown, the air thicker with humidity.

On the third day, he came to an area where the grass had been tamped down. The path seemed fresh, and it stretched off at an angle in both directions. With a shock he realized: This was his own path, from the previous trip. The grass was still a uniform 18 inches in height, but it hadn't yet sprung back up from his footsteps.

On the fourth day, he came across a few other spots where the grass had been trampled. He squinted and caught sight of the Apaga's settlement, off in the distance. He still wasn't ready to face them.

He swung left, away from their grid of farms.

Again, inevitably, he returned to the chestnut trees.

Curled up in the shade of the twisted trunk, he thought furiously. On the second trip, he'd become more accustomed to the rhythm of the days, so he'd managed to keep better track of time. Five days, roughly 14 hours' walk each day, average three miles per hour…that added up to a little over 200 miles.

Two hundred miles. The circumference of the Velt. The distance from any single point back to itself along a straight path.

He looked up, squinting through dappled leaves at the bright sky. What lay past the sun, beyond whatever mechanism held it fixed in the sky, past the cloud cover shrouding it? Now he knew: the other side of the world. Perhaps the exact spot where he'd crossed his own path, found his own tracks matting down the grass.

How many miles across the center, to that point on the other side of the world? Seventy, maybe. The sun itself was 33, maybe 34 miles above.

Not a sun at all. Not a world.

There had to be a way out. Somewhere, somehow. The alternative was unthinkable: life among Masika's herd of human sheep—or the even duller, pacifistic People.

He cast off again, along a fresh path. Striding, marching across the Velt, alone in his purpose. The sun seemed hotter now, the air thick and wet. *Does it ever rain here?* he wondered.

A day passed. Two. Again he crossed one of his own, barely visible paths—from which trip? He wasn't sure. The grass began to thin out, the soil giving way to red stone. Up ahead and to the left, he could see rock formations rising up.

The Canyon of Shadows.

He shivered and veered right. He wasn't ready to revisit that place. Besides, it was dead, barren. Full of ghosts—trapped souls with no way out.

No way out.

The grass shaded from yellow to brown. His throat was dry; he hadn't seen water for miles. The horizon seemed to curve upward more sharply now, dry grass rising up to stretch all the way around the world.

A sharp metallic smell brought him back to his senses. He shook his head, disoriented. He was facing a low warehouse with a familiar stylized "V" etched onto its door.

Ranium City. He was back in Ranium City.

He spent the night exploring the labs and high bays of the City. In the big open building, the one he'd visited previously, the strange humming seemed louder than before. He stood for a long moment, letting it soak into him, then ran back outside.

In another building, he pried open a hatch and descended into a cramped underground passage, barely big enough to crawl through. Machinery lined the walls of the tunnel, screens and buttons, all dark and unresponsive to the touch. Yet still something hummed in the walls. That same stubborn power, hidden deep within the Velt.

I'm below the grass, he realized. For some reason that seemed significant.

He coughed, gagging. The metal smell was strong here, the air stagnant. He scrabbled backward and returned to the surface.

In the morning, he resumed his travels. Ahead, from the expanse leading to the chimera's lair, he heard shouting. He ducked behind a palm tree and watched.

The noise grew louder, resolving into human voices. A dozen men and women came into view. They pumped their fists in the air, chanting rhythmically. He didn't know the words, but he recognized the crudely tailored clothing as they drew closer. The Apaga.

More of them appeared: two dozen, three. A hundred. They marched toward the caves, chanting and shouting.

The chimera hunt, Thanos remembered. Once every 17 years, the Apaga took on the savage creatures in a fierce, ceremonial battle.

The party drew closer, angling past Thanos's hiding place. Pagan strode at the head of the group, leading the charge. As he jabbed his knife in the air, the others mirrored his thrusts. The knives had been fitted with sharp metal attachments fixed over the blunt wooden blades.

Young and old Apaga marched together, men and women. He caught sight of Basi, his face stoic, hand clasped to Masika's. She looked as strong as ever, the sharp-bladed knife gripped firmly in her other hand.

Thanos felt a sudden wave of regret. He remembered Masika's words: *Maybe you can show us a few moves.*

The group vanished into the rocky caverns. Thanos stole out of his hiding place and swerved right, avoiding the caves. He was beginning to understand the three-dimensional geography of the Velt: This detour would take him close to the People's settlement. But that was better than facing the chimera.

Or Masika.

Night had fallen by the time he returned to the chestnut trees. He lay still, his mind whirling. Three circuits of the Velt; three different paths, all leading back to the same spot. There was no doubt now. No doubt.

He closed his eyes. Tried to picture the world, the Velt, as it might appear from outside. Was it some sort of starship? A generation ship, equipped only with sublight engines, creeping its way from star to star? Taking centuries, even millennia, to reach some forgotten destination?

Or a satellite? An opaque snow globe fixed in some remote orbit, its stark metal exterior lit to blinding radiance by the fires of an unknown star?

He made the fourth trip in a fit of madness. Three days, no sleep. He strode up and down the slopes of the Canyon of Shadows, marched straight through the ghosts. Barely avoided the caves. Heard the wail of the chimera, long and mournful on the wind.

By the fifth trip, he was dry and sunstroked. Throat

parched, skin baked red. He staggered across the grass, lurching like a wounded beast. Sounds, fragments of words, issued from his mouth. He felt like a wraith, a ghost, doomed to walk this half-world for all time.

Again the chestnut trees loomed ahead; again the sky grew dark. Dimly he registered that this was a different kind of darkness. The clouds were gathering and thickening, masking the relentless rays of the artificial sun.

As the first crack of thunder rang out, he ran for shelter. Huddled up to the enormous tree, he pressed his body against its ancient bark. He felt like a part of the tree—a branch, a single ring on its aged trunk. *This is home now,* he thought. *This is my only home.*

Rain fell in sheets. He huddled under the trees, but there was no escape. Soon he was soaked, his crude Apagan clothes clingy and reeking. He struggled out of them and threw them away.

He looked down. At the base of the tree, the water had washed away an area of soil. He knelt down, his bare legs sloshing in the muck. Reaching out, he shoved away a wet pile of mud.

An air vent. Thin, rectangular, like the one he'd seen on his first trip to Ranium City. Same stylized "V" in the corner.

A patch of grass grew alongside the vent. He reached down, carefully avoiding the vent, and scooped up another handful of mud. Then another, and another. The blades of grass stretched several inches down into the ground.

He lowered his face to the mud. Rain washed down his hands. He reached up and swept water out of his eyes.

Now he could see the base of the grass. Each blade, each razor-thin stalk, grew out of its own tiny metallic planting base. Like a million separate house plants, each in a pot so small it was nearly microscopic.

Above, the thunder cracked. The chimera's howl echoed it, borne on the sodden wind.

He grabbed a handful of grass and pulled. A dozen blades snapped free; he tossed them away in the air. He looked down, staring, as each tiny base sprouted a fresh spear of grass.

He let out a howl. Curled up his fists and *punched* the grass, as hard as he could. Pain stabbed up his hand, but he barely noticed. He punched the ground again, denting and scattering the tiny plant-bases, then swept them aside.

Grunting, snarling, he dug into the ground. Disrupted soil, dislodged small machinery, crushed worms beneath his bloody knuckles. Rain poured down onto him, unheeded. He had only one goal, one instinct underlying his actions: escape.

If he couldn't fly off of this world, maybe he could tunnel out of it.

His fist scraped on something hard and wide. He peered down, his eyes blurred by rain and fever. He swept aside mud, flinging it up to the surface in handfuls.

It was a hatch. Round and wide, and covered with an embossed, tarnished version of the familiar "V" logo.

He battered at it with his fists. He scrabbled and reached around its sides, struggling to find a grip to pull it open. Climbed down into the hole and kicked at the hatch with both feet, screaming and crying, howling into the wind.

She found him slumped over it, mumbling, naked and half conscious. Climbed down into the hole and took his chin in her hand, lifted it so she could look into his eyes. Her hair was drenched, her clothing soaked.

She was still the most beautiful thing he'd ever seen.

"'Sika," he gasped.

Her eyes looked older than before. She touched his cheek, then looked away.

"What?" He rose to his knees, took her by the shoulders. "What's wrong?"

"Basi," she said. "He didn't…the chimera got him."

"Oh."

All at once, his head was clear. Rain still poured down; his fingers still bled. The Velt was still a trap, a maze with no exit.

But now Masika was in pain.

"I'm sorry," he said. He reached out for her—an awkward, sincere motion.

"You don't understand." She pulled away, holding out a hand. "When he died, I felt nothing. I mean, I don't mean that. I grew up with him, I loved him like a brother. I mourn for him."

Thanos nodded.

"But I realized," she continued. "In that moment,

when his broken body landed next to me on the rocks. I looked at him, and I knew…"

Lightning flashed, bright as fire.

"…I'm not afraid of the storm," she said.

He stared into her eyes. He felt captured, trapped. But not like before.

"I am," he said. "I'm afraid."

"Of the storm?" She let out a little laugh. "Of death?"

"No."

He wailed aloud, startling her. She stumbled back against the side of the makeshift hole. Cast a quick, puzzled glance at the etched metal of the hatch beneath their feet.

He tried to calm himself, to stem the tide of tears. But it was impossible. All the fear, all the pent-up emotion of a lifetime, seemed to pour out of him in a long primal cry.

She reached for him. He bent forward, sobbing, and fell into her arms. He grabbed onto her, holding tight. A naked man, a drowning man gasping his last. She was air, oxygen, life. She was love.

She was his last chance.

"I'm afraid," he said again. His tears mingled with the rain, soaking into her shoulder.

She patted him softly, not letting him go. She would never let him go. His next words were so quiet, she had to lean in closer.

"I'm afraid of Life."

TWENTY-SIX

IT WAS said that when the Mad Titan came to the Velt, for the first time in his life he knew peace.

At first, he was hesitant to live in the Apaga village. Masika worked out a compromise. She set up house in an abandoned shack on the edge of the fields, and Thanos learned the art of tilling the land on her family's plot. In time, they made a home.

Aside from a few casualties, the chimera hunt had been a success. Pagan had led the Apaga to victory, slaughtering not one but two of the giant, fearsome beasts. The village ate meat for weeks—not stringy rabbit or the occasional cow, but dozens of rich, thick steaks spiced with tangy herbs. Thanos ate heartily, hungrily.

One of the heads—it looked like a lion with strangely curved tusks—stood mounted on a pike in the town square. Pagan had been named Kyros, the Master of the Hunt. The village, which had no actual political leader, revered him.

Yet Pagan seemed troubled. He began stopping by the shack belonging to Thanos and Masika, first once a week and then more frequently. He insisted on speaking with Masika alone; he seemed indifferent, even hostile to Thanos.

Thanos was jealous initially. Given Pagan's newly elevated stature within the tribe, it was conceivable that he wished to pursue Masika for himself. Steeling his courage, Thanos decided to ask Masika for an explanation. He kept his words soft, his temper controlled.

She looked him in the eye. He could tell she understood the effort he'd exerted.

"Pagan doesn't want me," she said. "I think that would be a violation of honor to him."

He looked at her, puzzled.

"He's consumed with guilt," she explained. "He blames himself for Basi's death. They were friends since childhood."

"The hunt is dangerous," Thanos said. "You told me yourself…the chimera always exacts a price."

"Pagan believes he should have trained his friend better."

Thanos nodded. He thought about it for a day and a night. When Pagan visited the next day, Thanos stopped him at the door and held out a blunt wooden knife.

"Teach me," Thanos said.

Pagan stared at the knife, then looked up into Thanos's eyes. He nodded.

So Pagan taught Thanos the art of the knife. It was a soft sort of combat, a more ritualistic fighting style than any Thanos had known. Over time, he began to appreciate the languid motions, the graceful thrusts and parries.

And from that day forward, Pagan was his friend.

Thanos and Masika grew closer. They explored each other, prodding and edging around each other's secret sorrows. She had a dark side, a wit that could turn cutting without warning. As she'd said, she wasn't afraid of the storm.

Sex with her was remarkably vigorous. Her body was quick, her mind searching. She brought him to his limits again and again, and left him happily spent. He had never paid much attention to a woman's pleasure before, but he soon learned to return Masika's attentions. The smile on her face afterward brought him a type of satisfaction he'd never known.

Whenever he grew too serious, she cut him down with a sharp quip. To his surprise, that made him love her even more.

A year passed. Masika asked him to help refurbish her family house. After the crops had been harvested, Thanos turned to this task. He reinforced a sagging wall beam. He carried stones to the front yard and arranged them to form a pleasing porch area. He got to know the neighbors: the burly farmer couple across the way, old Mako with his belligerent dog, the extended Yaza family.

Thanos found the physical labor soothing, and the knife exercises calmed his mind. He grew more skilled at farming, learned to maximize the output of a given plot of land. The Apaga grew oats and barley, kept pigs and sheep. He learned the least painful way to put down an animal, and how to strip and clean it in the slaughterhouse. But he didn't like to spend too much time there. It made him uncomfortable.

He continued to study the Velt. Whatever this place was, it had apparently been forgotten, abandoned by its designers. In his prior lives, Thanos had built machines and used them for many purposes. He knew that, left untended, they all failed eventually.

One night, after a long day in the fields, he sat with Masika in front of the family house. Her body touched his, swaying back and forth on the two-person swing he'd hung from an oak tree. A night breeze ruffled her hair.

"This is nice," she said, closing her eyes.

"It's quiet," he agreed.

Mako's dog let out a volley of yelps. The old man appeared and grabbed the leash, waving apologetically.

Masika turned to Thanos, a wry smile on her face. "Too quiet?"

He raised an eyebrow. Over the past weeks, pieces of his past had returned to him, scraps of memory rising to the surface. He'd doled these out to Masika carefully, told her a few mild anecdotes about the Infinity Gems and his time on Hala and Sacrosanct. But he always kept the worst details to himself. He didn't want to scare her away.

"Such power," she said. "It must have been wondrous."

"It was hollow," he replied.

To his surprise, he realized it was true.

She burrowed her head into his shoulder and made a soft noise. "Want to go inside?"

As they headed in, he realized they'd moved back into her family house. He hadn't even noticed. Masika could be a tricky one.

In the third year, a drought struck the village. The rainstorms grew shorter and less frequent. The crops began to dry up; water had to be rationed. The pond shrank to a tiny stream. A few cows died of dehydration.

Thanos vowed to help his adoptive people. He'd already determined that the normal rules of farming didn't apply here: There had to be drains hidden beneath the surface to absorb excess moisture, and pipes to feed the wells. Now the wells, too, were running dry. Some component of the system had broken down.

He consulted with Pagan, and together they led an expedition to Ranium City. Once again they searched for control centers, clues to the hidden network that kept the Velt alive. Pagan and Masika seemed skeptical, almost amused by his talk of *integrated systems* and *global irrigation networks*.

Again they found nothing. The humming in the large empty building seemed even louder than before, as if something deep within the world were building to an overload.

Thanos wasn't deterred. Under his direction, the Apaga raided the abandoned buildings for an assortment of pipes and disused pumps and engines. As Masika helped tote the equipment back to the fields, she turned to him with a smirk.

"More machines?" she asked. "Like the ones you say grow the grass?"

He cocked his head at her. "Do you still doubt it?"

"No," she replied.

They fitted together a network of irrigation pipes in the fields. They built catch-basins to collect the sparse rainwater, refurbished a pump to force the water through the system. There was some debate, even argument, about which fields should be serviced first. But they held a village meeting and agreed on priorities. As always, the Apaga were a cooperative people.

Thanos stood with Masika as the first water gushed out across the fields. She and the others let out a cheer.

Thanos smiled gamely. But he knew it was only a temporary fix.

In the sixth year, he opened up contact with the People. His initial plan was to enlist them as slave labor in an ambitious shared-farm network. Masika slapped that down before he could bring it to either group. Ultimately they began a pilot project to grow vegetables for both tribes, in a desirable plot near the People's village.

He even made friends with Poto. He sat in the old woman's modest kitchen for hours, drinking mead and listening to her chatter. Most of it was utter nonsense, but every now and then he thought he could glimpse the meaning behind her words.

"There is one certain thing only about a human mind," she said, hand pressed tight to her earpiece. "And that is that it acts, moves, works ceaselessly while it lives."

"It's a planned ecosystem," he said. "The farms don't have the little grass planters; the land returns to fertility much faster than it would in a natural setting. All of it was laid out purposely, a very long time ago."

He reached for the mead jug, poured himself another glass. *I'm a little drunk,* he realized.

"I crossed whole mountain ranges," Poto said, still clutching the earpiece. "Following the sun until we found the warmest of warm valleys on the sunward side."

"But it's all going to break down," he continued. "In a year, two, maybe a century. Then there'll be no air, no water, no—no people at all."

"On one of these nights I dream that the Captain is falling again. He is falling through the capsule into the center of the sun."

"It's the way of things." He shrugged and downed the whole glass. When he looked up, Poto was staring at him.

"What he needed," she hissed, "was an internal timepiece. A unconsciously operating psychic mechanism regulated, say, by his pulse or respiratory rhythms."

"Are you—are you talking about the Velt? About fixing this world, this ship, this rundown deathtrap we're all stuck on?"

She blinked, turned away. Looked up at the ceiling, seemingly hearing words from the earpiece. Her lips moved soundlessly for several minutes.

"He had tried to train his time-sense..." She paused, turned to stare at him again. "...running an elaborate series of tests to estimate its built-in error, and this had been disappointingly large."

"So there's no way to do it?" He felt suddenly small, helpless. "No way to save the Apaga, to preserve all these lives?"

"The chances of conditioning an accurate reflex seemed slim."

He fell back into a wicker chair. Shook his empty glass in the air.

"I can't save them." He thought of Masika, her strong body warm against him on the porch swing. "Can't save her."

I'm *really* drunk, he thought.

Poto grabbed his arm. He jumped—she'd never touched him, not once. Not since that day, years ago, when they'd come to blows.

She plucked the earpiece from her ear and held it out to him. "For strength," she said, her voice urgent. "Millions have felt the power of our oracle."

She slumped forward, her eyes rolling back in her head. The earpiece slipped from her fingers and clattered to the floor.

Thanos sat perfectly still, staring at a bald patch on the old woman's head. He felt an odd sense of loss, an awareness of time passing. As if parts of himself were being washed away, so slowly he hadn't even noticed.

He hadn't thought of Death for over a year.

Later, as the others carried away the body, he spotted the earpiece discarded on the tile floor. He bent down and plucked it up, held it to his ear. Shook it once, twice.

Nothing. Not even static. Its power was completely gone.

○————————○

IN THE eighth year Masika became sullen. She begged off walking with him, refused his advances. She rescheduled her sleeping periods so they were out of sync with his. Even her wit seemed blunter, more hostile.

I'm losing her, he thought. It was bound to happen. How could a monster hope to hold on to an angel?

One day he came home to find her in the small sitting room. She motioned for him to take a seat on a rough stool. "I have something to tell you."

He sat. He felt like his guts were being ripped out slowly, organs exposed to the cold of space. She's leaving, he thought. Those will be her next words: *I'm leaving you.*

"I'm pregnant."

"Oh." He stared at her. "Oh!"

He stumbled over to her, took her hands in his. He forced himself to smile. "I'm so relieved. I mean, glad."

She smiled back, a hopeful look in her eyes. But

he knew she could see. Part of him was glad, yes. But mostly, he was terrified.

In the weeks that followed, Thanos maintained his carpentry work, his knife training, his labor in the fields. But the memories, the old lives, threatened to rise up and destroy him. He'd been a father before, more times than he could ever admit to Masika. And every time...every one of his children...

He began to have dreams. Vivid, terrible dreams, visions of small mewling things writhing and bawling in his arms. There was spit and vomit and feces, and there was blood. Always there was blood.

Once he saw a green woman with scales, with lovely yellow eyes and a head-fin that curled behind her like a tail. She held out her arms and handed him a tiny, bawling creature. He accepted it in his hands. His gray, rocky hands. His powerful hands.

Just a twist. A single twist.

One night he had an argument with Pagan. Later, he couldn't remember why. But drinks were consumed, blows were exchanged. When Thanos stumbled home drunk, Masika grabbed him by the arm. She twisted him around and slammed him against the wall.

"Just tell me when you're gonna leave me," she snarled.

He blinked, tried to banish the alcohol-fog. Stared into her bloodshot eyes, lined with worry, and then down to her swelling stomach.

"I told you," he whispered. "I'm afraid of Life."

She gaped at him, astonished. *"Who isn't?"*

She released him. He stood against the wall, raised a hand to sweep hair out of his eyes.

"We can do this." She grasped both his hands, loosely. "But it has to be together. I need you with me."

He nodded.

"Can you do that?"

"Yes," he said. "I can do it."

"Good." She let out a long sigh and turned away. "Get me a rabbit steak, will you? Extra pepper."

But the days dragged on, and the nightmares continued. Once he dreamed he was in Ranium City, struggling and clawing at a hatch like the one under the chestnut trees. He found a starship spread open for repairs, its hyperdrive gleaming and exposed. Exposed. Exposed. Exploded.

When the day came, he stood watching as Masika lay on the bed. The healer, a middle-aged woman named Hara, checked a handheld device with blood pressure and heartbeat readings. Thanos himself had rigged up the small electric generator that powered the healer's equipment.

Hara poured water into a clay bowl and washed her hands. She glanced briefly at a tray of old, meticulously preserved instruments. Then she knelt down between Masika's legs.

Masika grunted and moaned. She caught Thanos's eye and beckoned him closer. When he reached out his hand, she squeezed it in a grip worthy of an Elder of the Universe.

"It's coming," Hara said.

He felt a rush of panic. But there was nothing to do except hold on—hold on and watch. Masika looked beautiful, a wingless angel screaming and grunting for dear life.

The baby was dark, tiny, and dripping wet. Hara snipped the cord with a scissors that must have been centuries old. She wiped the baby clean and handed him to Masika.

Masika bounced him up and down. The little boy opened his eyes and squealed. Masika smiled weakly and gestured for Thanos to approach.

He knelt down and studied his child. To his immense relief, he felt only love.

"Not such a monster," Masika murmured, tickling the baby's chin. "Not such a little monster at *all.*"

THEY named the baby A'Lars. Thanos knew it meant something, but he couldn't remember what. After the flurry of dreams, his past seemed to fade rapidly into the distance, like the memory of a bad marriage. A vague source of shame, banished and forgotten.

He studied the plates in the sky. Made charts, took measurements with the instruments left behind by Masika's father. The Velt's rotational period was precisely twenty-two hours and forty minutes—a bit shorter than Earth's day, a little longer than the cycle on Titan, where he'd been born.

A few years later, he decided to lead another party to Ranium City. In the interests of unity, he insisted on taking representatives from both the Apaga and the People.

Morak of the People, now gray-haired and slumped, was leery. "To set foot in the City means doom," he said.

Thanos smiled. "My son has but seven years, and he insists on coming. Do you think I would risk his life?"

Morak smiled back.

This time, Thanos was determined to leave nothing useful behind. If the Velt's secrets were hidden somewhere in those six buildings, he would find them. For five days the party combed through the ruins, covering every inch of the disaster site. They stripped buildings of copper and wire, of blankets and curtains. They ripped out the few batteries that still held a faint charge.

Pagan discovered a cryo-vault containing several hundred tins of food, labeled in English with drawings of smiling faces eating soup. When little A'Lars popped open the first can, he squealed with delight.

"Father," he said, dipping a finger into the can. "We should eat this forever!"

Thanos glanced at the pile of cans. Several of them read VEGETABLE or VEGETABLE RICE.

"We will share it with the People," he said, smiling.

Later, he sat with Masika on the swing in front of the house. It groaned a bit more now when it swayed; its chain had grown rusty. But it was still solid.

"So." She picked out a bit of tuna from one of the newfound cans. "I assume you've solved all the mysteries of the Velt? Where we came from, who built the City, what sort of godlike beings they've evolved into now?"

He smiled. "We've gathered supplies, some raw materials that can be used to expand the electrical grid. I think I can keep the irrigation system going another few years. But most of the hatches still resist our efforts. The few we managed to open led only to dead circuitry, lights that have given up winking altogether."

She laughed. "You make them sound like living things."

"All things come to an end. Living or mechanical."

She reached out and brought the swing to a halt. Turned and laid a hand on his leg.

"Your words are familiar," she said. "But your tone has changed."

He frowned. "How so?"

"You sound…softer. More relaxed?"

He rose and paced out onto the porch. Across the way, the new woman in Mako's former house nodded in greeting.

"Everything has its time," he repeated. "Some creatures, organic and metallic alike, live and die in a single place. Some cages are sealed; some traps have no escape."

A rhythmic thumping noise came from inside. Little A'Lars, practicing on makeshift drums.

Masika held out her hand. "Maybe that's all right."

He took the hand. "Yes," he said. "Maybe it is."

IN THE 17th year, he agreed to lead the chimera hunt. A'Lars asked to come, and when told he was too young, he threw a series of fits. Masika couldn't reason with him.

The thought of his son facing the giant predators of the Velt terrified Thanos. The dreams began again: young children, sons and daughters of all races and species, torn from their mothers and mutilated.

As night was falling, he took the boy outside and gestured at the house.

"I need you here," he said firmly. "To see to your mother."

A'Lars screwed up his face. "But—"

"She carries your little sister inside her."

The boy's eyes went wide. He glanced at the house, then past it, out at the expanse of the Velt. He squinted into the sky, staring at the night-plate hovering directly overhead.

Then he turned back to his father and nodded.

When Thanos told Masika, she laughed in his face. "He's supposed to see to me?"

"Don't tell him otherwise," Thanos begged.

The hunt was glorious. Pagan and Thanos strategized beforehand, weaving nets from the strong fabric they'd scavenged in Ranium City. They lured the chimeras with audio recordings of mating calls, and ambushed them expertly. Only one Apaga man was injured, none killed.

In the end they trapped *four* of the beasts—an

all-time record. Thanos himself slew the last of them, leaping from a parapet with both knives raised.

Later, in the town square, Pagan's eyes welled with tears as he proclaimed Thanos the new Master of the Hunt. "No man, no woman ever deserved this more," Pagan said.

Thanos bowed his head in humility. The cheering of his people was the most joyous thing he'd ever heard.

Years passed. As Thanos watched his children grow, fear sprouted now and again in his heart. *So fierce,* he thought, *so beautiful.* If something were to happen to them…. But nothing did. A'Lars grew into a fine man and took over most of the farming duties. The girl, Hether, resembled her mother. She had a sharp wit and a firm hand at the potting wheel.

Once, when his back was stooped and his hair thinning, Thanos paid a return visit to the Canyon of Shadows. He stayed there a day and a night. But he never spoke of what he saw, and Masika did not press him.

The shadows of his past continued to soften. He came to recall certain people, certain battles, and to forget others. He believed he could see a purpose in it all—a sort of higher power nudging him, all along, toward this place. A destiny.

Masika sat with him on the porch, her gray-haired head dozing gently against his shoulder. The swing was rusted in place now; it no longer moved. But its chains still held it to the tree above.

"I think it was the suffering," he whispered.

Her eyes fluttered. She muttered something unintelligible.

"So much of it." He closed his eyes, remembering. "On Sacrosanct, on Hala. People starving, dying. Selling their honor, their bodies, their dignity—all for a few coins. Throwing their lives away for rulers who laughed at their sacrifice."

Masika opened her eyes, sat upright.

"I couldn't bear it," he continued. "Couldn't sympathize, couldn't accept that such horror existed in the world. So I became *him* again. The monster."

She laid a hand on his. It was warm, but he felt cold.

"It's true," he said. "She was right. I fell into the patterns so quickly, so easily. I learned nothing."

Masika turned to face him. There was resolve in her wrinkled eyes, and a deep love that he'd almost come to take for granted. But something else, too. Something he couldn't read.

"That's over," she said. "Your life is here now."

He nodded, a tear rising to his eye. "It is."

"You are Kyros, the Master of the Hunt. You are the bringer of water and life, the uniter of the tribes. You have two fine children, and you are the love of my life. A life that is greater, deeper and more joyful, than a thousand thousand stars glittering in a gauntlet of jewels."

He smiled. "Yes," he whispered. Moved in to kiss her.

"However." She held out a hand. "There is something I must tell you."

IT WAS said that when the Mad Titan came to the Velt, for the first time in his life he knew peace.

But all things must end.

TWENTY-SEVEN

"**IT'S IN** her lungs," said Shara, the young healer. "Her stomach, too. Hell, it's in her spine."

She held out a small device, a flat screen with wide handles on either side. Thanos glanced at the image: an x-ray shot of a torso and chest with glowing spots winking up and down the lungs. The screen flickered, turned to static.

"Sorry. Doesn't hold a charge long." She walked over to a bulky, patched-together generator and plugged the x-ray device into it.

Thanos clenched his fists. The healer's chamber had barely changed over the years: the same rows of bowls and ointment jars, the familiar tray of instruments.

"Is there nothing you can do?" he hissed.

"The ancients had…well, not cures. Treatments— radiation, chemicals. But all that knowledge is lost." Shara gestured at the charging station. "I was only able to make the diagnosis because *you* figured out how to recharge the seeing machine."

He glared at her. Part of him, the rational part, knew that Masika's illness wasn't her fault. But Shara was the tribe's healer. And here she stood, shrugging and helpless.

"At least you know," she said.

Thanos lumbered over and glared down at her. Shara blinked, startled.

"You have only been a healer for a short time," he growled. "Perhaps your skills are not up to the task."

She gazed up at him, defiant. Then she turned and called, "Mother?"

Old Hara appeared in the doorway. She moved slowly, her limbs stiff with arthritis. But her eyes were as sharp, as knowing, as the day she'd delivered Thanos's son.

Shara explained the problem. Hara shuffled into the room, stopping before the instrument tray. She ran her fingers along the old scalpel, the forceps, the large and small syringes. She cast a glance at the x-ray machine, its screen flashing on and off in the charging stand. Then she turned to stare at Thanos and swept her hands across the arrayed medical supplies.

"*That's all there is,*" she said.

AS MASIKA grew weaker, the tribe rallied to her side. The neighbors looked in on her when Thanos and the children were away. Pagan, now retired from field work, brought her food and medicine.

A'Lars had grown into a tall, square-jawed young man. One day he was waiting outside when Thanos returned to the house. He looked like he'd been crying.

"Father," he said, "what can we do?"

Thanos looked up into his son's eyes. Realized, for the first time: He's taller than me.

"Take care of the fields," Thanos said.

He brushed past, into the house. Masika lay dozing in the outer room, muttering fitfully. He stopped and arranged a pillow under her head.

She patted his hand. "Turn off that ringing noise?" She smiled, as if sharing a private joke.

In the back room, he gathered up as many of her father's implements as he could fit in his pack. Tiptoed past her and out into the field, all the way to the edge of the family farm. The neighbors hadn't yet begun their farming day; even the slaughterhouse was quiet. No one could see him here.

When he dumped the instruments out onto the ground, he realized his back ached. This body, he thought, running his hand through sparse hair. It's aging. It's human.

Too human.

He ran his eyes across the assembled tools. Sextants, compasses, telescopes. Sample bottles, a pH counter. A tiny air tester that looked like a digital watch.

I can do it, he thought. I can solve the mystery.

He sat there a day and a night, running all manner of tests. A'Lars came out once, but let him be. On the second morning Pagan brought him a plate of food and left it silently on the ground. Thanos ignored him, concentrating on a soil sample.

In the end he learned nothing. A few details about

the movement of the night-plates; clues to the DNA tweaks that had been performed on the local animals. But the Velt remained a mystery, a puzzle with half its pieces missing. A locked room with no door.

When he returned home, Masika was sitting on the porch swing. "I failed," he said, throwing down the pack.

She smiled at him. There were new lines on her face, but her smile was as playful as ever.

"There's no way out," he said.

"I don't—" She winced in pain. "I don't want a way out."

He sat down next to her. His heart ached. He wanted to be strong for her, but he was exhausted. The words wouldn't come.

"Oh, cheer up," she said. "Get me some rabbit—"

She erupted into a coughing fit. He patted her softly on the back until she stopped.

"Make it tea," she said.

o———————o

IT'S CALLED cancer," Thanos said. "Am I right in thinking it's unknown among your people?"

Lorak looked back at him, puzzled. She was no longer a little girl; she had to be past 40. She was still missing a few teeth, but her hair was streaked with gray.

"Among *the* People, I mean," he said.

They stood in a house on the outskirts of the Apaga village. The walls were bare; a few of the People's primitive cups littered the table. Lorak had come here as part of a cultural exchange, along with a small group from her settlement. Thanos had reached out to her, knowing of her fascination with the Apaga.

"I…" Lorak paused. "I've never *heard* of cancer. That's true."

"I was thinking that your people…they still maintain a strict diet of leaves and vegetables, right?"

She nodded.

The door opened. Thanos turned to see his daughter, Hether. "Oh," she said. "Father." She looked around, as if she might try to escape.

Thanos frowned. Since the advent of Masika's illness, Hether had become withdrawn. She rarely saw her mother, and refused to talk to Thanos at all.

"Hether has been spending time here," Lorak explained. "We've been talking."

Hether fidgeted, staring at the floor. She was in her mid-teens now—an awkward age. Half child, half adult. She had her mother's wide features and lanky physicality.

"Lorak is an old friend," Thanos explained, though Hether already knew that. "She was the first person I met when I came to the Velt."

Lorak smiled. "He *really* wanted to conquer people back then."

"The People are…" He paused, took a step toward Hether. "Their diet is very different from ours. I thought perhaps…that protected them from certain illnesses."

Hether nodded, a sharp movement. She didn't look up. But she didn't leave, either.

He turned back to Lorak. "Perhaps your father would know more? I didn't see his name on the exchange list."

"He passed last year."

"Oh. I'm sorry."

Thanos remembered the slim blond man who'd greeted him in the People's village, so many years ago. How foolish Morak had seemed, how naïve. Thanos felt a pang of regret: I should have known him better.

"He had the Rot," Lorak explained. "It consumed his insides."

"Oh." And then: "Oh."

He muttered a hasty good-bye. When he stepped outside, he was surprised to hear the door open again behind him. Hether followed him out along the edge of the field, watching as the approaching night-plate cast a looming shadow on the grassland.

At length she reached out and took hold of his arm. "It was a good try," she whispered.

○────────────○

MASIKA grew weaker. Her muscular arms became lean and leathery. She slept long hours and cried out in the night. She had trouble holding down food, even tea.

She tried using her mother's loom to distract herself. But that, too, was beyond her power.

Thanos redoubled his efforts. He returned alone to Ranium City and searched every inch of the ruins. In a burned-out vault, buried under rubble, he found a small jackhammer. It was almost too heavy to lift, but he hoisted it aloft and pressed the activation button. To his amazement, it wheezed, rattled, and pumped its blade in the air.

He carried the jackhammer to the chestnut trees, the landmark he'd used on his long-ago walks around the Velt. He'd never told anyone but Masika about the trees. Their twisted trunks reached several feet higher than before, the helical leaf patterns thick against the artificial sun. At the sight of them, he felt a strange, nostalgic mix of hope and despair.

The hole, the ditch he'd clawed out with his bare hands, had been filled in decades ago by wind and erosion. By the time he'd dug it out again, the night-plate had slipped across the sun.

At last he saw it. The round hatch, the "V" etched into the hard metal.

Averting his eyes, he aimed the jackhammer straight at it and thumbed the "on" button.

Metal screamed and sparked. The hammer blade skidded along the hatch cover. He leaned down hard, pressing the jackhammer forward. The squealing noise filled the air, blocking out the aches in his arms and back, banishing all rational thought.

When he broke through the metal, he almost fell. He steadied himself, thumbed off the jackhammer, and tossed it away. Then he reached down and, with a great effort, yanked free the chipped hatch.

"No," he said. "Oh no."

He reached down with both hands, but it was no

use. The passageway stretched down into the ground, presumably descending into the bowels of the Velt. It was wide enough for a man.

But it was completely filled—up to the top—with dirt. Another dead end; another escape route sealed by time and decay.

Thanos hung his head, slammed the hatch back down, and trudged up out of the hole.

○────────────────○

THE DREAMS returned. People dying, singly and in the thousands. Bombs falling, germ vectors gliding in air. Knives sliding along skin, slicing veins. Throats snapping. Infants held underwater till their thrashing ceased.

He became afraid to see Masika. Her pain reminded him of his own helplessness. The helplessness made the dreams stronger, more ruthless and real.

You don't fear Death. You fear Life.

One night he lay in bed next to her, his eyes wide. Mind spinning. The Velt seemed to whirl around like a toy ball, lost in an abyss of stars. He saw all his paths—every journey he'd taken around its 216 miles—as the rings of a great twisted tree.

"I know," she whispered.

He turned in surprise. She lay on her side, staring up at him with piercing eyes.

"Don't try to speak," he said.

"I know who you are." A warm, loving smile crept onto her face. "My beautiful rocky man."

He opened his mouth, but no words came. She reached out and grabbed his hand with surprising strength.

"Your hands," she said. "Your rough gray hands…"

He turned away and wiped tears from his face. Her hand went slack. When he looked back, she had fallen into a deep, untroubled sleep.

ONE DAY, one terrible day, she beckoned him close. In a faint, pained voice, she asked to be carried out into the field.

He went to the healer and borrowed a stretcher. He carried one end and recruited A'Lars to take the other. Masika seemed light as the air, like the breeze blowing over the grasslands.

Like an angel.

They laid her down at the edge of the field, just beyond the fence. The day was clear and bright. The corn grew high behind them; the grass ahead was brown and patchy, sparse from years of drought.

A large boulder caught Thanos's eye. The same rock, he realized, where he'd first seen his angel, so many years ago.

Within him, a spark flared to life.

One by one, the neighbors filed out to say good-bye. The Yazo family, all 14 of them. Smiling, gap-toothed Lorak; Rina with the quick knife. The woman in Mako's old house—he could never remember her name. The two healers, old Hara and young Shara.

"Oh," Masika said. "Oh, I don't deserve this."

He couldn't tell whether she meant the pain or the attention.

When Pagan approached, Masika flung her arms wide. He knelt down and embraced her with trembling arms.

"Thank you," she said to him. "Thank you for all of it."

Thanos watched them all. He felt mesmerized, paralyzed. Made of stone.

Hether knelt over her mother for a long time. Their conversation was low, intense, and private.

"It's all right," Masika said at last. "Go now."

Hether hesitated.

Masika forced a smile. "Go make lots of mistakes."

Hether sniffled, smiled back, and ran off.

Thanos felt a touch on his shoulder. It was the young healer, Shara. Her eyes looked old, older even than her mother's.

"It won't be long," she said.

A'Lars was speaking to Masika. "I will," Thanos heard him say. "I promise."

Thanos looked up. The sun shone down, steady as always. Fixed at exactly the same point in the air, halfway across the center of the Velt. Just as it had been for centuries.

"Husband," Masika croaked.

He looked down. A'Lars was just walking off with the two healers, glancing back sadly at his mother.

Masika lay alone on the stretcher, beckoning to Thanos. Silently he lay down next to her, flattening the grass.

Then it was just the two of them. He clasped her hand and felt her warmth, imagined her moving fiercely beneath him once again. A lifetime of pain, of joy, seemed to flare between them.

She grimaced, cried out. He leaned in to hear her words.

"It was—" She cried out again. "It was enough."

She squeezed his hand, hard enough to hurt. The pain seemed to jump from his hand to his heart, feeding the flame inside him.

"No," he said. "It wasn't."

He squeezed her hand back. She recoiled at the pressure, turned sharp eyes toward him.

"It's not fair. I did everything." He squeezed his eyes shut. "I did everything *right.*"

She opened her mouth, began an urgent reply. Then her body went stiff. Her hand grew limp; her eyes rolled back. She collapsed onto the stretcher and was still.

Then Thanos was alone. Alone in his village, his cage. His human prison.

Alone with his rage.

The spark flared and caught fire, fear and anger feeding it like oxygen. His form began to change—his limbs growing, becoming hard and strong. Biochemical reactions surged through him, transforming his entire body.

He looked around at the Velt, at the grass and huts

and crudely cultivated fields. Forces sizzled within him, welling and pooling in his eyes, at his fingertips. Psionic power, plasma energy. His birthright as a Titan, a heritage he'd renounced long ago. Long ago and far away, for a promise that suddenly seemed utterly empty.

Death, he thought, you fickle mistress. You've stolen away my one chance, my final chance at happiness.

I did everything right.

Thanos the Conqueror, the Mad Titan, dropped to his knees, stared down at the grass, and screamed.

The first plasma blast burst through the outer layer of soil. The shockwave rocked the village, ripples stretching halfway across the Velt. The Apaga paused in their daily chores and turned with fear in their eyes.

The second scream punched a hole through nanotube-steel. Tiny grass planters shattered, clanking, to reveal deep tunnels lined with humming circuitry.

Thanos saw none of it. His eyes burned; his fists glowed. His thoughts were subhuman now, consumed by pure primal emotion.

With the third scream, the hole grew wider and deeper. The edge of the world came into view, hundreds of feet down—a thin outer layer of permaglass, leading to some unknown vastness. Bubbles rippled on the other side of the transparent layer, dimly visible from the surface.

The villagers were running now. Some hurried toward Thanos, crying out to him. Others fled. Pagan called to A'Lars, leading him back into the field.

Thanos staggered to his feet. His leg caught on something: Masika's stretcher. Her body tumbled free and fell into the abyss.

The next scream was the loudest. Pure cosmic energy blasted against the permaglass—shattering it in an instant. Within Thanos, some barely conscious part of him thought: At last. Take me, Death. Cleanse this wretched world in the cold vacuum of space—

A rush of water struck him like a hammer. He lost his balance and fell backward onto the quaking ground. The water smelled like salt. He'd broken a tooth; there was blood in his mouth.

A'Lars and Pagan stood nearby, shouting and pointing in astonishment. Thanos turned back to look at the hole.

Water spurted up like a geyser. It spread out to cover the farm, the grass. The hole was expanding, the soil washing away on all sides. Water poured in, faster and faster.

"I was wrong," he whispered.

He stared at the column of water. It seemed to rise for miles, reaching up as if to threaten the sun. It gathered in pools, surrounding him, drenching the landscape all around.

"About all of it." He shook his head. "All the excuses. The rationalizations."

Someone tried to grab his arm, pull him away. He slapped the hand away.

"I blamed the suffering, the horror. I thought I knew myself."

The water was rising now. All around him, it spread through the Velt. Gravity shifted, and he knew: The machinery was dying.

"I thought I could live with myself."

Water filled the world. Through filmed eyes, he saw his son go down, gasping. Someone reached for A'Lars: Hether. His beautiful daughter, eyes wide, cheeks bulging with the last breath she'd ever take.

Hether, he thought.

Masika.

Then the water swept over him. Gravity failed; the current shifted and reversed direction. The sun arced across his vision, blurred into a refracted red smear.

He tumbled headfirst into the hole, swept inexorably down on the tide. Gasped, choking, as fluid filled his lungs. Layers of world-stuff rushed past: dirt, machinery, sparking circuits, nanosteel barriers. More machinery. Finally, ahead and below, the cracked permaglass portal leading to the unknown.

The last thing he saw was the metal hatch, tumbling free in the vast sea beyond. Twisting and spinning like a coin, still branded with that etched-metal "V." And then he saw nothing at all.

EPILOGUE ONE

THERE were people living in houses and tents. There was a sun that shone; there were black plates in the sky. There was a burst of power; there was water. There were people, gasping and choking.

There was a field covered with water. There was a stretcher with a woman on it. There was a hole. There was no stretcher. No woman.

He cried out. Reached for her and dove, head-first, into the hole. Then there was no hole— just water. The current was harsh, fierce. It swept his hair back and blinded his eyes.

He saw her, dark and tumbling, limp against the tide. He reached out a hand, but she was too far away. He gritted his teeth and swam harder. Legs kicking, arms flailing.

"It's not fair." Somehow the words came out, though he was immersed in water. "I did everything. I did everything *right!*"

Then she was there. Masika. Her eyes opened, boring into his mind like lasers. Her mouth formed three words in a hiss of bubbles:

No, you didn't.

Thanos screamed and sat up.

The first thing he saw was a high wooden post with a carved serpent wound around its length. The post, one of four, surrounded an enclosed bed strewn with lush pillows. Dark curtains formed a canopy around the bed.

The curtains parted to reveal a familiar figure perched on the edge of the bed. Staring, judging him. Pale skin, large dark eyes.

"You," he said.

The mother-shade.

Rage boiled inside him. "What have you done?" he demanded. "You've taken it from me. Taken everything."

"No." She shook her head. "You did that yourself."

He moved to the edge of the bed. I'm back in the bedchamber, he realized. The inner sanctum of Death's shrine.

The dark mahogany form of the Infinity Wardrobe stood against the far wall. He moved toward it. Its doors were closed; full-length mirrors reflected his body from two different angles.

His body. His tall, broad, gray body. His impenetrable skin, tough and unforgiving as a block of granite.

The mother-shade glided to her feet as if she were weightless. "You've failed," she said. "Again."

An image rose to his mind: a dark lovely face staring at him with total understanding. He blinked, tried to hold onto the memory. But it was already fading.

"On Sacrosanct," the shade continued, "you searched for meaning. But the lure of power was too strong. You could not resist."

He turned away, clenching his fists.

"On Hala, you embraced the quest for power. Grabbed it with both hands, like a teat to be suckled." She laughed. "Look how *that* worked out. Then, in the Vault—"

"The what?"

"The Vault." She stared at him, amused. "One of a group of experimental retreats created by a team of Earth scientists to preserve the human race in case of global catastrophe. This particular Vault was buried on the bottom of the Atlantic Ocean, in the southern hemisphere."

He nodded, eyes wide. The bottom of the ocean.

"The Vaults were designed to encourage and accelerate human evolution," she continued. "That didn't come off so well, did it? The inhabitants stagnated. They forgot their past, devolved into a primitive state."

"They were people," he said softly.

"Guess it doesn't matter now."

"Wait." He strode over to her, pointed a rough finger at her chest. "Accelerate human evolution? How *old* was this 'Vault'? How long ago did the experiment start?"

"That's the genius of it." She gave him a condescending smile. "Inside a Vault, time moves more quickly. By a factor of several hundred, normally."

His mind reeled. Several hundred?

"Oh, that's not the half of it. Your particular Vault had an accident—the time distortion equipment entered into a state of geometric overload. By the end, time inside was moving at over 3,000 times the speed of the outside world."

Another faint memory: the empty building in Ranium City. The humming that grew louder every time he visited.

"So," he began. "While I lived in the Velt—"

"Vault."

"While I lived for decades…made a life, married, had children…"

She made a small, disgusted noise.

"…how much time *really* passed?"

"In the outside world?" She thought for a moment. "About a week."

He staggered back to the bed. Sat down, felt the mattress sink beneath his heavy body.

"A week," he repeated.

"Quite a feat of engineering," the shade said. "The Vault, I mean. The gravity manipulation alone…Bella Pagan and her staff were decades ahead of normal Earth science."

Pagan. The name struck some chord inside him, raised an emotion he couldn't name. But there was nothing else.

"In the Vault, you sought *peace*," the shade continued, "Imagine that. A creature of your appetites."

He closed his eyes. His thoughts whirled madly,

lost in a cyclone. He forced them away, banishing doubt to the farthest corners of his mind.

"Aww! Poor little monster." She smiled, mocking him. "Don't despair."

The Infinity Wardrobe began to open. Thanos caught a glimpse of bodies, familiar and strange, whirling and sweeping within. Tall men and short, blue-skinned women and lithe beings with no gender. Tiny clicking insects, slow-breathing mammals that filled an ocean.

Everything. Every creature imaginable, every life that had ever lived.

"Plenty more skins in the universe," the shade said.

He raised his hand, feeling the energy build. The plasma blast shattered the mirror first, then the dark wood. He held out his arm, perfectly steady, and increased the energy flow. It felt easy—natural.

The Wardrobe splintered, sparked, and imploded. It collapsed into a smoking pile of glass and wood, heaped against the peeling wallpaper of the chamber.

He didn't pause, didn't even glance at the mother-shade. He strode to the door, thrust it open, and marched out into the throne room.

She was there, as he'd known she would be. Seated atop her throne, above the bones and skulls, the broken remnants of the dead. Above the weapons of destruction, the knives and pistols and sabres hung in a line along the green stone wall.

"Mistress," he said. "No more games."

She shifted. Crossed long, pale legs. Turned dark eyes to stare down at him.

"I have returned," he continued. "Returned from my exile, my wanderings. From the *test* that you so cruelly set for me."

The mother-shade stood in the bedchamber doorway, watching.

Thanos kept his gaze fixed on Mistress Death. "On Sacrosanct," he said, "I sent you dozens of souls. I cut a swath through the Church of Universal Truth, exposing its dark nature. I killed a friend, someone I cared for, all in the name of your holy domain.

"On Hala, more died. I rent the Empire in two, spilled blood on the spaceport of the most feared race in the galaxy. Many perished; many more will die there, in the years to come.

"And in the Velt, I gave you everything."

He crossed to the weapons rack. The mother-shade shook her head in disgust. Death followed his motions from above, cocking her head in an insect-like motion.

"If you accept my love," he said, "I will give you more. I will reclaim the Infinity Gems, use them to deliver you souls beyond imagining. Worlds unknown will perish, sobbing, in blood and fire. And I will build you a home, a shrine so glorious it will shame this humble castle. A palace of terror to tower over Hell itself."

He paused. Ran rough fingers down the line of pistols, of knives.

"All this and more I pledge," he continued. "My fealty shall be endless, my devotion to you will know no bounds. We will stride across the bands of hyperspace, two souls with one will; our dark love will dwarf the stars themselves. We will blast a swath of destruction, make of the strings a symphony of blood and fire like nothing eternity has ever seen.

"The choice is yours. To know your love, I would grant you all that is within my power. But there is one thing, and one thing only, that I will never do."

He lifted a large energy-sabre from the rack and thumbed it to life. He whirled, lunged, and thrust its blade through the mother-shade's heart.

Her dark eyes went wide. Her tiny frame shuddered, shook. She reached for the glowing saber with both trembling hands.

Grunting, he raised the sabre, lifting her frail body up off the ground. Energy surged from the blade through its twitching victim. When she went still, he flicked the blade and shook her free.

She slumped to the floor, blood leaking from her chest. Eyes staring in horror. Dead at his hand.

Again.

He turned slowly, wiped the sabre on his leg. Then he raised the weapon aloft and fixed Death with a steely gaze.

"I will not change."

Death's eyes twitched. She glanced at the mother-shade's lifeless face, then turned to stare at the blazing sword in Thanos's hand. Her tongue licked dry lips.

Once again, she stood and descended the mountain of skulls. He watched, mesmerized by her beauty. Her every motion was grace; her skin was a pale, perfect canvas.

And yet he was calm. All doubt, all demons, had been driven from him at last. When she lifted her head to kiss him, he knew: She is mine.

Her lips were fire and ice, waking and dreaming. As hot as the heart of a sun, yet colder than the thin-spread atoms at the edge of creation. Within him, the flame burned bright.

He pulled away and raised his bloody sword. Clutched her bony waist tight and smiled a dark, foreboding smile.

"Let the game begin," he said.

EPILOGUE TWO

THREE figures converged on the body lying in the surf. A pair of thin but powerful hands, dark green in color, took hold of one leg. Unnaturally long fingers, at least eight inches from knuckle to nail, wrapped around the other leg. The third pair of hands—red-gold, armored, powered by an arc reactor—seized the body by the shoulders.

"Ready?" Tony Stark said. *"Heave."*

Tony's servos clicked and whirred. Reed Richards stretched out two legs to plant himself in the sand, pulling as hard as he could. Slowly the body began to move.

Gamora let out a groan. "All that time growing up," she gasped, "I never knew how *heavy* he was."

The three of them stepped back, breathing hard. The thick body of Thanos lay still on the sand. His torso was as wide as a barrel; his arms were like tree trunks. His dark eyes, chiseled deep into his gray stone face, stared upward, devoid of life.

Tony indicated the wet trench leading down to the sea, marking the path where Thanos had been dragged ashore. "I'd hate to see the one that got away," he said.

They paused for a moment, gathering their thoughts. The Brazilian island was unusually quiet; the local police had cleared away most of the tourists. Down the beach, a single pier led out across the water. The police stood manning a perimeter at the upper edge of the beach, near a line of trees.

Reed knelt down next to Thanos. He pulled out a small electronic device and started waving it over the body.

"Le Titan Fou," Tony said, flipping open his faceplate. "Looks like Drax was right after all."

"He'll be happy when I tell him," Gamora replied. "He got kind of depressed when we lost the energy signature. Again."

"No life signs," Reed said. "Ergo, no energy signature."

"Where's your big Destroyer pal now?" Tony asked.

"At the resort." Gamora indicated a hotel complex overlooking the beach. "I think he's discovered Moscow Mules."

"Well, that ought to take the edge off. Speaking from bitter experience."

Reed snapped off his device. "I wonder what Thanos was doing underwater," he mused.

"Bunch of civilian corpses have washed up on the mainland," Tony replied. "None of 'em identifiable as yet, but they seem to have surfaced from some depth. S.H.I.E.L.D.'s sending a submersible down for some deep recon."

Gamora stared at the body. "Are you sure he's gone?" she asked. "Thanos has always had an odd relationship with death."

"No heartbeat, no detectable brain activity." Reed seemed almost professionally offended by the question. "I will admit, however, that his rocky skin is so thick, there's an element of doubt."

"Hold up," Tony said. "What's that?"

He knelt down and pointed at Thanos's hand. The thick fingers were curled into a tight fist, but a glint of metal was visible within.

It took them five minutes to pry the hand partway open. Reed flattened his own hand, reached between the thick gray fingers, and pulled out a small, half-crushed electronic device. It looked like a cross between a flip phone and a remote control.

"I'll be dipped in Adamantium," Tony said. "An image inducer."

"Yours?" Reed asked.

"I built it, yeah. Years ago." He reached out and took the device. "This was the very first model."

"I don't understand," Gamora said. "What does it do?"

"Allows the user to disguise his appearance. You know, camouflage. Kurt Wagner used to use one—Nightcrawler, from the X-Men. Whenever he wanted to fit in with normal-looking humans."

"It's completely burned out," Reed said.

"Yeah." Tony flipped the cover open and closed. "Looks like it was in continuous use for decades."

"Huh." Gamora stared at the Titan's unmoving form. "What else does it do?"

"Nothing," Reed said.

"An image inducer just affects other people's perceptions," Tony explained. "Bends light into preprogrammed patterns. It doesn't change who you *are*."

He tossed the device away, into the sand. A wave washed over it, carrying it out to sea.

"I've seen Thanos do a lot of things," Gamora said. "But I've never known him to hide his identity."

"He does tend to wear his accomplishments on his sleeve. The more delusional, depraved, and psychotic, the better." Tony winced as a series of chimes sounded in his ear. "Crap."

"What is it?" Reed asked.

"S.H.I.E.L.D. just sent me a barrage of texts—looks like the submersible found something. I better go see if I can help."

"Ben's on the way with the Fantasticar," Reed said, indicating Thanos's body. "We can handle the cleanup."

"Great. You guys get the easy jobs." Gamora grimaced up at the resort hotel. "I've got to wrangle a drunk Destroyer back into orbit."

"The hero business," Tony said, smiling. "Nobody said it'd be easy."

He flipped down his faceplate with a mental command. He fired his boot-jets, rose up from the sand—then froze.

"What?" Gamora asked. "What is it?"

Jets flaring, Tony glided over to Thanos's body. Reed and Gamora followed. Tony dropped to a crouch, flipped up his faceplate, and studied the Titan's gray countenance. When he turned toward the others, there was a strange look on his face.

"I'm sure it's nothing," Tony said. "But was he *smiling* before?"

ABOUT THE AUTHOR

WINNER of the Eisner Award for Best Editor, Stuart Moore's comics and graphic novel work includes the original science-fiction series *Earthlight*, *Shadrach Stone*, and *PARA*. He has written *Web of Spider-Man*, *Namor*, and *Wolverine Noir*, the adaptation of the bestselling novel *Redwall*, and two volumes of the award-winning *The Nightmare Factory*. He wrote *Civil War*, the first in a line of prose novels from Marvel Comics, and *Thanos: Death Sentence*.

ALSO AVAILABLE FROM TITAN BOOKS

BLACK PANTHER
WHO IS THE BLACK PANTHER?
A KINGDOM BESIEGED

In the secluded kingdom of Wakanda, the Black Panther reigns supreme—until a savage villain called Klaw invades with a grudge, a super-powered army, and the support of western nations. Now the Panther must defend his homeland, his family, and his very way of life against overwhelming odds. An all-new novel based on Reginald Hudlin and John Romita Jr.'s groundbreaking Black Panther tale!

TITANBOOKS.COM

MARVEL

ALSO AVAILABLE FROM TITAN BOOKS

DEADPOOL

PAWS

EVIL. POWERFUL. CUTE.

Marvel's hyperactive assassin in his first full-length novel!
His target: puppies that booome giant monsters. Wait. Puppies?
Is that right? Can we do that?

TITANBOOKS.COM

ALSO AVAILABLE FROM TITAN BOOKS

AVENGERS
EVERYBODY WANTS TO RULE THE WORLD

An all-new, original prose novel by the *New York Times* bestselling author of *Guardians of the Galaxy: Rocket Raccoon and Groot—Steal the Galaxy!* and *Guardians 3000!* In Berlin, Captain America battles the forces of Hydra. In the Savage Land, Hawkeye and the Black Widow attempt to foil A.I.M. In Washington, D.C., Iron Man fights to stop Ultron. In Siberia, Thor takes on an entire army. And in Madripoor, Bruce Banner battles the High Evolutionary! Only one thing is certain: This confluence of adversaries isn't a coincidence. But what larger, deadlier threat lies behind these simultaneous attacks on Earth?

TITANBOOKS.COM

ALSO AVAILABLE FROM TITAN BOOKS

ANT-MAN
NATURAL ENEMY

Meet Scott Lang: ex-con, single father and part-time super hero. Scott and his teenage daughter, Cassie, are just settling down in a new city when a criminal from Scott's past comes gunning for them. But is the killer really after Scott, or the secrets of the Ant-Man tech? And just how far will Scott go to protect his only child?

TITANBOOKS.COM

MARVEL

ALSO AVAILABLE FROM TITAN BOOKS

CIVIL WAR

THE EPIC STORY THAT BLOWS THE MARVEL UNIVERSE APART!

Iron Man and Captain America: two core members of the Avengers, the world's greatest super hero team. When a tragic battle blows a hole in the city of Stamford, killing hundreds of people, the U.S. government demands that all super heroes unmask and register their powers. To Tony Stark—Iron Man— it's a regrettable but necessary step. To Captain America, it's an unbearable assault on civil liberties. So begins the Civil War. Based on the smash hit graphic novel—over half a million copies have sold in print and digital formats.

TITANBOOKS.COM

MARVEL

ALSO AVAILABLE FROM TITAN BOOKS

SPIDER-MAN
FOREVER YOUNG

Hoping to snag some rent-paying photos of his arachnid-like alter ego in action, Peter Parker goes looking for trouble—and finds it in the form of a mysterious, mythical stone tablet coveted by both the Kingpin and the Maggia! Caught in the crosshairs of New York's most nefarious villains, Peter also runs afoul of his friends—and the police! His girlfriend, Gwen Stacy, isn't too happy with him, either. And the past comes back to haunt him years later when the Maggia's assumed-dead leader resurfaces, still in pursuit of the troublesome tablet! Plus: With Aunt May at death's door, has the ol' Parker luck disappeared for good?

TITANBOOKS.COM

MARVEL

OFFICIAL MARVEL STUDIOS' COLLECTIONS

**CAPTAIN MARVEL:
MOVIE SPECIAL**
On Sale Now • $24.99
ISBN: 9781785868115

**MARVEL STUDIOS:
THE FIRST 10 YEARS**
On Sale Now • $24.99
ISBN: 9781787730915

ALSO AVAILABLE!

**AVENGERS:
INFINITY WAR**
THE OFFICIAL
MOVIE SPECIAL
$19.99 • Hardback
ISBN:
9781785868054

**ANT-MAN AND
THE WASP:**
THE OFFICIAL
MOVIE SPECIAL
$19.99 • Hardback
ISBN:
9781785868092

**BLACK
PANTHER:**
THE OFFICIAL
MOVIE COMPANION
$19.99 • Hardback
ISBN:
9781785866531

**BLACK
PANTHER:**
THE OFFICIAL
MOVIE SPECIAL
$19.99 • Hardback
ISBN:
9781785869242

**THOR
RAGNOROK:**
THE OFFICIAL
MOVIE SPECIAL
$19.99 • Hardback
ISBN:
9781785866371

THE ULTIMATE COMPANIONS TO MARVEL STUDIOS' LATEST BLOCKBUSTER MOVIES!

Only available in the U.S. and Canada.

MARVEL
© 2019 Marvel

AVAILABLE IN ALL GOOD BOOK STORES AND DIGITALLY AT
TITAN-COMICS.COM